FIERY GIRLS

A Novel of the 1911 Triangle Waist Company Fire

Heather Wardell

Part One

CHAPTER ONE

Rosie
August 22, 1909

"ROSIE LEHRER!"

Fear holds me still for a moment, then I realize that if I take too long, I might lose my chance. If I even have a chance.

My legs shaking so much I feel almost as though I'm still on the ship, I manage to walk forward to the girl, a little older than me, who called my name.

"I'm Cecilia Greenstone, Rosie, and this man here is your inspector," she says in Yiddish, gesturing to the stern-faced man in a black suit who sits, perched on a high stool, with one hand resting atop a messy stack of papers on a small desk before him. "I will be your interpreter. Unless you speak English?"

"Not well enough— I mean, I did try to learn, but—" I bite my lip. "Yiddish, please." Not that it'll matter what language we use, once she learns the truth about me.

She nods. "Yiddish is fine. Please do speak as loudly as you can."

I already was.

"Have you any relatives here already?"

"No," I admit, trying to hide the trembling of my hands in the folds of my skirt. "No, I do not."

Should I keep my eyes on Cecilia? It would ordinarily be polite, since she's the one speaking. But I know that the questions she asks aren't hers, they're the inspector's. He's the one who matters. But he terrifies me.

Cecilia moves a little closer, cupping her hand around her ear. "Will your husband—no, you're only sixteen. Your father, then? Will he arrive soon? Or perhaps a brother?"

I shake my head, misery sweeping over me.

She moves closer still and lays her hand on my shoulder. "Rosie, it's all right. Answer the questions and I'll be able to help you."

"You won't," I say, fighting back a sob. "I'm not allowed."

"Not... what do you mean?"

"I am *alone*," I admit. "I came here alone. My parents didn't know... we thought I could... but... on the ship..." I stop, unable to find words to describe the horror I felt when, on the very day my ship departed, I learned that a girl alone would not be permitted into America.

Cecilia squeezes my shoulder. "It is all right, Rosie. No, you can't leave Ellis Island alone, but you won't have to. If you do well, if you answer my questions carefully, I have people who can help you."

I want to believe this. I *need* to. But I've only just met her.

"Trust me," she says, looking into my eyes and nodding as if she can see what I'm thinking. "Trust me, Rosie. I promise you. I work with the National Council of Jewish Women, and we can find you a room and a job and—"

The inspector barks a few words, which I can't quite hear, and Cecilia turns back and answers him. He pulls his mouth to one side as if he doesn't like what she said, but he gives a sharp nod.

"We must go through the questions quickly, Rosie. Do your best."

My father would call me foolish, but I find myself trusting her. "All right."

"And be loud!"

I've been raised to be a quiet girl, a good girl. But here, I must be different. With so many potential immigrants in this huge high-ceilinged hall, each with an interpreter helping an inspector decide whether they should be allowed to enter America, everyone's almost shouting to be heard over everyone else, and I need to make myself do the same. I need to take a deep breath and shout my answers, though the air stinks of the fear of people who haven't bathed for weeks.

But how, when I'm so scared I can hardly speak at all?

Cecilia nods encouragingly and gives me a small smile, barely a twitch of her lips, and I try to calm myself by looking only at her gentle face below her thick brown hair swept up beneath a pretty gray hat.

I think she cares about me.

I think the inspector does not.

Men in uniform never care about Jews, it seems to me, unless they're deciding how to get rid of us, and his cold eyes and set jaw frighten me.

"Rosie, tell me, why have you come here?"

I take such a deep breath that my corset creaks then push out my words as loudly as I can. "I am here to earn the money to bring my family to America. My parents, my brother, my two young sisters."

She raises her eyebrows and I know she's thinking the same thing I am: it will take me years to earn passage for five people.

She doesn't say it, though. Instead, she asks a few more questions, about my background and what I know about America, then gives me a smile that reminds me of how my mother can tell me I have managed to impress her without speaking a word.

As my heart begins to fill with hope, she turns and says something to the inspector.

Though I can't hear her, he obviously can, because he answers her then waves his hand toward the staircases behind him as if shooing away a fly.

"You passed," Cecilia says to me, still in Yiddish. "Welcome to America, Rosie."

To my shame, my eyes fill with tears and I barely manage to hold back a sob.

I have spent nearly two weeks worrying in every waking moment. Though I tried to be optimistic, I couldn't. I was certain that once we reached New York I'd be put right back on the stinking horrible ship and forced to return to Belostok, to Russia. To the Pale of Settlement, where we Jews are forced to live. I've had nightmares every night about it.

But Cecilia told me I would be allowed in, and she was right.

I trusted her, and I was right to do so, and the relief is almost too much to bear.

The inspector looks unimpressed at my reaction, so I swipe at my eyes and find a few English words. "Thank you, sir. Thank you."

He nods and again waves me away, and Cecilia takes my arm so she can guide me past the inspector who is now calling another hopeful immigrant from the endless lines.

Once we reach the head of the stairs, she says, "I know it's frightening being an immigrant, Rosie, I am one myself, but you are a heldish maydl. You will do well here."

Nobody has ever called me a brave girl before, and it fills my heart with sunshine. "I want to. I..." I have so many questions swirling in my mind. When my parents told me I would be moving to America, I somehow never thought about how it would all work. They told me to go, so I went. Now that I'm here, though, everything I don't know overwhelms me. How am I to do this alone?

"So, let me tell you how I can help you," Cecilia says, leading me toward the staircase. "I know a house for immigrant girls, with good food and clean rooms for a fair price. The workers there will help you find a job, and they also have classes to teach you English and other things about America."

The money my parents sent with me felt like a fortune at the time, since I'd never had any money of my own before. But after hearing people on the ship talk about how much they brought, and what they would have to spend, I feel like a pauper. "How... I would pay how much?"

"Only two dollars a week," she says with a smile.

I feel my shoulders relax. I heard people expecting to pay three or even four dollars.

"Yes, it's good, isn't it? We have some rich ladies who help us, so the cost isn't too much. Do you have dollars with you?"

I grimace. "Roubles. I'm sorry."

"It's all right, there's a money exchange here."

She pauses as we squeeze past a woman dragging several crying children and a huge old suitcase down the stairs. I wonder if we should offer to help, but Cecilia doesn't, so maybe that's not done in America.

Once we can walk together again, she says, "You'll need a job. Can you sew?"

I nod. "My mother is a seamstress. She taught me everything, starting when I was six."

"Excellent. There are many garment factories near the house, so that will work perfectly."

She sounds relieved, and I didn't even tell her that my mother taught me to sew every seam perfectly because that felt like I'd be bragging. Knowing how pleased my parents will be when I use my skills to begin sending money back to them, I can't help smiling.

Cecilia pats me on the shoulder. "I have someone from the home here." She stretches up to look over the mass of people, some anxiously staring up the stairs and others loudly reuniting with newly-arrived loved ones. "Where *is* she... oh, there. Come with me."

We struggle through the crowd until Cecilia stops in front of a girl of about my age with her hair, nearly as dark as mine, pinned up under a straw hat with a red ribbon. "Rosie, this is Julia Kessler. She came here a year ago, and now she works and lives at the home I told you about. Julia, Rosie Lehrer is here from Russia on her own. She needs to exchange her money, and she'll need a sewing job once she's settled in."

"Of course, Cecilia," Julia says, giving me a shy but sweet smile.

Cecilia nods at Julia then at me. "Good luck, Rosie. And again, welcome to America!"

Before I can find so much as one word to thank her, she's heading back toward the stairs.

Going up to help another immigrant, no doubt. Without her, I could never have answered the inspector's questions. Cecilia saved me from being sent back to Russia, and she'll save others today too. Though she's not much older than me, she is a young woman while I feel very much a girl. Will I become like her? I hope so, but it's hard to imagine.

Julia clears her throat and says, "Are you ready?" and I nod and follow her. She helps me get my two leather-handled cases back from where they were stored while I waited to be inspected, then guides me to the money exchange and watches carefully to make sure I get what I should for my roubles. Only ten dollars, which doesn't seem like much after how hard my mother worked to save those roubles, but since I get half of it in coin it looks like more.

Julia and I carry my two cases out of the building and onto a wooden ferry boat. It's like the one that brought me from the ship to Ellis Island, but this time, instead of everyone yelling only in Russian or Yiddish, people are yelling in every possible language. Yelling, and crying and laughing too, and pointing with great excitement at the enormous Statue of Liberty.

I'm not yelling. I'm too stunned. I am finally here. America. New York City. Those magic words have appeared in so many letters sent back to Russia from girls who left home for a better life, and now *I* will be writing those letters.

"So, Rosie," Julia says into my ear, "why did you come to America?"

"To earn money to bring over my family." That was the only answer I gave during my inspection, but I'm more relaxed now so I add, "And because of my aunt."

"Oh, is she here? Or coming soon?"

I shake my head. "She died two months ago." The first and only time I ever saw my father cry was when he told me and my brother of his sister's heart attack, and I have to blink back my own tears as I realize how very far away I now am from my family.

Julia squeezes my arm. "I shouldn't have asked."

"No," I say quickly. "I like talking about her. I miss her. She worked in a garment factory, as I'll be doing here, and she was loud and exciting and fun."

Julia leaves a quiet respectful pause then says, "And why did that make you come here?"

"My parents decided to send me, two weeks after Aunt Ida died. Because she wasn't that old, and they think she might not have died if she'd been in America. They think it's safer than Russia so—"

"Which it is."

Julia gives an embarrassed giggle at having interrupted me, but I don't laugh with her, because she sounded both angry and sad when she spoke. "Was Russia not safe for you?"

"I didn't mean to tell you, not now, but I came here to bring over my family, same as you." She swallows hard. "But then... six months ago there was a pogrom at home. My whole village..."

Horror sweeps over me. The word means "devastation", and from what I've heard about the violent riots against Jews, it is the right word. "There's nobody to bring over now? I'm so sorry."

She nods and whispers, "Thank you," then takes a deep breath. "But America has been good to me. I've learned English, and so much more. You will too, at the home. Girls get to learn here."

I'm still shaken by Julia's loss, but I am happy to hear this.

Back home, the czar allows only three Jewish children for every one hundred boys in a school, and those places are all taken up by the richest people. My family isn't rich, so none of us have been to a school. My brother Meyer spends all day at the synagogue studying Torah, as my father does. For my two younger sisters and me, the only education available, other than a little reading and writing, was learning to sew skirts and shirtwaists at our mother's side as she toiled for factory owners.

Of course, that's all we need, since we'll have the same lives as every Jewish woman: get married, raise children, take care of the home, and earn as much money as we can to support our husbands in their religious studies. Aunt Ida, at thirty-five, was the oldest unmarried woman I've ever met, and my father frequently told her it was more than time she found a husband, so she would have done so eventually.

Once I make enough money and my family arrives in America, my father will talk with the men at our synagogue here and find me a suitable husband, and I will take care of everything while that husband studies.

But until then, I am alone in America, able to do whatever I choose. At home, when I so much as expressed an opinion Mama would snap, "Don't you be like Aunt Ida!" I never understood why, since I thought Aunt Ida was wonderful, but there's nobody to snap at me here. I can have my own opinions.

I briefly thrill at the thought, but then fear sweeps me at the idea of choosing my own way.

Luckily, Julia nudges me. "Ready for your first English lesson in America?"

I nod, happy for the distraction and also for the chance to test myself. From the day my parents told me I'd be coming here until the day I boarded the ship, I spent every possible moment trying to learn English from a book, but I'm not sure I'm pronouncing things properly.

"I," she says, poking herself in the chest, "am Julia Kessler."

"I," I repeat, poking myself as she did, "am Rosie Lehrer."

"Gut!" She smiles at me, then translates the Yiddish to English though they sound nearly the same and says, "Good."

"Good good Julia," I say, being silly and hoping she will realize I know that.

She giggles, and I do too, and by the time our ferry reaches the dock we have practiced saying, "I'm hungry," "please help me", "thank you", "you're welcome," and "I can sew very well."

"Those will get you started," she says, returning to Yiddish as we clutch at the rail to keep from falling on the rocking deck. "And don't forget the classes at the home too."

Lessons from the book are coming back to me, so I say carefully in English, "That is good. I go to classes. I can sew very well, so I work in a factory. Thank you."

"Nearly. You *will* go to classes and you *will* work in a factory."

"I will," I repeat, recognizing what she's added to my words. "I will do those things."

"Well done." She grins and grabs one of my cases. "Let's speak English, then. I will carry this for you."

Hauling my other case, I follow her off the ferry into a crowd of men shouting about things to buy or places to stay in every language. I do my best to keep up with her, but when we're briefly separated a man grabs my arm and says in Yiddish, "Little girl, you want a place to sleep? A job? I have both. Very good. I'll take care of you. Come with me."

I try to pull away, but he won't let me go. Scared, I push my case against him as hard as I can, and I manage to free my arm from his grip just as Julia arrives and snaps at him, "She's with me."

The man turns away without a word and begins making the same offers to another girl behind me.

Julia catches that girl by the hand and pulls her along with us until we're out of the crowd. The other girl breaks away and runs off, and Julia calls, "Wait!" after her but the girl doesn't look back.

"What was he going to do with us?"

I forgot to speak English but Julia's staring after the departing girl and I'm not even sure she noticed. "If you were lucky, a lot of sewing for almost no money."

"And if we weren't lucky?"

She turns to me now, her eyes sad. "Nothing good."

I take a breath to ask her to explain, then decide that maybe I don't want to know, especially since we don't know where the other girl is going and how she got off Ellis Island alone. It must be hard to do Julia's job and only be able to help a few of the thousands of immigrants. It must feel, as my father always says of an impossible task, like trying to empty the ocean with a spoon.

Instead of upsetting Julia and probably myself too by asking for more details, I say in English, "What happens now?"

What happens, I soon find out, is that we take a subway and a streetcar, my first time on both, to a teeming street which would, except for its smell of rotting garbage and sweating bodies, fit in perfectly back in Belostok.

If it weren't so busy.

I've never seen so many Jewish people in one place, more than the entire population of my tiny village. Street peddlers shout about how theirs are the crispest pickles or the most attractive eyeglasses, and throngs of old women in black skirts and long-sleeved shirtwaists pick through the wares. Men of all ages, also in black but with thick beards and payot curls on each side of their heads below their hats, stand in groups talking, and children laugh and shout as they play tag and stickball among the crowds and the horse-drawn wagons.

"Good to see something familiar, right?"

I nod, but Julia is wrong. I want everything here to be different, and so do my parents. More, I want *me* to be different, and how can I be if my world is the same?

The other workers at the clean bright house are as kind as Julia and Cecilia, and soon I find myself in a room with a narrow white metal bed with brown blankets, a wooden bedside table topped with a gas lamp, a pink-flowered pitcher and bowl sitting on a washstand with a white towel and washcloth hanging on its side rack, and a small wooden cabinet. Though none of these things are large, they almost completely fill the tiny room so only a bit of the scuffed hardwood floor shows.

I look around, amazed that this space that smells so clean and fresh is all for me.

"It's all right, I hope," Julia says in English, staring down at her black leather boots. "We don't have any larger rooms."

"Oh, no, it is good! I never had a room... alone," I say, not sure how to word it in English. I shared a room even smaller than this with Rachel and Tessie at home. It will be strange to sleep without my sisters' snoring and muttering at night, but probably wonderful too. "It is very good."

"I'm glad, Rosie. I'm glad you now have a room to yourself."

"To your—to *my*self."

She nods. "That's right. Well done. Now, we won't be eating dinner for another hour, but I can get you something right away if you're hungry."

I shake my head. Seeing the bed, the first one I'll ever sleep in alone, has made me realize exactly how tired I am. "I think I might sleep a little."

"I did the same thing when I arrived here myself two years ago," she says. "A rest would be good for you, but you'd like to wash up first. It'll feel good."

I'd rather sleep, but I haven't had any hot water to wash with since I left Russia. "Thank you."

She grabs the washstand's pitcher. "I'll be right back."

I've only managed to take off my battered hat and pull my two skirts out of my first bag when she returns, and looking at my clothing makes me compare it with hers.

Julia's skirt, a deep rich brown that swirls at her ankles as she turns away from replacing the pitcher on the washstand, isn't so different from my black ones although its color is prettier. Her waist, though... while it has long sleeves and a high collar like mine, it's pure white with beautiful lace and pleats on the front, not plain like the three black ones I made and brought. I know I need to send home most of my earnings, but I would love to buy at least one piece of American clothing to store in my new cabinet. But would my parents approve?

Julia flutters around, fluffing the pillow and blanket on my bed and helping me shake out my clothing and spread it across the cabinet to air, but long after all of that is completed, she still lingers.

Why? Doesn't she realize how tired I am?

I'm about to ask her why she hasn't left when I remember that she was an immigrant too. Maybe on her first day in America, she wanted someone to stay with her. That's not what I need, but how can she know that?

Warmth fills my chest at her kindness and concern and I say, in Yiddish because it's easier to find words, "Don't you have something else to do, Julia?"

My face goes hot as I realize how abrupt my words sounded, not at all as I meant them, but our eyes meet and she smiles.

"I know, I should let you sleep, and I should go back to Ellis Island in case Cecilia has found another girl for me to help, but I remember how scared I was on my first day."

I smile back, relieved she understood what I meant even though I didn't say it well. "I'm grateful for your help. And I'm not scared anymore. Because of you. If everyone in America is as kind as you, it will be a wonderful place to live."

She blushes. "Well, you rest now. Come down whenever you wake up and we'll find you some food."

I promise her I will, and she turns down the gas lamp and at last leaves me alone.

The moment the door closes, I free my heavy black cotton stockings from their clips on my corset and roll them down and off, then give my legs a good scratch. That done, I pull off my skirt, waist, and corset cover, then unhook my corset and drop it with a sigh of relief onto the bed.

After a few deep breaths, I remove my drawers and my chemise, which are sweat-stained and smelly from being pressed against my skin by the corset since early this morning, then use the hot water and soap Julia provided to clean myself as best I can.

She was right, it *does* feel good to wash, though I can't stop yawning throughout.

Once I've dried off and put on the cleaner of my two cotton night-gowns, I draw back the blanket and settle into bed.

And before I can reach to turn off the lamp, I am wide awake.

Wide awake, in a bed in America, all by myself. It's so hard to believe: I am here, alone, for at least two years. In that time I will need to work hard, of course, but I will also make all of my own decisions for the first time.

Thinking of decisions makes me sit up, slip out of bed, and dig in my bag to find the letter my father wrote for me to read on the ship, my frustration rising again at all his rules.

Only work for a Jewish man. Never be alone or in a compromising situation with that man. Never work on the Sabbath. Keep kosher.

I know all of this, Papa, I know.

That last one, though, I might have broken on the ship. The crew began providing us meat on our eighth day and I ate though I didn't know what it was because I was nearly out of food. What would my father have had me do, starve?

Not wanting the letter to come into my new life with me, I wrap my hand in my night-gown's fabric to carefully remove the possibly-hot glass shade from the gas lamp, then turn up the gas until the flame is at its largest.

Shocked at what I'm doing but not wanting to stop, I ease the paper's edge into the lamp.

The flickering light begins to lick at the letter's corner.

Then, far faster than I expect, the fire bites at the paper like I bit at the meat on the ship in my hunger, and flames race toward my hand.

I drop the paper to the floor and snatch up one of my shoes, crushing the fire like a meshugener until the leather sole of my shoe has defeated it.

Then I fall onto my back on the bed and laugh until tears pour into my ears.

Yes, I might indeed be a crazy person. That *was* a crazy thing to do. And I destroyed my father's words, which I would never have done at home. If he knew...

But of course, he never will. And for the first time in my life, I have solved a problem all by myself. One I caused, yes, but still.

Besides, I tell myself as I wipe up the paper's ashes with the already-filthy hem of today's skirt, it's like they say at home.

Whenever bad things happen, when the people who hate Jews attack us and set fire to our homes and businesses, even when people's wooden houses simply burn down, everyone talks of how wonderful it would be to move to America.

And they have one big reason why:

"In America, they don't let you burn."

CHAPTER TWO

Maria

August 9, 1909

ALONZO'S HANDS SLIDE UP MY NOW-BARE LEGS, and I moan and roll my head on the pillow he made of my stockings.

"Bella," he murmurs, pushing up the loose leg of my drawers and pressing his mouth to my thigh. "Beautiful girl."

I grab his hair and pull him up so we can kiss, and as he rises he takes hold of my skirt and pulls it up too, all the way to my waist.

With his mouth locked to mine I'm surrounded by his clean soapy scent, which blocks out the aroma of horses and hay warmed by the blazing sun. I'm almost sorry: those once-disliked smells have come to remind me so much of my time spent kissing and touching Alonzo here in the spare stall of his parents' stable that I insist upon taking care of our own horse at home simply so I can breathe in the scent and remember how wonderful every moment with him is.

His hand slips under my gathered-up skirt's hem and moves under the waistband of my drawers, and as it slides lower I whimper and clutch at his back.

"You can't, Alonzo," I make myself say. I always have to stop him, and I never want to. "You shouldn't..."

"I should," he murmurs into my ear. "I love you."

The whole world seems to stop for an instant then delight floods through me so I feel like I'm glowing even brighter than the sun. I love him, and I have for months, but I never once thought... "You do?"

"Of course," he says against my neck. "And you're leaving Italy tomorrow so this is our last chance." His hand moves a little lower. "Do you really want me to stop?"

"I..." A wonderful shiver runs through me. "Do you truly love me? Will you marry me? Will you—"

He kisses me, stopping my words, then whispers, "I'll do whatever you want."

"Then no," I say, so happy I can hardly breathe. "No. Don't stop. Please."

I feel his other hand fumbling at his waistband, trying to free himself. We're going so much further than we ever have before, and though I know what I should do, what any good girl would do until she's married, I can't, I *can't* stop him as I should. I saw him watching pretty Serena yesterday while she flirted with his best friend and I don't want to lose him to her. Or anyone. Besides, this feels too good to stop.

And he loves me, I know that now, and I love him so much, and tomorrow I leave for four long years away from him. Before I go, I so badly want his touch and his kisses and—

"Maria!"

I gasp and push at Alonzo's shoulders to get him away from me, but he's already scrambling away on his own, leaving me exposed so I have to struggle to get my skirt down while still on my back. "Vincente," he says, clutching his half-undone trousers and looking up at my furious brother, "we weren't doing... I mean..."

"I know exactly what you were trying to do," Vinnie snaps, his anger making him look much older than Alonzo even though they're the same age, "and you won't with my sister. Get out of here!"

I expect Alonzo to tell Vinnie what we agreed to here, to tell him that it's all right. He doesn't, though. He turns around, without even looking at me, and runs out of the stable.

"You don't understand!" I get quickly to my feet and straighten my skirt. "Vinnie, we're in love, we're going to get married, and—"

"Idiot," Vinnie says. "Little idiot. You know nothing."

"I do! I do know."

"Get your—" He waves at my stockings. "Whatever you took off, put it back on. And fast. Before they get here."

"They?" I read the answer in his eyes, and horror makes my body shake so I can barely grab the stockings and rush to hide behind a wall to put them on. "Mamma and Papà are coming in here?"

"Not if we get out first, so *hurry*."

I do hurry, as much as I can, but getting my stockings' black cotton fabric attached to their clips and then tying the laces on my shoes seems to take forever, so when we leave the stable we meet our parents at the door.

"Maria, you didn't—tell me you didn't let him—"

My mother sways as if about to faint, and Papà grabs her arm as Vinnie says, "No, I got here before he could."

"He's going to marry me!"

Mamma closes her eyes, her lips moving without sound as they do when she prays, then she opens them and turns on me. "Stupid fool! That will never happen. His parents expect him to marry Alessandra. You know this."

I do. I also know that Alonzo thinks Alessandra is dull and ugly, and I know that his parents only want him to marry her because her money and social position will make theirs even better. He won't do it. He loves me. He will marry me. He said so.

I tell them this, and Mamma's hand flies out and slaps my cheek.

Hot pain races like wildfire over my face. She's never hit me before, nobody ever has, and though she is much shorter than me, and so old at forty, her blow hurt.

She doesn't seem sorry, either. "Thank God you're leaving tomorrow and won't see that boy again for years. And you won't see him when you come back either. I won't allow it. He'll never marry you, and you'll be his... his..."

Papà squeezes her arm, and she stops looking for a ladylike way to call me a most unladylike person as he says, "It's all right, Francesca. In four years, everything will have changed, and while they're in America, Vinnie will take care of her."

Papà didn't want me to go with Vinnie to America, saying that four years without his little principessa would be too long. Mamma, who's never once thought of me as a princess, insisted that I go with Vinnie and make money too. She says four years is enough time for us to earn enough to buy a much bigger restaurant for Papà and improve our current one for Vinnie to take over.

Vinnie is going to work at building tunnels for trains, which the Americans call "subways", beneath the roads, and I am going to sew. I don't mind embroidery work or helping to make my own dresses so I'm sure I won't hate having a job, and I do like the idea of coming home rich. Everyone says the streets in America are paved with gold, and even the seamstresses can earn five or ten dollars a week which is a fortune compared to what they earn here.

But Alonzo! I will be twenty when I return and he'll be twenty-two, and—no, I won't wait that long. I have to find a way to fix this now, not in four years, because I cannot leave Alonzo for Serena and Alessandra and all the other girls to fight over. He loves me, but—

"Maria, you won't see Alonzo again," Mamma says, giving me a look so ferocious I'd almost rather she'd hit me once more. "You will not. You will go home and take your bath and finish packing and practice your English and you will *not* sneak out to see that boy. And don't you even think about trying to bring him to America."

I blink hard as if I'm about to cry, using that action to hide my sudden delight at having a plan presented to me, then hang my head and look up at her, letting my lower lip tremble. "I know, Mamma. I'm sorry."

Papà, who always believes me, wraps his arm around me and pulls me close. "She's a good girl, Francesca. And she'll be a good girl in America too. And then in four years she'll come back to us."

ONCE I'M SURE EVERYONE IS ASLEEP I slip out of my bedroom and move quietly toward the front door, ready to claim I need to use the privy if anyone wakes. I am lucky, though, and in moments find myself alone outside in the dark silent night.

I did finish packing, although I only had a little left to do because I've been steadily doing it for weeks while also making sure Vinnie did *his* packing, and Vinnie and I spoke English all evening while our parents sat beside us with no idea what we were saying until we translated for them, and I even let Mamma scrub my back in the bath as she always wants to.

I *am* a good girl for doing nearly everything she said.

Besides, I probably wouldn't have thought of sneaking out if Mamma hadn't mentioned it, so really it's her fault that I'm out here now.

I'm glad to be out, and not only because I'll see Alonzo soon. The rich black sky is full of stars, and the spicy-sweet smell of the tomato plants I brush past in our garden mixes with a hint of sulphur from Mount Vesuvius, on whose western slopes my village rests like a meatball on a plate mounded with Papà's spaghetti. I will miss this, in America. It's a good memory to take with me.

I hurry along, letting one foot stay on the dirt road and the other on the grass beside it so I don't get lost, until I reach Alonzo's house, where I use the shadows of the lemon trees to get myself unseen to where I can toss a pebble at his window.

It takes four pebbles to get one up high enough, but the window finally opens and his face appears like the gorgeous moon in the dark sky.

"Who is—Maria?"

I move closer. "Oh, Alonzo, I'm so glad to see you."

He shoots a quick look back over his shoulder. "You can't be here. You—How'd you know which room is mine?"

I feel my face growing hot but know the dark will hide my blush. "You said once yours is the only one on this side of the house."

He didn't say that *to* me, only in front of me, and it was over a year ago, and I see his smile grow as he realizes how much attention I've been paying to him. "Well, you found me," he whispers, his voice making all of me feel as hot as my face. "Why?"

I wasn't expecting such a blunt question and for a moment I can't find words. Then I say, "You... you said we'd get married."

He draws himself a little back into the house. "Now? We can't."

"Of course not now," I say, surprised at his foolishness. Why don't men have any sense? "It's the middle of the night! No, in America. Once I have earned enough money from my job there, I'll send you a steamship ticket and you can come over and marry me, and we'll stay there and have children and be together every day and it'll be wonderful. Won't it?"

The darkness around us must be playing tricks with my eyes because his face seems to change, to grow hard and cold, as I speak, but before he can answer me I hear his mamma from inside the house call, "Alonzo, what are you doing at that window?"

He looks back over his shoulder. "Nothing, Mamma, just getting some air." Turning again to me, he whispers, "Go now!"

"But will you—"

"Yes, yes." He flaps his hand at me while also glancing over his shoulder again. "I will. Please *go*!"

I scurry off into the deep shade beneath the trees as Alonzo shuts the window and disappears, but I don't leave. Instead I wrap my arms around myself and pretend he's holding me.

He will be, as soon as I earn the money we need. I'm supposed to come home with that money, in four years, but I won't. I'll stay in

America and send Alonzo money for his ticket. Then he'll come to me and we'll marry and start our lives together. In America. The land of freedom, of gold-paved streets and happiness.

I can't wait.

CHAPTER THREE

Rosie
August 23, 1909

"Are you sure?"

I nod at the worried Julia. "I have a very good..." Unable to find the English words I want, I say, "I won't get lost."

"Good sense of direction?"

I smile at learning a new phrase. "Yes. A very good sense of direction. And I could use some air."

"But it would only be another hour or two before I could take you."

I have been waiting since the morning for her or one of the other workers at the home to have time to guide me around the neighborhood, and after the train and the ship and Ellis Island I've had more than enough waiting to last me a lifetime. "I'll be fine. I'm itching for a long walk."

"After all that sleep, no wonder."

We both laugh. When I woke up this morning shocked that I had slept right from the late afternoon into the next day, she admitted that she did the same thing on her first day in America.

Her laugh fades, and she looks at me with a frown for one more moment then gives in. "If you get lost or anything else goes wrong, ask at a shop. Tell them you're at the immigrant girls' home on Grand Street. They'll know how to find us."

I nod and hurry out before she can change her mind.

Standing on the crowded street, I take a few deep breaths. The air isn't exactly fresh, what with the sun heating up all the people, plus the smells of the delis and butcher shops and the horse droppings on the road. But it's air that's not in a house, or in the steerage class of a ship or in the crowded spaces of Ellis Island, so I like it anyhow.

A strange humming sound fills my ears, familiar but also not, and it takes me a moment to realize it's a sewing machine. No, not a machine, but hundreds. Thousands? Julia told me that many of the buildings in our Jewish neighborhood contain garment factories, but I didn't expect to be able to hear their machines from the street. How loud must it be inside one of those factories?

Knowing I'll need to find out soon, I make my way along the sidewalk beside the dirt road, looking at the signs on the shops and buildings as I pass. Here one advertises a luxurious bath for thirty-five cents, over there are hats for two dollars all the way up to the amazing sum of my full ten dollars, and across the road furnished rooms can be had for fifteen cents a day.

I frown at that last, wondering if the immigrant home is taking advantage of me since I'm paying more, then realize the fifteen-cent room likely does not include food or the English classes and other activities I can get at the home.

But though it seems like a good place for me, I can only afford it for five weeks, and even then only if I don't spend my money on anything else. That'll be difficult, because I will need money for lunches at work and to get to and from work, and because I've already seen that my clothes from home are different from what most of the girls here are wearing.

So has a peddler near me, apparently, because when she catches my eye she calls to me in Yiddish, "Wouldn't you like this lovely waist of mine? Only fifty cents."

She holds it up toward me so its long sleeves spread out to both sides and don't hide the front of it, and it *is* lovely. The fabric is pale blue, and the garment has lace and tucks on both sides of its pearl-like buttons and more lace at the cuffs of its long sleeves. It reminds me of the one Julia wore yesterday, except hers was white. So much prettier than the black ones I brought.

My feet move me closer to her cart without my deciding to go, and she says, a smile creasing her wrinkled face, "And this beautiful belt maybe? I can give you both for only sixty cents, a good girl like you."

One of the girls at breakfast was wearing the exact belt she is pointing to, I think, brown with three lines of gold thread running its length, and I'm tempted. It, along with a new shirtwaist, would make my dull black skirts look so much better.

But I've got only twenty-five cents in my pocketbook, and I know I should haggle. At least, I would at home. Here? Maybe people don't do that in America.

Feeling again the weight of everything I don't know about my new home, I mumble an apology for wasting her time and turn to go.

"Fifty, then," she says, "though I'd lose all my profit for the day."

Peddlers in Belostok use that exact line, and I have to fight to hold back a smile. She *is* expecting me to haggle, and she might be sorry because I'm good at it. I can always tell somehow when a peddler really is at their lowest price.

I turn back slowly and take my time running my eyes over her wares. "Fifteen," I say, "and not a penny more."

"And I thought you a good girl! Forty."

"Hmm." I keep studying the waist and belt and don't say another word. She does want to sell, or she wouldn't have dropped her price so much, so in a moment or two she'll—

"Thirty, though my daughter will starve tonight."

She probably doesn't even have a daughter. "Twenty, more like."

She heaves a dramatic sigh. "Twenty. It'll be the death of me, but twenty."

A little flicker of satisfaction at my victory rushes through me, but it's gone the moment my fingers touch the coins in my pocketbook. It's a good price, but should I be shopping at all? I have no job and I don't know how long it'll take to get one, and I know my father would consider this wasteful since I have clothes already.

Her "Well?" makes me realize I've frozen in indecision.

"I..." I withdraw my hand from my pocketbook. "I'm sorry, I can't."

"I won't go lower," she says, although I'm not sure she's telling the truth.

"It's not—I'm new here, just yesterday, and I don't have a job, and—"

"And you're wasting my time," she says and turns away, but though her words are sharp, her tone isn't, and I think she understands.

"I'll come back when I get a job," I say.

"With sixty cents you'll come back," she retorts, and I can hear laughter and kindness in her voice though she's pretending to be angry.

"Fifteen, maybe," I reply, and walk away chuckling as she calls, "Sixty-five!" after me.

My amusement fades almost immediately, though. When my mother sent me to buy fabric or bread or a hat for my father, she gave me the money and told me exactly what to get. I've never had to choose how to spend money before. How will I survive alone in America if I can't even decide when to spend twenty cents?

I walk on, wishing I had a new waist and belt in my hands, then almost trip over my feet at the sight of a beautiful straw hat with vibrant red roses in a shop window. I've always loved red roses, and the hat has the softly up-curled brim of Julia's hat from yesterday. Hers looked so wonderful on her dark hair, and I'm sure this one would on mine. I would walk so proudly, with that on my head. I would look like an American girl even with my black waist and skirt.

I peer in at the tag.

Four dollars?

I turn my back on the shop, feeling an almost physical pain, and make myself a solemn vow: I will not go back to the home today without a job. I'm sure Julia would help me later, but I want to do it alone. It will be part of learning to be a strong confident American. One who can afford to buy herself clothes, even if she doesn't do so. One who knows whether she *should* buy herself clothes. One who can make choices and feel certain they're the right ones.

By the time I had my breakfast this morning, there were only a few girls who were not already at their jobs, those who were ill or pretending to be for a rare weekday of freedom. While we ate our dark bread and drank our coffee, they wanted to know about me. I did feel strange, having several girls listen to me at once, but though I stumbled through my words with embarrassment I managed to tell them why I had come to America. In return, they told me all about working here, and especially that the English factories pay better than the Jewish ones, mostly because they are generally bigger and not crammed into one apartment.

My father wants me to work for a Jewish man, so I should, but he also wants me to earn as much money as I can. Those two wants, I don't think I can fulfill them both at once.

As for what I want, since my work with my mother was in our tiny house I want something different, and I want the most money for my labors.

Excited and scared, and hopeful I'm making the right choice, I walk up and down the streets looking at the factory signs until I see a sign reading 'Imperial Waist Factory" in front of a large building with several men speaking English outside.

"Hello," I say, terrified, then blush despite myself as they all turn.

"Hello," one says, but I feel that he's making fun of me. Then he says a lot more, all in English I don't understand.

"I can sew very well," I say, then manage to add, "Job, please?"

He speaks again, but I get none of it. Wishing I had waited for Julia, wishing myself anywhere but here, I say, "Job? Please? Sewing?"

The man snaps something at a younger man near him, then he turns and walks back into the building followed by all the other men as the younger one tells me, in Yiddish, "He says you should learn English properly first. Learn English, come back, and maybe."

"How much does he pay?"

He blinks, obviously not having expected that. I don't know why: of course I should know what I would earn. "Four dollars a week. If you sew as well as you say, maybe five. Only maybe."

"I will learn and come back," I say, dazzled by the idea of five dollars a week all to myself. Then I add, in English to prove I can, "Thank you."

He nods and disappears into the factory.

I walk on, saddened by my failure then saddened further when I realize I will never have five dollars 'to myself'.

My parents borrowed nearly fifty American dollars from their bank in Russia for my travel here, and I have to pay that back as soon as I can. Once that's done, what I send to them will go toward bringing over my family. To have them all here will cost over two hundred dollars, and that doesn't even count renting an apartment for us and buying food and American clothing for everyone once they arrive or what I'll need to survive on my own during the time I'm here alone. It's an unbelievable amount of money to earn.

Apparently I must learn English, and learn it well, in order to get a good job, but that'll take time too. I'll have to work for one of the Jewish sweatshops until I manage it. So no big factory for me now, just the same cramped home workshop in which I've toiled my whole life.

My head, topped by its old dull hat, hangs as I walk sadly on down the street. But when I see a little boy hauling mounds of black fabric on his shoulders I remember what I heard at breakfast about how the shlepper boys carry garments-in-progress back and forth between various apartment sweatshops. Hoping this one might lead me to a factory, I speed up and follow him for a few blocks until he drags himself into a multi-story building.

I don't quite reach it before the door closes behind him. But fortunately the front door doesn't have a lock so I can get into the building, and his burden makes him slow enough on the dark steep stairs that I follow him easily up the three flights to where he knocks on a door.

A man opens the door and says, "It's about time you got here, Hyrum," in Yiddish, then takes the fabric from the boy before loading him up again with black garments from a pile inside the door. "See you tomorrow. Earlier tomorrow."

The boy nods and departs, and the man looks up and sees me. "And you? What do *you* want?"

"I'm Rosie Lehrer," I say, feeling more comfortable since I know I can speak Yiddish to him. He doesn't seem kind, but I don't need kindness, I need a job. "I am looking for work. I have been a seamstress since I was six. Do you have a place for me?"

He narrows his eyes and pulls at his long black beard. "What do you make best?"

"Skirts." It's not true, I'm better at waists, but I suspect the boy was carrying away skirts, and I *can* make them. Hoping he believes me, I add, "My mother in Russia trained me."

His eyes narrow further, then he says, "New to America?"

"Yesterday," I say, scared he knows I lied about the skirts but hopeful.

"Very new! Then welcome, and a job you shall have."

My knees feel weak but I don't think he'd like me grabbing the wall of his apartment. "Thank you. Thank you, sir."

"I am Mr. Saltz. And you will be here at eight o'clock tomorrow morning, Rosie," he says, pointing back into the apartment. "And every day but Saturday. Yes?"

"Yes," I say, my heart soaring. I have done it, and all on my own. The first step toward becoming... well, whatever I will become. "Yes. I will be here."

"Good," he says, and closes the door. I hear him telling someone inside, "I've hired a new girl. She starts tomorrow," and a woman answers, "Finally," but I turn and hurry away down the stairs before he comes out again and sees me listening. I don't think he'd like that.

I have done it: I am an American girl with a job, and I will make money!

As I stand blinking after emerging from the dark hallway onto the bright busy street, I realize I forgot to ask how much money. Well, I will find out tomorrow. And even if it's only three or four dollars a week, that is all right for now. Everything is all right. I will work during the day and study English at the home in the evenings, and eventually I will have earned all the money I need and I will bring over my family and we will be happy.

And maybe, if I do *very* well, when I marry the husband my father finds for me I'll be wearing that lovely hat with the red roses.

CHAPTER FOUR

Maria

August 25, 1909

"Is my hair all right? I need to look my best."

Vinnie stares at me, his face blank.

"Well?"

My annoying brother blinks twice. "Sorry," he says in English, not sounding it. "I didn't understand that."

He was the one who decided we would speak only English in America, not me. I hate letting him tell me what to do, but I want to know I'm properly put together before we leave the ship and go to be inspected. I sigh, so he'll know I'm frustrated with him, then say in English, "Do I look all right?"

He smiles. "You look like a girl about to walk on American ground for the first time."

"Yes, but..." I set down Mamma's silver hatpin, which she got from her Mamma when she turned sixteen and which I was delighted to receive on my birthday in April, then slide both hands up over my dirty hair, trying without a mirror to make sure the shorter pieces are tucked into my topknot. The movement brings my sleeves into my line of sight and I gasp at how untidy they are. "My shirtwaist, it's all wrinkled..."

Vinnie takes my hands as I reach to smooth my clothes. "Put on your hat. Don't worry. They know we've been on the ship sixteen days. It's all right. They will let us in."

I'd feel more comforted by his words if I couldn't feel his hands shaking.

Once we've made our slow way with the other passengers up onto the ship's deck, a man pins a slip of paper with the number 18 onto our coats then points toward the gangway where we board a crowded stinking ferry and leave our ship forever.

At least, I hope it's forever.

If we don't pass inspection, we'll be back on the ship and returning to Italy. That *would* get me back to Alonzo, but it's not how he and I want to be reunited.

The ferry docks eventually, and we follow the other passengers, our legs wobbly from being on the ship so long, up the big gray stone steps and into the huge red-brick Ellis Island building where our fitness to be in America will be judged.

Inside, a man in a black suit with gold fabric on the shoulders is pointing in various directions as he calls out, "Men this way, women and children that way, leave your baggage over here."

I stare up at Vinnie, even more terrified. We need to go separately? I want to stay in America with Alonzo until I die, and going through inspection by myself means I might say the wrong thing and be rejected. Or what if *Vinnie* says the wrong thing and I can't help him?

My brother, his face pale as a white marble statue beneath the stubble of the beard he tried to shave off this morning, takes a sharp deep breath and says in English to the man, "My sister and I, we can't stay together? She's so young."

While I don't usually like being called young, I do feel like a frightened child right now, but before I can so much as hope, the man shakes his head. "Men this way," he repeats, "and girls that way."

Vinnie and I lock eyes for one moment, then he raises his chin and says, "Do as he says. I'll meet you at the Kissing Post. After our inspections. We will both pass."

I nod, but I know he doesn't believe his own words because he spoke to me in Italian.

Vinnie nods back, then I turn away and follow the women and children toward the correct stairs, dropping my baggage as I go in the big open room where everyone else is leaving theirs. As we climb the stairs, I see men in black uniforms at the top, watching us take every step. They watch, and sometimes they go to a woman, one who's struggling, when she reaches the top of the stairs and mark something on her shoulder with chalk. I don't know why, but it can't be anything good. I *am* a little out of breath when I reach the top, but I do my best to hide it, and nobody marks me.

Relieved at passing the very first test, I follow the slow-moving line of women and children into a big room where each of us has our eyelids lifted and their undersides examined. I don't know what the man is checking for, but whatever it is, he finds it on the woman before me.

Over her cries, he shouts to another man, and though I can't understand everything because the English is drowned out by the woman's misery, I do hear "hospital". This woman is not going to reach New York City. Not today, and maybe not ever.

The man washes his hands in a bowl of water then beckons me forward. I stand before him, the woman's sobs fading behind me as she's led away, and he gestures at me to raise my face so he can reach my eyes. I do, then have to hold back a gasp as he roughly turns each of my eyelids inside out. I've never felt anything so strange, but fortunately it only lasts a moment on each eye before he nods and waves me forward.

I continue along, blinking to soothe my eyes, and soon my line blends into the line of men as we all sit down on long wooden benches. I look around for Vinnie but cannot see him through the crowd, and if he can see me and is calling me I can't hear him over the babble of voices. I recognize English and Italian, but there must be a thousand other languages as people talk to their neighbors and shout across to those further from them.

I don't shout, and I don't talk. I sit silently, making sure not to breathe through my nose because the stench of so many nervous people who've been on ships without bathing for days or weeks is so strong I almost think I can see it in the air like a great brownish-green cloud, and I think of Alonzo, of his sweet mouth and sweeter words. I will get through this, for him.

I move up a little every time someone at the start of the bench leaves to be interviewed, and eventually, when I'm hungry and tired and have to fare la pipì so badly I'm afraid I'm going to wet myself, it's my turn and a man calls me over to where he sits on a high stool at a tall desk.

I stand before him, with my shoulders back and my head held high so he might not know I'm terrified, and he looks at the number pinned to my coat, shuffles through an untidy stack of papers on his desk, then says something to me. I know it must be English, since it's certainly not Italian, but I can't understand it.

He shakes his head and shouts, "LaGuardia!"

I flinch, not sure what this means, but a short man hurries over to his side and gives the papers on the desk a quick glance before saying something to me in what might be that same language I don't know.

I stare at him, willing myself to somehow make sense of his words.

He looks down at the papers on the man's desk again then pushes aside the top one and points at the next. The man says, "Yes, LaGuardia, yes" with frustration in his voice, and the short one, whose name must be LaGuardia, says in Italian, "Mi scusi, I was looking at the wrong page. You are Maria Cirrito, yes? You are here from Italy?"

Hearing words I understand makes me so excited I can't control myself. "Yes, sir, I'm Maria, and my brother Vinnie is here too and we—"

He raises a hand to stop me. "I have some questions. Are you ready?"

I nod.

I am wrong.

He asks his questions so quickly that even hearing them in Italian I can barely get an answer out before he asks the next.

Are you married?

Have you ever committed a crime?

Are you an anarchist?

How much money do you have?

Do you have a job?

What is your final destination in America?

What are the colors of our flag?

What is the fourth of July?

I do know how to answer them all since Vinnie and I rehearsed the possible questions from letters previous immigrants had sent back to us in Italy, which is good because otherwise I wouldn't know what the fourth of July meant other than the day before the fifth. But I never expected to have to do this without Vinnie, or so quickly that I can't take a moment to be sure I'm saying the right things.

I can hear my voice shaking on my first few answers, but then I realize I am finding the right words, all by myself, and pride fills me.

After several minutes of questions, during which I know I've given all the right answers, the little man turns to the first one and says, in English, "She has done well."

The first man looks me over then nods. "Go down the stairs. Left side for New York City. Wait for your brother down there."

"Thank you," I say, to the short one and then the first one. "Thank you so much."

"You're welcome," Mr. LaGuardia says, giving me a quick smile before hurrying off to help someone else.

The first man raises his eyebrows and stares at me, and I rush to the stairs before he can change his mind about letting me in. Not that he should. I have done well. Mr. LaGuardia said so, and I know it's true. I shouldn't have been so afraid. I always know what to do. I am Papà's principessa, after all.

Down at the bottom of the stairs there are more people milling about, more languages being spoken, but I cannot find Vinnie. I do find a toilet, thankfully, in the area near where the ferry will take the lucky new immigrants over to New York City. But long after I've taken care of that need, I am still alone in the crowd.

I don't know how long I wait, but it's hours after my pride and happiness in myself have faded away, and my feet are aching so much I wish I could sit somewhere. I don't, though. I stand close to the Kissing Post, the spot where newly arrived people meet their relatives who are already in America, and keep my eyes on the staircase where Vinnie will eventually appear.

As I wait, I realize that not everyone coming down the stairs is being allowed into America. Those on the middle stairs are being detained, and the weeping from people waiting at the Kissing Post when they realize their husband or sister is not free to go is unbearable.

What will I do if Vinnie appears on the middle stairs?

He is the one with the strength to go to work digging the subway tunnels. People have sent letters home saying the Americans like to hire Italian men for that because they work hard, and so Vinnie is sure he can get a job quickly. I of course can't do that work. Even the best sewing job won't pay anywhere near as well, so I wouldn't be able to support myself and also earn the money for Alonzo's ticket on my own.

So before Alonzo can arrive, I need Vinnie to, and as I wait and wait my worries grow and grow. My brother is healthy, or at least I always thought so, but maybe the inspectors saw something in him, something bad.

What will happen if—

I see him.

His head bowed.

On the middle staircase.

Feeling as stunned as when I fell off my horse last month, I stare for one long moment until the man raises his head and I realize it's not Vinnie.

Relief makes me so dizzy I have to sit down right on the floor, and that is when my brother does appear, on the same staircase I took.

"Vinnie," I cry, jumping to my feet and running up to him. "Oh, Vinnie!"

For the first time I can remember, he grabs me in a hug. "I was scared for you," he admits in Italian. "So scared."

"Me too, for you," I mumble, squeezing him tight.

We hold each other for a moment, then he clears his throat and pushes himself back from me. "Well, enough of this," he says in English, sounding happier than he has since we left home. "Let's go see New York City!"

CHAPTER FIVE

Rosie
August 24, 1909

I MAKE MY EXHAUSTED EYES FOCUS ON MR. SALTZ. "Not fast enough? But—"

"You should have been able to baste together at least thirteen dozen skirts today and you only managed eight. I can't have you taking so long. You make them perfect and there's no reason to do that. The other girls do big stitches, just enough to hold the pieces together until they can be machine-sewn somewhere else. Why can't you be like them?"

My boss of one day gestures at the other five basters squished into the tiny living room with us, all girls my age or younger looking down as if afraid he'll turn on them next.

He doesn't. Instead he holds out a few coins to me. "Be faster tomorrow."

I take the money and total up the unfamiliar values as quickly as I can.

Twenty-five cents.

He told me when I arrived that I would be paid five cents per dozen skirts. "Sir, I will, but since I finished eight dozen skirts should I not have..." Seeing his sudden fury, I trail off.

"You think I owe you more, do you? What about the thread you used? And the needle, and the gas for the lamp you turned up twice, don't think I didn't see it, and the bread and coffee I gave you for lunch? You... you *shtunk*!"

"I'm not an ungrateful person," I say quickly, hoping to calm him. "I'm not. I'm very sorry. Twenty-five cents is fine for today and tomorrow I will do better."

"Tomorrow you will be somewhere else! I need you like a hole in the head, little girl, so go away and make some other boss miserable. Go on, get out."

Horrified, I obey before he can think to demand the money back from me, rushing out of the apartment then down the steep stairs and out onto the nearly dark street. I don't know how late it is, but the mantel clock chimed eight while I was still working away at the pile of skirts, so it's no wonder my eyes hurt.

But they don't hurt as much as my heart.

I thought I would be a valued employee right away because I know so much about sewing. But I made the skirts too perfect. Mr. Saltz warned me about it at lunch so I tried to go faster, but even that wasn't enough. My mother wouldn't believe there's such a thing as too-perfect work: almost every day she made me go back and correct some tiny mistake I could barely see. The stitches I made today, she'd have been furious at how huge they were. Perfectly even and tiny stitches, that's what she insisted on. But here in America, I need to be fast not perfect.

Can I do that?

And *where* will I do that? Does it matter that Mr. Saltz made me leave? Will he tell other employers? Am I in trouble now? If a Jewish man won't treat me properly, will any employer? Have I ruined my family's hopes on my second full day in America?

I plan to ask these questions of Julia once I have dragged my sad self home, but I don't get further than telling her who had fired me today and how little he'd paid me.

She laughs. "You picked *him* of all the bosses you could have?"

Yesterday, I was so excited about finding a job that I'd grinned at her and said she didn't need to worry about me because I had taken care of myself. Now, I feel like a fool.

Her eyes soften and she stops laughing, instead giving me a gentle smile. "You're lucky he gave you twenty-five cents, you know. I've seen him keep more than half a girl's wages for his expenses. Don't worry, it doesn't matter a lick. Tomorrow I will take you to a factory, a real one not a tenement sweatshop, and we'll find you a job you can keep for more than a day."

I AM AFRAID JULIA WILL TAKE ME TO THE IMPERIAL FACTORY, where I was told to learn English first, but she leads me past it without slowing. She shows me good places to shop, and places to avoid because they're too expensive, as we walk a few blocks along Grand Street toward the elevated train station at the Bowery. I'm pleased to see that she thinks the peddler I met yesterday is a fair woman.

"I bought the white waist I wore the day I met you from her."

"I thought so, she offered me the same one in blue. Once I'm making money, I'll go buy something from her," I say, wondering if I really will.

"You should. You deserve a little treat."

My parents don't believe in treats, but I fell asleep dreaming of that pretty belt so... "But I need to send my money home."

"Well, of course, but a few cents here and there for a treat, it's not too much." She gives my arm a squeeze. "It's good to do what you ought to do, but it's also good to be kind to yourself sometimes."

I've heard variations on the first part of that sentiment often, but never the second. Is it true? Is it all right to spend a little of my earnings, once I'm at a good job, on myself?

Before I can decide, Julia pulls me over to a pushcart. "Speaking of treats, we must have a knish."

"But we just had breakfast!"

"I know, but you can't miss out, Rosie. Nobody makes them quite like Mr. Schimmel," she says, smiling at the man busily gathering our balls of baked dough from the depths of his cart.

"True," he says, handing us each a knish and accepting Julia's dime in payment before nodding to us and moving on to the next customer.

Julia was right. The outer crust is perfectly browned and the mashed-potato filling inside is hot and delicious. I try to pay Julia the nickel I owe her but she refuses, so I insist on paying her train fare so my debt is repaid.

The elevated train, which Julia says I must call "the El" like an American, rattles along above the roads, and I peer down at the various shops and factories as we pass them.

"What's happening there?" I say, pointing at a part of the road that seems to be a big pit with boards across it.

"Men are putting subway tunnels underneath the road."

I turn to stare at her, sure she's joking or I've misunderstood her English.

She nods. "I know, but they really are. They dig a huge ditch in the road and put boards across it so it still can be a road, and underneath they build a tunnel and connect it to the other tunnels."

I twist around on the yellow woven horsehair fabric of the bench to see as we begin to leave the pit behind. "That must be so much work! And so dangerous too. If the boards collapsed... how can they do that day after day?"

She shrugs. "They get two dollars or even more a day, and I suppose they get strong after a while. I wouldn't want to do it, though."

I shake my head, glad I'll be working at a garment factory. Sewing for hours at a time is hard on the neck and the eyes, but at least I don't have to worry about being killed.

We leave the El at Eighteenth Street and walk over to Seventeenth and Fifth Avenue. Julia makes sure I notice the direction we turn after leaving the station and the various street signs as we go along, so that

I will be able to travel on my own today after work and for as long as I keep this job.

Of course. I don't *have* the job yet, so after we enter the factory I am nervous as we stand before a Jewish man in his thirties and Julia explains that I am new to America and looking for a job.

"Rosie's very good, Mr. Rosenthal," Julia finishes, nodding as if she has seen me sew and can't imagine anyone else could do it better.

He runs his eyes over me. "If you say so, Julia, then it must be. Well, girl? Come over here and show me how you'd assemble a waist."

I follow him to a small table and demonstrate how I would put together the pieces of thin white fabric, explaining in Yiddish because my English isn't good enough yet for all the technical terms of basting and sewing and finishing, and when I am done he nods at Julia and says, "She'll do, I think. I'll give her a trial." Then he turns to me. "If I decide to keep you you'll need to join the union since we're a union shop. Your dues will be $1.35 per year, but they only take ten cents now and the rest in installments. That's not a problem, is it?"

"Union shop?" I don't know what that means.

"She's all right with it," Julia assures him, and I nod since she must know what's best for me.

"And you'll work Saturdays, yes? We're closed Sundays unless we're very busy but we do work Saturdays."

I can hear my father's voice telling me to say no, but I take a deep breath and say, "Yes, Mr. Rosenthal." Finding a job on my own didn't work out, even though it was with a Jewish man, so I will take this one though my father would disapprove.

I want it to feel good, choosing what I want. I want to feel strong. But instead I feel as nervous as if I were standing before him saying, "Tateh, I *have* to take the job, even working Saturdays. And Mr. Rosenthal is Jewish after all, as you wanted, and—"

My new boss's voice interrupts my thoughts. "Well, you might as well start now." He points at an empty chair in one of the long rows of girls who sit feeding white fabric through sewing machines. "The forelady will get you something to work on."

"Yes, sir," I say, but I don't move. I don't want another situation as I had with Mr. Saltz.

He raises his eyebrows. "Something wrong, girl?"

Though my knees are shaking, I say, "I was just wondering, sir, about my pay. Is it by the piece or—"

Julia grabs my arm and says quickly, "Never mind, Mr. Rosenthal, I will explain it all to her. She's very new to America."

He frowns at me, says, "Fine, but hurry," and stalks off.

Julia shakes her head. "Do as you're told, Rosie! You can ask questions later, of the other girls at lunch time or at the home, but never of the contractors, and certainly never of the boss if you meet him."

If... "Isn't Mr. Rosenthal my boss?"

"He's a contractor," she says, speaking so fast it's hard to understand her even in Yiddish. "He works for Mr. Leiserson who owns this factory. *He's* the real boss, and remember that if you see him you keep your head down and you keep quiet."

"I will," I say, confused by her anger and wishing I hadn't tried to stand up for myself. "Is Mr. Leiserson a bad man?"

"No, but he's the *boss*. Bosses don't care about you and they never will unless you make them, and if they care it will be bad for you, so you don't want them to notice you. Do as Mr. Rosenthal tells you and you will be all right."

"Why couldn't I ask about the pay?"

"He doesn't know yet," she says, starting to walk toward my waiting chair so I follow her. "It will depend on how well you work and on how much the bosses are paying him for each bundle of waists."

Puzzling this out, I say, "So if he gets twenty dollars a bundle..."

"More like ten, probably, and out of that he might use eight or so to pay his girls. Depending on what they're worth to him. He'll decide what you're worth on Saturday."

I frown. "So until then I work for free?"

"No, on Saturday he will tell you how much you'll get, and on the next Saturday you'll be paid for the work you did this week. So you'll always be a week behind but you'll be paid every week, whatever he says is fair." She pushes me down into the chair. "Which will be nothing if you keep talking! Now, goodbye and I will see you tonight. You can get yourself home, right?"

"Yes," I say, looking up at her. I didn't get the chance to find out what a union shop is, but I'll ask her tonight. "And thank you. And I will be quiet."

She gives me an 'I hope so' nod, then her face softens and she flashes me a smile before leaving me alone with girls I've never met.

"Hello, I'm Rosie," I say quietly, in English. Surely greeting the others is all right?

Their heads dart in my direction, but they look away back to their sewing machines when Mr. Rosenthal shouts, "Quiet and work!"

So we are and we do. I sit for hours, hearing only the steady growl of the sewing machines, as I fold and seam sleeves and attach them to the already-sewn bodices of waists. At least with Mr. Saltz I worked on all parts of the skirt, though it was only basting. I could have done this sleeve work when I was eight years old so I am soon bored, but I make sure I do good but not perfect work and as much of it as I can.

At the end of the day, Mr. Rosenthal comes to see what I have finished. He checks my seven dozen waists with sleeves neatly but not perfectly attached, and his eyebrows rise. "Well, Rosie, you might be more than just a pretty face." He gives my shoulder a squeeze then runs his hand down my arm. "I will see what you can do tomorrow."

His touch makes me feel awkward and uncomfortable, but I force myself to smile. I know, from the tiny bits of conversation the other girls and I managed to share at lunch and in the moments when he was too far away to hear, that he often takes liberties with the girls. If all he does is touch my arm, I will be all right.

If I'm lucky, that's all he will want to do.

CHAPTER SIX

Maria
August 28, 1909

"WAKE UP. MARIA, WAKE UP. MARIA!"

Vinnie's voice eventually becomes so loud that I can't pretend I'm still sleeping, and I open one eye and mutter, "Why?"

"We have to start working, so you need to go with Margherita to get your job."

No part of this sentence appeals to me. "What time is it?"

"Time to get up."

I roll my eyes and push myself up to sit on the middle one of the three hard wooden chairs whose seats I used as a bed. A terrible bed.

Mamma called it lucky that my parents' old friends the Billotas moved to New York last year with their two children and could take us in as boarders for only five dollars a week, but it doesn't seem lucky to me. Their fourth-floor apartment is tiny, with only a small bedroom and kitchen and an even smaller parlor, and my shock at seeing such a cramped place when I had my own bedroom back in Italy grew even more when I found out they already had two boarders.

The Billotas use the only bed and the bedroom themselves, their daughter sleeps on the parlor's small couch and their son in its only armchair, and the boarders usually sleep on the floor on thin mattresses but have been spending the nights two floors up on the roof because the weather is so hot.

I wanted to sleep outside too, to get even a little fresh air instead of the stink of all the people inside, but Vinnie said it's not the right place for a girl and Mr. Billota glared at me when I took a breath to argue. So Vinnie and I made do with the chairs.

I didn't come to America to sleep on chairs.

"Vinnie, I don't want to live here. I want a home for just us. A *good* home."

"Shh," he whispers, frowning at me. "Don't be rude. We'll have a better home, some day. When we have more money. But we can't have money without jobs. We've had two full days to relax in America, and now it's time to work."

Those days weren't relaxing, not to me. I was so tired from the trip I wanted to sleep all day, but Mrs. Billota insisted on showing me how to use her sewing machine so I'd know how for my job. She made me help with the dishes and the cooking too. Since we're paying, shouldn't we be treated as guests?

But even that was more relaxing than getting up this early. On Thursday and Friday everyone leaving for work woke us up, but Mrs. Billota let me and Vinnie sleep a little longer once they'd gone. No more, though. Now we must leave with them. I'll be at work by eight every day but Sunday, and I really don't want to even for Alonzo. Though I'm sure I'll get plenty of breaks during the day, it's still going to be tiring. And I don't like to be tired.

I sigh, knowing there's no point in telling any of this to Vinnie because he won't care.

"Don't *sigh*, Maria. Just get ready for work."

I roll my eyes at him then tip my head from one side to the other to stretch my neck as he turns on the kitchen sink's faucet. The water takes a moment to arrive but then he's able to dip his hands into the stream and splash his face.

I giggle at the gasp he can't hold back as the water hits his skin, and he rubs his face dry with a cloth then turns to me with a mock glare and says, "You think you can handle the cold better than me? Get over here."

I turn out to be no better, gasping as he did.

"Told you," he says with a chuckle.

"Do you think," I say after I've scrubbed off the water, "there will ever be hot water in an apartment, coming from the faucet, instead of only ice cold?"

He shrugs. "I don't like to think too far ahead, you know that. For now, there's cold, and even if there is hot someday, there won't be any for us if we don't make money."

I nod, but I can't help imagining a home, a home for me and Alonzo and our children, and a beautiful kitchen far larger than this tiny cramped one, with hot and cold water in it and in a proper bath room. No tub in the kitchen corner for us then, like there is here.

But I'll need to work to earn money before that can happen. Last night, as the eight of us sat on the fire escape to get a little air before bed, the Billotas' daughter Margherita, a pretty girl who's sixteen too but seems older because she's so confident and so much more American than me, told me about working at the Bijou waist factory. She promised me other Italian girls to talk to and fun walks in the nearby park at lunch and work I could do sitting down instead of the hard labor ahead of Vinnie, and it doesn't sound all that horrible.

But I still don't *want* a job. Not yet, anyhow.

Nobody but Papà is ever concerned with what I want, though, and he's not here to help me, so I give in. Margherita and I dress with her mother in the tiny bedroom while Margherita's brother and father and Vinnie and the two boarder men wait in the hall outside the apartment for their turn to use one of the two toilets on our floor. Then Margherita's mother starts water boiling for coffee and we girls use the toilets while the men dress. We *could* walk down the four flights of stairs to use the privies outside then walk all the way back up, but naturally everyone prefers the indoor flush toilets.

Once we've all eaten our breakfast of a small hard roll and a cup of black coffee, Vinnie gives me a few coins for the trolley and for my lunch and says, "Be good, all right?"

"When am I not?" I glare at him as he snickers. I wasn't trying to be funny. "You be quiet. Oh, and good luck getting a job."

"You too," he says, though Margherita has assured us I won't have any trouble. "And behave yourself after work."

I roll my eyes, and Margherita laughs and says, "Don't worry, Vinnie, I'll take good care of her."

"That's what I'm worried about," Vinnie mumbles, but he smiles at her then leaves with Mr. Billota and the men to get a job on their work crew building subways. They won't be back until eight o'clock or even later tonight, but Margherita and I will be done by six because it's Saturday. My day will be shorter than Vinnie's, but it's still a longer work day than I want to do or have ever done before.

Though I'm not interested in working, I find myself excited as Margherita and I ride the trolley several blocks to the factory. I look around in all directions, seeing restaurants and tenement buildings like ours and shops of every description, but though I enjoy seeing new things I am still disappointed that the streets aren't actually paved in gold like everyone said back home. Maybe they only are in the richer neighborhoods. It's still all new and different, though, and I squeeze my hands together against my chest and imagine someday showing it to Alonzo. When he arrives he will be impressed by how much I know and so happy to have me as his wife.

But I need money for that, and getting a job is the only way I can get that money. So after Margherita has rung the bell to stop the trolley and we're standing before the Bijou factory building, my nerves make me hang back from the crowd of girls trying to get inside. What if Margherita's wrong and the bosses won't hire me?

"Stay with me," she says, looking over her shoulder in aggravation. "If we're even a minute later than eight they won't let us in, and I don't want to lose that pay."

I rush forward, ignoring the complaints I hear from the girls behind as I pass them, and ask Margherita, "They won't let us in if we're late?"

"If we're later than eight we don't get to start work until noon. As punishment."

I nod, but not having to work doesn't seem like punishment.

We shuffle forward several steps, then wait, then shuffle again, and I am about to ask why when we get inside the building and I realize we are taking an elevator. I've never been in one before, and my excitement about trying something so new wipes away my fear.

The elevator full of girls buzzes with conversation. Some is in Italian, and I hear talk of moving pictures and vaudeville shows and places called "Coney" and "Steeplechase", all of which sound wonderfully exciting. I don't recognize the other languages around us, but Margherita leans in and whispers, "We have Italians here, of course, and a few American girls, but mostly it's Jewish girls from Russia. They'll probably make you sit beside one."

I turn to her, but before I can ask why they would do that, the elevator jerks to a stop, the operator opens its doors, and we pour out.

My nervousness returns as Margherita leads me up to a man standing, with his arms folded, studying the girls as they take their seats.

"Mr. Berger, I have a friend with me who needs a job," she says to him in English, her voice meek and sweet instead of her usual brisk tone. "This is Maria Cirrito. She's a wonderful worker. Very quiet and careful."

"Is that so?" He turns to me. "You speak English, girl?"

I nod. "My brother and I learned together."

"And did you also learn together to sew?"

I can't hold back a giggle at the thought of Vinnie sewing, and he smiles at me as I say, "No, sir, but I can sew by hand, I embroider very well, and I know a little how to use a machine." A very little: only what Margherita's mother has taught me since I arrived. She doesn't go out to work, instead making money at home by keeping boarders like us and by assembling skirts on her machine. I will probably do the same when Alonzo comes, because men seem to want their wives to stay at home.

"A little," he says, narrowing his eyes at me. "A little you know? Well, I'll give you a try. Because of Margherita. But if you don't work well, out you go."

"Yes," I say, since this is obvious. "Thank you, Mr. Berger."

"You can sit beside Margherita today," he says, his tone like he is granting me a huge favor. "She will show you how to sew sleeves. But after today, you do it alone. I won't have you girls sitting together and chatting."

I realize that the room has indeed become silent except for the roar of sewing machines. We might not be able to chat over that sound even if we wanted to, but clearly it is not allowed. That must be why Margherita thought he'd put me beside a Russian girl: unless she speaks English we couldn't talk.

We thank him again, and he points out two chairs for us then grabs two bundles of fabric from a box and hands one to each of us before walking away.

When we've settled into our chairs and unwrapped our bundles, Margherita's is of sewn-up sleeves and almost-completed waists to attach them to. Mine turns out to be of strangely-shaped pieces of fabric. I point at them. "What do I do with—"

"No talking," a woman says behind me, making me jump.

"Sorry, Anna, but Mr. Berger said I could teach my friend today," Margherita says.

"All right," the woman says, sounding like it's all wrong. "But only today. And whisper."

We both nod and the woman walks away. Her shoes have rubber soles, I realize, so she can creep up on us quietly, like Alonzo's stable cat slinking around on its soft feet.

"Anna is the forelady," Margherita whispers in Italian. "We all hate her. Anyhow, give me one of those."

I do, and she quickly folds it to show me that it makes a sleeve. After whispering instructions on how to use the sewing machine and how not to sew the sleeve together inside out, she does one to show me. She pushes down on the foot pedal attached to a huge bar running the length of the table, her hands guide the sleeve forward toward the fast-moving needle and then under it, and then the sewn sleeve passes right through and into a trough at the middle of the table. She breaks off the thread, leaving a few inches dangling from the fabric, then tosses the sleeve into my area of the trough. "All right," she whispers. "Your turn."

"Don't you have to trim the thread?"

She shakes her head. "They hire little children to do that. They're not supposed to but they do. Try a sleeve."

My first few are not very well done, but then I begin to understand how fast to push the fabric through and exactly the kind of curve I need to make to keep the seam the right distance from the edge.

And then I am bored.

I wish I could talk to Margherita to keep myself entertained, but instead I let myself think about Alonzo, his hands and his mouth and the feel of his body on mine, and I dream up every detail of the home we will have. A whole apartment to ourselves, with real leather wallpaper in the hallway like rich people have instead of the red-painted burlap that imitates it in the Billotas' building's halls. A comfortable bed we share instead of sleeping on chairs. And of course, hot and cold running water. Our children can share a room, at first, but once Alonzo gets a job...

What will he do? I can't imagine him digging subway tunnels as Vinnie must be doing right now, he's too elegant for that, and he obviously can't sew with me. Could he maybe have a restaurant like Papà does? No, he wouldn't like being on his feet all day. Maybe he could be a—

"Maria!"

I jump, and Margherita says, "Mr. Berger is talking to you. Pay attention!"

How long has he been standing beside me? I have no idea. He will be furious.

Instead, to my surprise, he is chuckling. "I like a girl who focuses on her work. And how is that work?" He picks up the last sleeve I did and examines it. "A good start, Maria." He drops the sleeve back into the trough. "For a learner. I'll pay you three dollars per week."

"Thank you, sir," I say. I'd like more, but Margherita told me this factory always starts new girls at that rate so I am not surprised. I'll be a learner until Mr. Berger thinks I know enough to be paid by the piece.

He nods and leaves, and Margherita whispers, "Just two and a half hours until lunch."

And then another five after lunch! Is this what it is to be in America? All day spent inside sewing sleeves? No breaks until lunch? Vinnie's lucky to be outside in the air and sunlight, not trapped indoors like me.

I don't want to sigh in case the forelady is again nearby, so I nod and go back to working and dreaming of how I'll spend my earnings for Alonzo.

WHEN AT LAST MR. BERGER CLAPS HIS HANDS AND SHOUTS, "The day is done, girls," my neck is stiff and my eyes are dry and I can't imagine how I'll come back here day after day and work even longer than I did today. We only got one break, and that wasn't even an hour long, and being forced to sit still all day does not suit me at all.

Margherita, though, couldn't be more bright and happy if she'd spent all day resting on the softest of beds, and the other workers seem the same.

"So lovely to finish early, isn't it? And tomorrow off! What now, girls?" Margherita looks around at the others as we take the elevator back down.

"Steeplechase," a pretty blonde says, and several others agree at once.

Margherita glances at me. "How much money did Vinnie give you?"

I check my pocketbook. "After buying lunch, I've got twelve cents left."

She grimaces and shakes her head. "It costs ten, and you need five for the trolley. Maria can't go. A nickelodeon, maybe?"

The blonde girl says, "No, I want Steeplechase," and three others nod.

"Well, Fanny, you and the others go there then," Margherita says, her tone cold. "I'm going with Maria. Anyone else?"

Two other girls, both Italians, agree to go with us, and the groups separate once we're outside without saying goodbye.

Margherita gives a disgusted snort, and another of our girls says in our shared language, "She's at that amusement park every chance she gets, that one. And she's not paying for it herself. Treating's all well and good, but a different man every day?"

The other two agree, and I say, "Treating?"

"You fresh off the boat?"

Margherita laughs. "She is, Rosita, she is. Maria and her older brother arrived this week."

"Sorry," Rosita says, not sounding it, and Margherita turns to me and says, "When you get a man to buy you a meal or a show ticket or maybe even a new coat, that's treating. Girls can get more than they can afford, that way."

"But why does the man buy all those—"

I cut myself off, realizing too late what the men receive in return for their money, and the girls laugh.

Rosita wraps her arm around my waist. "Get it now, Maria? You're probably too young to know anything about men, but—"

"I'm not," I say, indignant. "I have a man back home, and he'll be here soon."

They urge me to tell them all about it, and since I love talking about Alonzo I don't hold back.

When I finish, Margherita says, "He sounds handsome, Maria. I look forward to meeting him when he arrives."

She and Rosita exchange a quick look, which I don't understand but which seems mocking, and I'm about to ask about it when the other girl says, "And your brother? Is he handsome?"

I take a breath to say of course he isn't when Margherita says, "Oh, yes. Handsome and smart and a hard worker. Tall, with the same brown eyes as Maria but his hair is a little lighter brown. And I met him first, Lucia, don't forget."

Lucia rolls her eyes and says, "Maybe I'll meet a man at the nickelodeon. But first, should we get some food?"

The others agree, and I do too although I'm shocked by what Margherita said. Vinnie *is* a hard worker, but handsome? I've never thought so. But then, he's my brother.

Margherita looks around then leads us to a peddler holding a metal tub on his head and shouting, "Pizza here, two cents a slice!"

Munching on a not-so-hot but still tasty slice of pizza with tomato, oregano, garlic, and extra virgin olive oil, I walk along with the others debating whether the marinara pizza Margherita and I have or the margherita pizza of Rosita and Lucia is better.

We don't find an answer, although it's hard to argue with Rosita's belief that mozzarella improves everything. But regardless of which pizza is the best, we're all full and happy when we begin to hear a man yelling. His voice is strangely loud, which confuses me, but when we get closer I realize he's holding some sort of machine in front of his mouth to make his words carry better.

"Five cents, just five cents, for an hour's entertainment! Come on in and watch the show!"

We don't go in, though. I'm ready to, but the other three stand on the road in front of the small theatre and look around like they're waiting for someone to arrive.

"What are we doing?" I whisper to Margherita.

She shakes her head and smiles past me.

Turning to see where she's sending that bright smile, I see a group of four young Italian men approaching us. They wear black suits and white shirts, and have their hats tipped down over one eye, but none is as handsome as my Alonzo.

"Girls, interested in seeing the show with us?"

Rosita blinks up at one of the men as Lucia and Margherita move toward two of the others. "That would be lovely, thank you."

She and her chosen man walk to the ticket seller and I notice that he pays for her. Lucia heads off too with her man, and Margherita starts to then looks back at me. "Well?"

I look from her to the remaining man and back again, shocked. They explained treating, but I didn't expect to see it happen right in front of me. "I... Alonzo... he wouldn't like..."

"If you've got a fella already," the man says to me, "never mind," and before I can answer he walks over to another group of girls and is soon escorting one of them inside.

Margherita shakes her head. "Oh, Maria. You have so much to learn." To her man she says, "She only arrived this week. And Alonzo is her brother, not a fella. Poor girl, she knows nothing."

I want to protest this and also deny that Alonzo's my brother but I don't get the chance because the man is saying, "Well, then, to welcome Maria to America, might I treat you both to the show? Just this once, of course."

Margherita slips her arm through his. "Of course, and how kind of you," she says, and before I know it, I am sitting in the pitch-dark theatre with the three girls and their new men.

We walked in at the end of an illustrated song, but its last picture is removed from the screen as its final notes die out. After a brief pause for the attendants to spray the air with water scented of fresh-cut flowers to cut down on the stink of so many people crowded together in the August heat, a moving picture starts up.

We're soon all howling with laughter at it, watching as the men on screen become increasingly furious about women with huge hats sitting in front of them blocking their view of their own screen. But when a strange grasping metal clamp comes down and lifts the hat right off one woman's head, I stop laughing and stare in confusion. How could that happen? I've never seen such a—

The clamp returns and picks up a whole woman!

The others clap and cheer, but I can't help nudging Margherita and saying, "Will that happen here?"

"What?"

"Will that clamp come and—" I shiver. "I don't want to be carried away."

She bursts out laughing, then turns away and I hear her telling her man I'm afraid of the clamp. He leans around her toward me, slipping his arm around her shoulders as he does, and says to me, "It's all make-believe, Maria. Don't worry, little girl."

Margherita laughs once more then cuddles into the man as he leans back into his own seat without removing his arm from her shoulders.

Her laughter hurts my feelings. I've just never seen a moving picture like this before, one with things that aren't real. I'm not a little girl, either. I'm the same age as Margherita, and in love with Alonzo. Why does nobody take me seriously?

I pout for a bit, but since nobody seems to notice, I give it up and watch the rest of the films, singing along with the Italian songs between them when I know them. I'm shocked, though, that

Margherita lets her man kiss her a few times, right on the mouth. She just met him!

Alonzo, far more handsome than any of these men, would be able to convince a girl he just met to let him kiss her even more easily.

My stomach clenches around the pizza I ate, and I take deep breaths and try to calm myself. Yes, he *could*. But he wouldn't. He loves me, and we will be together.

I don't like working so many hours, but I will. For him. Then he will be here with me.

And I will never have to be treated by a strange man again.

CHAPTER SEVEN

Rosie
August 28, 1909

ON SATURDAY AT NOON, MR. ROSENTHAL COMES TO ME and draws me away from the other girls. "You did well this week, Rosie." He runs his hand down my arm then takes my hand in his. "Very well. I'm glad to have you here."

I'm not sure I'm glad to be here, since he's been touching me like this every day and I don't know how to stop him.

But when he adds, "I've decided to keep you on and pay you four dollars a week. And if you continue to be a good girl, if you're good to me, I might be able to give you a raise soon," I make myself smile at him and say, "Thank you, Mr. Rosenthal."

He pats my cheek, while I try not to flinch, then releases my hand and walks away.

Four dollars. It's not wonderful, but at least it's more than I would have managed to earn with Mr. Saltz.

The money I must send my parents to repay my trip to America comes to mind. At four dollars a week, it would take me over twelve weeks even if I sent every last penny I earn, and I can't do that or I won't be able to pay for my lodging or trolley fares or lunches once my original ten dollars runs out.

Julia told me to go after work today to get an account at the Jarmulowsky Bank, from which I can send money and also letters to my parents. The one I wrote last night to let them know I arrived safely is in my pocketbook to be mailed today. I can't send any money yet since I haven't been paid, but I know with my next letter they'll expect me to receive everything I don't need to survive.

But how am I to know what I need to survive? I haven't even been here a week yet.

Send it all? Send nothing? Send a single dollar until I know how much I need? All the options feel wrong, and I wish I could ask my parents for advice without waiting weeks for a reply. I'll ask Julia later, but no matter what I end up doing, I'll be better off if Mr. Rosenthal does decide to give me a raise.

The words "if you're good to me" rise in my mind, and I wonder what he meant. I am good. I have been careful to work quickly while also doing a nearly perfect job. Not perfect, because perfect is too slow, but close. I've been on time every day and I don't slip out early like some girls do. I'm even working Saturdays, though I know my parents would be unhappy with that. What else could Mr. Rosenthal want from me?

I turn toward the dressing room to pick up my hat and pocketbook, and see him in a corner with a pretty girl who'd been working near me. She giggles as he fiddles with the lace at the neck of her waist, twisting away from him but not so far as to stop him.

I look away, feeling sick inside. Is that what would make him call me good? If I let him touch me or do whatever he wants to me?

Not *whatever*. There are things no unmarried girl should do. But a touch here and a tickle there? Is that what it takes to——

An elbow digs into my side and I jump.

"Sorry," Clara says, a smile in her voice. "Were you sleeping?"

I smile back, remembering how we and the other Jewish girls were joking at lunch yesterday about all putting our heads down on our tables at the same time to take a nap, laughing at how angry Mr. Rosenthal would be if we did. "Not by myself, I wasn't. I'm not that brave."

She chuckles. "You mean you're not that foolish." She waves her pay envelope at me. "He must have told you what you'll earn. Are you happy?"

I shrug. Clara works as a draper, turning a designer's idea for a waist into a pattern by cutting and shaping fabric on a tailor's dummy, and with such a skilled job she certainly earns far more than I do. My pay would seem pathetic to her.

"It will get better," she says. "As you get more experience and show what you can do. At least it's a union shop. Could be worse."

"How could it be worse? He's giving me only four dollars. I thought unions made sure their employees got paid well." That's what Julia told me when I asked.

She smiles. "Well, it *is* part of what we do. But remember, you're done at noon today while most shops work until six on Saturdays, and you didn't lose pay for your thread or anything else you used. Mr. Leiserson promised us he would only hire union workers, and that makes this one of the fairest shops around. Only four dollars now, yes, but soon you'll earn more, and in these conditions too."

I nod, feeling embarrassed for not thinking of all that. I knew other girls at the home had to work later today, but I didn't know that was because they're not in the union. I'll add a note about this to my letter: if my parents know anything of unions, they'll be pleased to learn I have such a good job.

Clara starts toward the dressing room and I go with her as she adds, "What are your plans for the rest of the day?"

"There's an English lesson at my home this afternoon, and then I thought I'd study a little, maybe go for a walk, then go to bed early." It sounds boring after my long days of work this week, although I really am tired, and I wish I had plans to do something more exciting like go back to the nickelodeon Julia took me to last night.

But Clara nods approvingly. "Good girl. The more English we know, the better. Although the union runs in Yiddish mostly, so you'll have no troubles there. I have a union meeting tonight, in fact, at seven. Do you want to come with me?"

I like Clara, who is a few years older than me but fun to be with, so I want to say yes. But I'm sure the whole meeting will be men talking and girls listening and I don't want to do that. "Thank you, but I won't today," I say in English. "I need to study."

"Studying is good," she says back in English, with less of an accent than me. "Unions are good too."

I smile at her, then stare as she puts on a hat that makes the one I saw in that window look like something you'd find on the street behind the horses. "Your hat is beautiful."

She grins and pats the cluster of pink roses atop its brim. "Thank you. I saved up and bought it just last week. We have to be responsible but we also have to have a little fun sometimes. Right?"

"Right," I say, promising myself to work hard at my English and at my sewing so I can get better pay and afford a hat like hers.

Guilt sweeps me, and I add to my promise in my head, "And so I can send more money home."

We leave the building with a crowd of other girls, and none of them have working hard on their minds. Clara is invited to a vaudeville show, more nickelodeons than I can count, and a place called Coney Island within moments. I'm not invited directly, but the girls smile in my direction and I'm sure I can go along if I want to.

And I *do* want to, but before I can agree to any of the invitations Clara says, "Rosie and I are going to be good students today, I'm afraid. She's working on her English and I have a great stack of union reading to do before tonight's meeting. But you girls go and have fun."

The girls give me looks that say they know they should be learning English instead of wasting their afternoons in fun, and I give them one back that says I wish I were going with them.

They feel flighty, and I feel boring.

Is no girl ever happy with the decisions she makes for herself?

AS I NEAR MY HOME AFTER OPENING MY BANK ACCOUNT and sending my letter, I have convinced myself that spending the rest of the day in learning and studying is a good use of my time, and not only because I don't want to go back to work on Monday and tell Clara that I wasted my day. To be someone who can earn more than four dollars a week, I must put aside foolishness and work hard.

Feeling proud of that decision, I walk up the front steps of the home and am nearly knocked over by Julia and a group of giddy girls rushing out the door.

"Oh, Rosie, I'm so glad you're here," Julia says, grabbing my arm to keep me from falling. "We're going to Steeplechase! You know, the amusement part? I was hoping you'd make it back before we left."

"I... what about the English class? I was going to go there then spend my day studying."

"We'll practice as we go," Julia promises. "Don't you want to have some fun?"

"I do," I admit, and fall in with them, vowing to myself that I will put aside foolishness tomorrow. Or Monday.

We do indeed speak English nearly all the way, and the others sing a few English songs too though I don't know the words, as we walk to the trolley then take the El to Ninth Avenue and Forty-Second Street where we pick up the steamboat that will take us around Manhattan and to Coney Island. But we have to return to Yiddish when Yetta asks me, "Why were you going to study all day? Don't you deserve a rest?" and I can't find the English words to explain about Clara and how she inspired me with her union talk to study hard.

"Clara? You can't mean Clara Lemlich? You *know* her?"

I'm surprised that a girl who doesn't work at Leiserson's has heard of Clara, then even more surprised when I nod and everyone begins asking me what she's like.

"How," I say when I manage to break through their chatter, "do you all know about Clara?"

Yetta says, "Everyone knows about her. She's one of the highest-ranking girls, no, *people*, in the union. Our union, Local 25."

"Highest-ranking? More than some of the men? But surely the men wouldn't listen to her." I've never known men to listen to girls.

The others laugh, and Yetta says, "Oh, they do, because she doesn't give them a choice. I've seen even big men back down when she has something to say."

"But she's tiny!"

"Tiny but determined," Yetta says, and the others agree.

I ponder this the rest of the way and while we sit on a park bench and eat hot dogs before heading into Steeplechase Park. Little Clara, barely five feet tall, is important in the union? I thought nobody would listen to a girl like her, like me, but it sounds like everyone does. Maybe I should be going to the meeting with her tonight after all.

It's too late for that, though. I have spent my five cents to get to Coney Island and another three for my hot dog, and so I might as well pay for Steeplechase and walk in under the huge "ten hours of fun for ten cents" sign and see exactly how much fun I can have for ten cents.

Within an hour, I've already had more than ten cents' worth. We start fairly calmly with the Ferris Wheel, but soon the Human Roulette Wheel spins us around and flings us out into a pit of sand, the Dew Drop sends us shrieking down a steep twisty slide until we topple out at the bottom in a tangle of arms and legs, and both Julia and I have fallen off the Razzle-Dazzle because we couldn't keep our balance sitting on the large wooden circle while several strong young men rocked it back and forth.

My sides hurt from laughing and from screaming, and I can't believe I almost missed out on this. I'm young. I can study later. Ten hours of fun won't hurt my future, and ten cents spent on that fun won't make a difference to my parents.

Would it?

Before I can begin to worry, Julia says, "Here you go, Rosie," and hands me my hat which fell off my head when I fell off the ride.

I thank her and put it back on with more attention to how securely my hatpin holds it to my topknot, as she shakes out her skirt to remove the sand we fell into then says, "Where to now?"

"Steeplechase ride," several girls say at once. One adds, "And then the—" but is cut off by Julia slapping her arm playfully.

"And then the what?" I say, but they just grin and promise I will see and lead me up a long flight of stairs to where eight wooden horses attached to rails await us. Julia and I mount one together, struggling with our heavy skirts, and the other girls pair up too, and other people settle onto the four horses we aren't using, and then the worker yells, "Good luck!" and pulls a lever and our horses all lunge forward and down a hill, picking up speed as they go.

I scream and laugh, and Julia waves her hat in the air and begs our horse to go faster. But despite her best efforts, after we've gone up and down all the little hills we arrive second-last.

Feeling wobbly from the ride and the laughter, I wouldn't mind taking a rest, but the workers order us forward and into a tunnel. The tunnel quickly gets smaller and smaller, until we're actually crawling along the ground, but as I start to wish myself anywhere but here, the tunnel ends and we come out to where we can stand.

This new area is not well lit at all, and the floor doesn't seem level, and I find myself stumbling as I walk back and forth through roped-off lanes that remind me of lining up at Ellis Island to be inspected.

Then, to my shock, a midget with a red mustache, wearing a red-and-blue clown costume, appears before us and shakes a padded club at us threateningly.

We all squeal and leap out of his way, landing on a piece of floor that is somehow moving back and forth. I fall over, knocking Julia and two other girls down as I do, and we lie laughing in a heap for a moment before scrambling to our feet.

"Are you all right?"

I look over with the others to see a young man standing smiling.

Not at all of us.

At Julia.

"I am," she says, staring at him like she's never seen anything so wonderful before. "Thank you."

"It's hard to walk in here," he says, offering her his arm. "Would you like to—"

"Yes." She slips her arm through his. "Thank you."

They walk off, and I realize Julia has forgotten that the rest of us exist. We remaining girls exchange surprised glances, then giggle and follow the new couple.

The floor continues to move at unexpected times but now I'm more ready for it and don't fall, and watching Julia and her man ahead of me means I see what's coming up.

There are several more midgets in our path waving their clubs, and one even hits Yetta on the shoulder. She shrieks, but once we're past him, she admits it didn't actually hurt. "But if you don't scream, they hit you again."

A tall skinny man dressed as a farmer is our next obstacle, and somehow as we pass him a gust of wind shoots up from the ground beneath my feet and raises my skirt several inches above my ankles.

I blush, and my friends laugh, but I think I can hear laughter beyond them. Then I'm sure I can, when the farmer pulls a pair of bright pink drawers from a fake tree covered in hot dogs near him and offers them to me as if mine were blown off by the wind. I throw my hands over my face, not sure who's laughing at me and embarrassed to have my underclothing in people's minds, and scurry off.

Finally we near the end, which I know because I can see Julia and her man sitting on a bench watching us and laughing. Two more midgets stand at an open gateway, swinging their clubs at people passing, but we manage to get through without being hit and collapse onto the bench beside Julia.

Then I look behind us and realize there are rows of benches, set like a theater so everyone can see.

People *were* laughing at me, the people who came through first and became the audience for the next people. It feels wrong, but I am soon laughing too. It's just so funny to see people falling over and women frantically trying to tug their skirts back to the floor and men being paddled by the midgets. Those people come out and join the audience, and the earlier audience members leave, and it's the strangest thing I've ever experienced but the funniest too.

We watch for quite a while, then Julia says, "Ready to move on?"

I assume that once we're outside she'll take her leave of the young man, but if anything she holds his arm more tightly as we depart the theater. Two other young men who were sitting nearby come out with us, and while at first they're friendly with all of us, two girls quickly attach themselves to them and get most of their attention after that. Julia and her man, who while we sat I learned is named Israel, pay attention only to each other.

I'm not sure how I feel about all this. I don't think I want a "fella", as the girls at work call men, at least not yet, but I would still like a man to *want* to be my fella and none of these men do.

But this is only my first week in America. If I want a fella later, maybe I can find one.

And maybe I won't want one. The girls at work who talk so much about men don't seem to do anything but go to dances and parties and amusement parks in pursuit of those men. Clara doesn't talk about men and she's an important union girl. I probably should be following her path, since it's the one that will lead to making the money I want and need, but it *does* seem like Julia and the other girls are having more fun than Clara possibly could at a union meeting. I do want money for my family, but I want fun too, while I'm young and unmarried.

So it's hard to know for sure what I should do, but I can't become a union girl here at Steeplechase, so I can't do anything but enjoy myself today.

At about nine o'clock, after we've ridden so many rides I am dizzy and my throat hurts from screaming, we take the steamboat and El and trolley back home. The two young men leave us before we board the trolley, and I notice that the girls they were escorting don't seem too upset to lose them, but Israel stays with us all the way back to our house. He and Julia stand together, away from the rest of us, on the crowded trolley, and walk a few steps ahead of us to the house.

Yetta nudges me and points, and I realize Julia and Israel are holding hands.

"Did she know him before?" I whisper.

Yetta shakes her head. "She's usually like us," she whispers back, "meeting a man someplace and having a bit of fun then never seeing him again. But this time seems different."

It certainly does, since when we reach the door Israel and Julia are finishing up making plans to meet for lunch tomorrow.

We all say goodbye to him politely, and somehow manage to keep from squealing and pelting Julia with questions until we are inside the house and he probably can't hear us.

She just smiles, a far-away and dreamy look in her eyes, and says, "I've never been so happy to fall over in public."

CHAPTER EIGHT

Maria
August 29, 1909

I BRUSH SWEAT FROM MY FOREHEAD beneath the brim of my hat. "Can we walk more slowly, please?"

My brother does relax his pace a little, although not as much as I would like in the afternoon heat. "Sorry, I'm eager for that bath."

I am too, since we left Italy nearly three weeks ago and this will be the first time since then that my skin has been touched by hot water I didn't have to boil myself on the Billotas' stove. "We really don't have to pay?"

"That's what the other men at work said." He looks down at his hands, still with dirt under the nails though he scrubbed them in the kitchen sink last night and again today before we went to church with the Billotas. "We will see. Now, I want to talk to you about that nickelodeon yesterday."

I try to hold back a sigh. I had hoped we'd be home before Vinnie returned from his first day of work, but Margherita had insisted on letting the men who'd joined our group of girls take us out for dinner. Well, not 'us'. The man who'd paid for me to attend the movie hadn't even hinted that he might pay for my dinner too, and so I'd had nothing but a cup of water and a small roll since I could afford nothing else. When we'd arrived home and Vinnie had discovered I'd been out with what he called 'strange men' I'd known we'd be discussing it. I just didn't, and don't, want to. "If you must."

"I must. Tell me exactly how it happened that you went to a nickelodeon and a restaurant with men whose names you didn't even know."

I knew them after we were at the dinner table, but I don't think saying that will improve Vinnie's mood, so I explain how we met the men outside the nickelodeon and how they stayed with us through the movies and dinner.

"And did they... was there anything... I mean..."

Though I don't like any part of this conversation, I feel a smile tugging at the corners of my mouth at his attempts not to use any words to describe what the men might have done. "Did any of them kiss or cuddle us?"

"Maria!"

"Isn't that what you want to know? What we might have done with the men?"

He tips his hat a little further down over his eyes but I can still see that he's blushing. "Not about all the girls, no. Just you. And... no, just you."

"Well, 'just me' didn't do anything, of course." I consider pointing out I love Alonzo, but he knows so I don't bother. "I didn't so much as shake a man's hand. So don't worry about me."

He nods, but he doesn't seem comforted.

After we walk on a little more, I realize why. "You're also wondering about Margherita, yes? What she did?"

He turns to look at me. "When did you get so smart?"

Ignoring this foolishness, I say, "Well, don't tell her parents, but she did kiss the man. A little bit." More than that, really, but I don't want to get her in trouble. Any more trouble: her father was already furious with her for keeping us out so late. "But he *did* pay for both of us to see the show so maybe she was just thanking him."

Vinnie no longer looks like he thinks I'm smart. "Could have said the words," he mutters. "Didn't have to kiss him to thank him."

A surprising thought makes my forehead wrinkle up like a sleeve seam when the machine's tension isn't right. "Vinnie, do *you* want to kiss Margherita?"

He turns sharply toward me. "What? No. She's a child. Like you."

"I'm not a child," I snap, "and neither is she. She's sixteen. Nearly seventeen. And—oh, I just had a thought." I turn to him, feeling excitement washing away my irritation. "Wouldn't it be perfect if you and Margherita fell in love and got married? Two Italians meeting in America instead of at home. And then when you've earned enough money, you could take her home and it'd all be wonderful."

He rolls his eyes. "Now you *are* being a child. Margherita doesn't think that way about me at all."

"Oh, no?"

"No, she—wait, she does?"

"I don't know," I say in my best sweet voice. I don't actually know, except that she said he's handsome, but that's a good start. "I'm a child."

"Yes, you are," he says, but he's grinning.

Once Vinnie has some money, I have a feeling Margherita won't be waiting outside the nickelodeon for someone to treat her, and though it'd feel strange to see her with my brother I think it would also be good. Every girl should have a man like my Alonzo.

After a few moments, Vinnie clears his throat and says, "Well, anyhow. You've had one day of work now. How is it?"

I sigh. "All right."

"Doesn't sound all right."

"I'm bored," I admit. "All Mr. Bernstein let me do was sew sleeves together. I knew everything there is to know about that in an hour at the most, but he didn't give me anything else to do. I liked talking to the girls at lunch, and teaching English to the ones who don't know it well and making sure they would practice later, but doing the same work over and over again is dull."

"Did you ask for something different?"

"Margherita said not to." I sigh again. "She said he likes paying me a learner's wage and having me sew sleeves well."

Vinnie frowns. "I don't like him taking advantage of you. What does Margherita think you should do?"

"She says I should stay for at least a few weeks to get even better, but that after that, if I want to make more money I need to go somewhere else and learn a different part of the waist. I would be a learner there too, but then I could move somewhere else again and learn a different part, and do that again and again until I can make the whole waist."

"What happens then?"

"I could be a sample maker, or work at a factory where girls make the whole waist themselves. Either way, I'd be paid much more."

"Then you should leave that place after a few weeks, as Margherita said. The more money we can make, the better our lives will be here and back home. Where would you go next? Did Margherita say?"

I shake my head. "I'll ask her when it's time." Realizing I haven't yet told him my plans, I add, "And I won't be going back home."

Vinnie stops walking to stare at me. "What? Why not?"

I grab his arm and tug him along, since he stopped right where several old ladies were trying to go and they're giving him that glare that only old Italian ladies know how to give. "Keep walking."

We do, and he says, "Why do you think you're not going home?"

"Once I've made the money to bring him here, Alonzo is coming. And we're going to stay."

He shakes his head. "Oh, Maria," he says on a sigh.

"Oh, Maria, what?"

I know I sound defensive, and I am right to be because he says, "He's not coming here. No matter how much money you make, he's not coming. Don't you know that?"

"Of course I don't, because he *is* coming. He loves me and I love him and when he gets here we will be married and we will have a wonderful life together."

"None of that is going to happen."

His voice is gentle, but his words hurt. They hurt, and they make me furious. "It is, it is! He told me and I believe him and you will never make me think otherwise. Never!"

"I can see that," he says. "We won't talk about it any more."

"I will write him another letter tonight. And I will mail it and the one I wrote yesterday tomorrow. And you will see. He *will* be here soon! I asked him, in the stable and again that night, and he said he would. Why can't you understand this?"

"That night? Wait, did you go to—Never mind that. Maria, it's you who doesn't understand. Alonzo... men... we're not like girls." His face goes redder than the tomatoes Papà grows at home. "You asked him, and he said yes, because... well, he wanted to—"

Luckily, we arrive at the public bath as he says this, so I cut him off with, "My line is over there," and stalk away to join the girls and women waiting to get inside.

I can feel Vinnie watching me from his own line but I ignore him. My brother has never been in love. He might like Margherita a little but it's not love. So he doesn't understand. At home I even heard him say he was proud of not letting a girl make a fool of him, as if being too cold to fall in love is a good thing.

I am not so cold. And Alonzo is *not* making a fool of me. I know what he wants. He wants to marry me and have children with me and be together forever. Yes, he also wants to kiss me and touch me, but what of it? I want that too. He wants everything I want.

And soon Vinnie will know this.

When my love arrives so we can be together forever.

CHAPTER NINE

Rosie
August 31, 1909

I AM PREPARING TO GO HOME after another long day of sewing when I hear whispering but angry voices behind me, mostly male but a few female, and turn to see Clara and two other girls in a group with at least five men.

"He promised," Clara hisses, her hands clenched into fists on her hips. "I really thought he meant it."

"Maybe he did at the time," a red-faced man says, "but he's broken it now."

Another man, calmer than the others, puts in, "Are you sure? It would be bad to be wrong."

"Oh, I'm sure," the first man says. "Leiserson opened a new factory in secret and is hiring only non-union workers for it. He said he'd always only hire union, but I guess that only meant here."

"No, he meant it everywhere." Everyone nods at Clara's statement. "He's broken his word."

"So we will strike," the first man says. "Starting tomorrow. He won't get away with this. All the men need to go out."

"What about the girls?"

The man glares at Clara, his face growing even redder. "They don't matter."

She glares back, though she's so short she needs to look up nearly a foot to do it. "It needs to be everyone. If the girls stay in, you won't have the same leverage."

"We don't need girls," the man says, turning away from her. "Girls work cheaper than men, and they just leave when they get married. We don't need them in the union. Now, men, how will we—"

"You *do* need us," Clara insists as she moves herself back into his line of sight. "None of us are getting married right now, and we only work cheaper because we can't get paid more. But we want to. We want the same as the men. That's why we're in the union, and why we must strike with you. If we all go out together, all the workers together, we'll have more power." She looks at the others, both men and girls. "You know it's true. Solidarity matters."

I see them all agreeing with her though they don't speak.

The man sees it too, and doesn't like it, because he begins to say again that girls aren't needed.

Clara doesn't let him finish.

I watch my friend arguing with a man who could easily pick her up and throw her across the room, as articulate as if she's spent days preparing her words when I know that can't be, and I understand why I've heard people in the factory referring to her and the other Jewish union-organizer girls as 'farbrente maydlakh'. They *are* fiery girls. They're fiery and determined and not afraid of anything.

Me? I am so not fiery that I couldn't even decide for myself how much money to send home. When I asked Julia for advice, she suggested I start with a dollar and work my way up from there, so that's what I did. But it's such an obvious solution that I should have been able to find it myself. I did, actually, I did think of it, but I didn't have the strength to decide it without someone else telling me it was all right.

And now the union might strike! Clara has explained to me at our lunches what a strike is and what it means, and it sounds horrible. I am only earning four dollars a week, but I'd get next to nothing as a striker. Clara insists that if the union achieves its goals all workers will have better wages and shorter working hours, and that would indeed be wonderful. But how long will it take, and would me being on strike make any difference at all? Does one more girl on the picket line matter? I could sacrifice so much and gain nothing.

I look at Clara still telling the man exactly what she thinks, I see her fire and energy, and I know I simply don't have them. I wasn't raised to defy authority like her, to stand up and tell the world what I believe, and I don't even know how to start. I'll end up being like this until my father arrives in America and marries me off.

On Saturday instead of studying I went to Steeplechase, and then I spent part of Sunday with Yetta as I haggled with that peddler for the new waist and belt I wanted. The rest of the day I was with a group of girls from the home, picnicking at Central Park and walking through the Menagerie looking at the sea lions and elephants and polar bears and all the other animals in their cages.

I enjoyed my time off work, but I feel guilty about it now. Instead of being out having fun, I should have done as my parents would expect and as Clara would do: spent my time learning English and spent no unnecessary money. I did get the new clothing for only twenty cents, but still.

Dejected, I turn away to head for the dressing room for my hat but see the new girl Josephine in a corner with Mr. Rosenthal. She joined me and my friends for lunch today, though usually the Italians go on their own just as we Jewish girls do, because she wanted Clara to tell her about the union, and she was sweet and shy and always smiling. She's not smiling now, though. Mr. Rosenthal is stroking her cheek and leaning in toward her as he speaks to her, and she's clearly trying to lean away without upsetting him.

He hasn't touched me since he saw that I spend my lunch breaks with Clara, but watching him interfere with a girl even younger than me makes me furious.

Before I know what I'm doing, I spin around so my back is to them and shout out at the top of my lungs, "Where's that Josephine? She promised to walk to the trolley with me!"

"Oh! Here I am," I hear from behind me, and I turn as if I don't know where she is to see her hurrying over.

I say, "Well, finally! I didn't know where you'd gone!" loudly enough that Mr. Rosenthal will be sure to hear. I don't look directly at him, afraid he'll realize I called Josephine on purpose, but I see him leave the corner where he'd trapped the poor girl.

"Thank you," Josephine breathes when she reaches me. "You rescued me."

I slip my arm through hers and murmur, "You're welcome," then we begin chattering away lightly as we leave the building.

I'm smiling and laughing, but inside I'm still picturing Clara standing up to that union man. That's the image of who I want to be, someone who makes a difference, someone who could change a million people's lives with her words.

Will I ever become that person?

CHAPTER TEN

Maria
September 20, 1909

AS I GET READY FOR WORK ON MONDAY, yawning after a late night spent at a dance with my work friends, Vinnie says, "Maria, maybe it's time you move on from Bijou. You've been there nearly a month now. Get a new job, learn new things. Make more money."

I set my hat on my head and carefully push in my beautiful silver hatpin to secure it. "But my English group. I'd miss that." After I'd been at the factory a week, two girls asked me to help them learn English during our lunch breaks, and now there are five or six girls with me each day. Already they speak far better than they did before, and not just because they know I'll tease them if they don't learn. I've been creating practice exercises for them, keeping them on track and working hard, and I do enjoy sitting before them while they listen raptly to what I have to say.

He shrugs. "Couldn't you start one at the new factory?"

"I suppose."

"You could," Margherita says, sounding a little too eager. One of her good friends has recently joined my group, and I suspect she doesn't appreciate having her friend eating lunch with me not her. "You really should move."

Her wanting me to go makes me want to stay, and I'm about to say so when Vinnie makes a face like he's bitten into an unripe lemon and says, "And... anything you earn above four dollars a week you can save up to bring that... boy... here."

I've been wondering how I will save for Alonzo's passage since Vinnie and I combine our earnings, so this thrills me, but I don't want to give in too easily. "Don't call him a *boy*. He's going to be your brother-in-law."

"Don't remind me. Well?"

I consider for a moment, then turn to Margherita. "How do I get a new job?"

"Oh, good," she says, then hastily adds, "For you, I mean. So, let me tell you what to do."

She seems to enjoy telling me what to do a little too much, but I know she knows more than I do about this so I reluctantly do as she says. Instead of going to Bijou with her, I take the subway and a trolley a little further north to get to Triangle, a bigger waist factory on the top three floors of a tall building near Washington Square Park.

If they don't want to hire me, I'll do what Margherita suggests and go back to Bijou tomorrow saying I've been ill. I don't want that, though, both because I need to make more money soon and because Margherita would laugh at me for not being able to get a new job on my own.

I'm a little late because it's further away and I didn't leave any earlier than usual, so I have the freight elevator to myself on the way to the eighth floor. The operator doesn't speak to me after asking what floor I want, which gives me the time to determine how I'll ask for my new job here.

I have my words ready, but when I walk off the elevator and through a narrow hallway into the main working area a man snaps, "You're late. No pay until noon," before I can so much as breathe.

"Oh, I'm sorry, but I'm new, sir," I say, pretending to be nervous and sweet, as I know the bosses want us to be, instead of annoyed that he spoke to me in such a way. "I'm Maria, and I'd like a job."

"Can you sew?"

"Of course, sir, I have sewn many sleeves and I know how to set them into waists." I have seen it done, anyhow.

He narrows his eyes. "Are you a union girl?"

"Certainly not, sir," I say, not having to give a pretend reaction this time. Many girls came to work at Bijou from the Leiserson strike line, unable to afford to continue receiving only two dollars a week of strike wages instead of what they can earn by working, and I told them that I couldn't understand their foolishness. Why stand in the streets with a picket sign when you can be in a factory sitting down? "I don't believe in unions. And neither does my brother."

He bursts out laughing. "Well, that's good. Neither do I." His eyes run down my body and back up. "How old are you?"

"I'm sixteen, sir," I say. "My big brother is eighteen, though." I emphasize *big*, not liking how he's looking at me, and it works: the boss takes a half-step back from me and his smile goes away.

"Well," he says, looking confused, then straightens up and adds, "Well, you're still late, so no pay until noon. And you're clearly a learner at setting in sleeves so only three dollars a week."

"Of course, sir." It doesn't matter. I'll stay only until I stop learning and then I will change jobs again. Once I have had the chance to sew side seams and hems and buttonholes, and attach buttons and cuffs and lace or embroidery, I will know how to make the whole waist and will be able to be paid much more, and even before that I should be able to earn more than four dollars a week.

Once I've saved fifty dollars, I can bring Alonzo here and all my dreams will come true.

Why would I waste time with unions when I can work hard and get what I want most in life?

CHAPTER ELEVEN

Rosie
September 23, 1909

I CLING TO JOSEPHINE AND SHE CLINGS TO ME, and I'm not sure I know which of us is holding up the other. We're not crying, unlike two other girls near us, but I've never been so upset.

Josephine pulls away from me and demands of the man who brought us the news, "Will she be all right?"

He grimaces. "I think so. But broken ribs take a long time to heal, not to mention her cuts and bruises."

"What kind of man would beat a girl on the sidewalk?"

"There were two of them," he says quietly, seeming ashamed of his sex. As he should be. "Two thugs."

"But *why?*" Josephine nearly wails.

"Isn't it obvious?" One of the girls who's been crying swipes savagely at her eyes. "To make her stop. They don't want union girls, especially not ones who can talk like Clara. Not ones who'll go out on strike and encourage other girls to do the same."

My hand tightens involuntarily on my pocketbook's handle. Inside is a cable from my parents, a cable I received a week ago at the bank. All it says is, "Forbid you to be part of any union. Letter to follow." Is this why? Are they afraid that someone will hurt me like they hurt Clara?

"Well, it's not going to work," the other girl says. "We'll all be even more determined now. Won't we, girls?"

Josephine and the other girl agree, and I nod because I don't know what else to do.

I haven't gone on strike yet, most of us haven't because the union doesn't have enough money to support us, but I had been helping Clara at the union hall. Since the cable arrived, though, I've been trying to avoid all union talk and even hiding from people at lunch to make sure I don't get involved. I'm sure Clara thinks I've lost my wits with how I've been avoiding her. How do I tell the girls, how do I tell *Clara*, I can't go against my parents?

I don't know, but I also don't get a chance.

"We're having a special union meeting tonight at Cooper Union," the man says, "right after work. We won't let this stand."

I spend the remaining hours at work alternating between longing to go to provide support for Clara, even though she surely won't be in attendance, and knowing my parents have forbidden that action. When the day is done and I'm filing wearily down the stairs with everyone else, I still haven't made up my mind.

"Come on, Rosie," Josephine says. "Why are you just standing on the sidewalk?"

"I... I don't know. What to do, I mean."

She slips her arm through mine. "I do. Come on."

So I go. I go because I am here and my parents are not and because poor Clara doesn't deserve what was done to her. I go with my stomach clenched with fear at what my parents would say, but I go.

I forget all about my parents, though, when the man running the meeting says, "Here's someone for you to see," and Clara herself appears from behind the stage's drapery.

She moves slowly, with a limp, and I see her wince as she goes, but she moves without stopping up to the microphone. She takes a deep breath so she can speak, then her hand flies to her side and we all flinch with her.

"Oh," Josephine whimpers. "The poor girl."

I bite my lip and nod as Clara says, in English, "I was walking, last night, home from an English class. My English is not too bad but it could be better, so I was learning. Then, two men..." Her eyes close for a moment, then she reopens them and says, "They attacked me. They kicked me. They punched me. And they told me it would happen again, if I did not leave the union."

The hall full of people is absolutely silent, everyone's attention straining toward Clara.

"I will never leave the union."

So quietly said, but with such conviction and certainty.

The audience erupts in cheers and applause, but Clara raises a hand for silence, then drops it quickly as though the movement pained her again. "I will not leave, because I know we are in the right. Being beaten will not stop me. Please, please do not let it stop you. Do not let anything stop you from doing what you know is right."

Cheers and applause again, but I do not join in.

Do I know what is right?

I've always done what my parents wanted.

Could what my parents want me to do now be wrong?

How am I supposed to know?

CHAPTER TWELVE

Maria
September 24, 1909

"HOW CAN YOU *SAY* THAT, MARIA?"

I shrug, surprised at the girl's shock. "Isn't it true? What happened was awful, yes, but she was foolish to be out on her own. Things happen to girls alone."

"Only because men do those things!"

Another girl gives her arm a squeeze. "Don't shout, Santina. You're right, but don't shout."

"And why shouldn't I?" Santina says, only a little more quietly. "Shouldn't we all shout? Isn't that what a union's for?"

A man standing nearby clears his throat, and as we all turn to look at him he says, "Wouldn't talk like that. Not..." and jerks his head in the direction of the Triangle.

Santina snaps, "If you don't like it, go somewhere else."

He rolls his eyes and wanders off, and I have to say, "He's right, though. It doesn't seem like the bosses would approve of union talk."

"Oh, the bosses, I don't care a lick for them." But she says it so quietly, I know she really does.

"Well, I don't much like it either," I say. "It all seems a lot of nonsense to me. If people just work hard, they'll get along all right."

"Poor Clara's not getting along all right," Santina points out.

That is true, and the group's outrage rises again over what was done to her.

I share some of it, but not all. I do feel angry and disgusted that a girl was beaten by men, and I'm also outraged that men who would do such a thing are here in America while Alonzo, whose answers to my letters have not yet reached me, is still in Italy. He would never hurt a girl, me or any other, and it's wrong that all men are not like him.

But to be outraged that some men aren't what they should be? That a girl who speaks up isn't to every man's taste?

I might as well be outraged that water is wet and the sun rises every morning.

When our break is over, we return to the Triangle, where we wait in line for the slow-moving elevators because one of our number has a sore ankle and cannot manage eight flights of stairs. Even here, there are whispers about Clara and the attack on her, and about the union meeting last night and how something must be done.

I don't think anything needs to be done. This factory is better than the Bijou, with huge windows to let the light in and high ceilings so it doesn't feel uncomfortably crowded even with so many of us at work. True, that narrow hallway I entered through on my first day turns out to be how we leave as well, herded out through it to be searched one by one in case we have stolen a bit of lace or fabric, while the other exit door is locked so we cannot sneak out. The searching doesn't take that long, though, and we can chat while we wait our turn. We work long hours, yes, and I am often tired since the breaks I thought I'd get do not exist, but my job is still easier than Vinnie's.

Unions and strike lines are not my concern.

But they become my concern at about seven o'clock, when the power to the machines is shut off unexpectedly and the foreladies tell us to walk up the two flights to the tenth floor for a meeting. The ninth-floor girls join us for the second flight, which makes it even harder to move forward with so many girls in the narrow stairwell. But soon, we are all standing in the much cleaner area where the bosses work and where waists are pressed and then packed for shipping, staring at the two silent men by the windows.

Mr. Harris, his thin face serious, looks back at us all. He's walked the aisles on the eighth floor nearly every day I've been here, checking whether our work is right and telling girls how to do better when needed. He knows a lot about making waists, I can tell. The larger man must be Mr. Blanck, but I don't know what he does or what he knows, because although I've seen him check that the exit door we aren't permitted to use is locked near the end of the day, I've never heard him speak.

I don't hear him now either, because Mr. Harris clears his throat and says, "Mr. Blanck and I have learned that many of you attended last night's meeting at Cooper Union."

Several girls near me gasp in shock, and the man says, "Yes, of course we found out. Now, we are not angry. We are sad, girls, sad that you felt you needed to go there. We work hard to take care of you here, and we thought you were happy working for us. You do know there are many other girls who *would* be, if you are not. Don't you?"

I glance around to see the rest of the girls keeping their faces as expressionless as they can. He is right that other girls would take their spots, and though he says he is sad, I think he is more trying to threaten the union girls.

To my surprise, that bothers me. I don't agree with the union girls, but they *do* have the right to be in the union. I can tell them what I think because I'm a girl like them, but he is a man and a boss and he shouldn't try to stop them.

"Not all of you went," he says, "and we are glad of that. For those of you who did, though, you need to think about your jobs here, about the money we pay you and the good factory. You don't want to be back in a cramped little sweatshop, do you? No, you must want to be here. If you do want that, if you recognize that we are better for you than any union could be, we are happy to have you."

He doesn't say what will happen if they do not want to be here on his terms, but he doesn't have to. We all know. There are always more girls arriving in America looking for jobs.

He waits for a moment, as if he expects one of us to answer, then says, "Well, that's all, girls. Think about it carefully. Back to work now."

As we shuffle down the stairs, I can feel the girls around me looking back and forth at each other, thinking as instructed. I am thinking too.

I am thinking that I don't like union talk, but I also don't like how Mr. Harris talked to the union girls.

I want to earn money, and that's all I want.

But he should let the girls make their own decisions instead of pressuring them.

CHAPTER THIRTEEN

Rosie
September 25, 1909

MY THREE FRIENDS AND I STAND IN THE DARK BATTERY PARK amid a crowd of people awaiting the seven o'clock naval parade. As part of the Hudson-Fulton Celebration, military ships from all over the world will be joining American ones in a journey from Governor's Island up the Hudson River. Those ships will be lit up by searchlights from various tall buildings along the river and also from the Statue of Liberty which we can see before us in the glare of its own searchlight. On our way here we made sure to ride the trolley along Fifth Avenue, to see all its buildings lit by electric lights for the first time, and since our world is aglow in a way it's never been before we should be excited and chattering like the people around us.

Instead, we are quiet, staring out at the Statue instead of so much as glancing at each other, and I know we're all thinking of the fifth girl who should be with us. She should be, and she would be if it weren't for those two awful men who attacked her. Instead she's at home in her bed applying all her drive and determination to healing her injuries.

As we moved to where we now stand, I heard people in the crowd talking about Clara and what was done to her. None of them know her like we do, know how sweet she is when she's not arguing with someone and how she always says that no matter how many newspapers she reads in a day she must have "a book for dessert" at night and how lovely her voice is when she sings with us at lunch time. All they know of her is that she is a union girl and was beaten for it.

Beating girls is apparently not a crime in America. The policemen have done nothing about Clara's attackers though everyone seems to know which of the thugs who harass the strikers they are. None of the people I heard talking tonight seemed outraged by what was done to her. At most, a few older women expressed sadness that she'd been hurt, but immediately followed that with, "But she should have left all that to the men. Girls aren't meant for strike lines, or for unions, everyone knows that."

We might not be meant for unions. In a perfect world, we would not need to be in them. But this is not a perfect world, not even here in America. Maybe especially not here in America.

The men here are not taking care of our interests. Mr. Rosenthal made us work on Rosh Hashanah and today on Yom Kippur, though he too is Jewish and should have allowed us the holy days, and the policemen don't have any concerns for Clara. Nobody cares for us girls. So we need to take care of our own interests. And despite what "everyone knows", despite what my parents would think, perhaps the only way to do that is to—

"Did you see this?"

I turn with the others to examine the program Josephine is holding out to us. It's difficult because she's shaking it in her fury.

"Hold still," I say, catching her wrist. "What is it?"

"I can't believe this, any of this." Her emotions make her Italian accent stronger than usual, but after weeks of having lunch with her I can still understand her English. She points at the program. "To spend like this, when we have nothing, and poor Clara..." She bites her lip. "Well. It's horrible."

I peer at the program with the others, and have to agree. "They spent a quarter of a million *dollars* on this entertainment?"

Josephine nods at me, her eyes blazing. "All to celebrate two dead men."

"Three hundred years ago Hudson discovered this dull old river—"

"And one hundred years ago Fulton ran a steamship up it—"

"And now they pay that sort of money to celebrate it all."

"And charge us a quarter for this program. While we barely have a single dollar to our names, never mind a quarter of a million dollars."

We four stand, united in our anger, for a long moment, then Josephine says, "Well, I'm not staying for it. They've wasted their money on me. I won't let them entertain me and make me forget about—well, everything. I won't. Who's with me, girls?"

The rest of us say, "I am," together, and we grin at each other and begin making our way back out of the crowd. I am a little sorry to be missing what sounds like it will be a great spectacle, but I think they all feel the same way. We are doing it anyhow, though. Doing it for Clara.

This must be what going on strike feels like. Strikers turn their backs on their immediate desires, such as receiving usual wages instead of just strike pay, to fight for a better future.

Joining together with my friends feels good, actually. Brave and strong and good.

Fiery.

I like it.

Maybe if I concentrate on this feeling, let it grow, I'll know what to d—

"Be careful, please!"

Josephine has bumped into a tall young man, and he wasn't shy about telling her so in Italian-accented English.

Though it was clearly her fault since the man wasn't moving, the already upset Josephine gasps with fury and lets loose a loud and ferocious stream of Italian words I of course cannot understand.

The girl of about my age with the man must understand, though: her eyes widen and she moves closer to the man for protection.

Seeing the girl do this makes me angry too since no men protected Clara, and I raise my chin and stomp past them as the man gives Josephine a sharp retort in their shared language.

Our eyes meet, mine and his, as I pass. His dark ones flash with annoyance at Josephine but when he sees me a hint of admiration creeps into them. He's handsome, and he might think I'm pretty.

Well, what of it? I tell myself crossly and keep going. *Why should I care what a man I don't even know thinks of me?*

I should not.

Which does not stop me doing so for days.

CHAPTER FOURTEEN

Maria
September 27, 1909

STILL GIDDY AND FLOATING FROM THE AMAZING SIGHTS and sounds of the festivities to which Vinnie took me on Saturday night by the Hudson River, which weren't ruined at all by one rude girl who dared to yell at Vinnie when *she* bumped into *him*, I arrive at Triangle Monday morning and am quickly brought back down to earth.

"Why are we all—" I begin to ask the crowd of girls milling about on the sidewalk, but before I can finish, one near the front calls out, "The doors are locked! We can't get in."

We stand a moment, wondering and murmuring to each other, and then someone else chimes in with, "It's because of the union."

The union locked the doors?

Fortunately another girl asks that question before I can, so she receives the ridicule that would otherwise have been mine.

"Of course they didn't. Don't you have a lick of sense? How could they have? No, it's the bosses. After that little speech they gave us on Friday, they decided to close down."

One girl calls, "Forever?" and the quaver in her voice echoes my own nerves. I've lost my job? But I've only had it a week. I'm not yet ready to look for a new one.

"How would we know? But I doubt it," the first one says, as other girls begin whispering their fears and concerns to each other.

The one who said the union was the cause clears her throat and takes a deep breath, then begins shouting over us all. "No, they'll reopen. The bosses won't want to lose their money. But they're showing us that they have all the power. That they have it and we don't. And they'll be right unless we all join the union and prove them wrong. I say we join right now. Come on, girls! Who's with me?"

A cheer goes up and a great many of the girls follow the shouting one away down the street. When their noise has died off, I'm left with a small group of silent girls. We glance at each other, then look down at our feet, then turn and walk away alone to return to our homes.

I feel embarrassed and ashamed. I don't know why, but I do.

THE NEXT DAY, AFTER SPENDING MONDAY working with Margherita's mother and realizing that staying home all day is not as relaxing and comfortable as I'd thought it would be, I am again at Triangle at eight o'clock.

This time, the doors are open as they usually are. Unusually, though, the managers and foreladies are talking to each girl who tries to enter. They let some pass into the building, but more are turned away.

Worried that I will be as well, I shuffle along with the crowd until eventually a forelady says to me, "And are *you* in the union?"

"No," I say, confused.

She gives me a single nod. "Hurry on in, then. There's much work to be done."

I go in, but I don't hurry. Wanting to know what's going on, I pretend to be adjusting the ribbon tie of my shoe so I can listen to the next few girls being questioned, and soon realize that any girl who admits to being in the union is turned away.

The next girl answers the forelady's question with, "I was not in it, but I will be now. Sending away the union girls is wrong!" and then to my horror adds in Italian, "You there, playing with your shoe, you agree with me. Come out with us!"

I look over, panicked, and shake my head. The forelady is staring at me, her eyes narrowing, so I quickly say in English, "No, I am not in the union. I want to work here."

The girl tosses her head and turns away without another word to me, and the forelady says, "Get to your machine then."

I nod and rush over to the stairs since the elevators have already gone up so walking will be faster.

Climbing the steep stairs, I take deep breaths to calm myself. Refusing to let the union girls in is wrong, but I am still working at a good factory. I am earning money for me and Vinnie, and soon for Alonzo, and he will come to me when I've earned enough.

Nothing can go wrong for me.

I will not allow it.

CHAPTER FIFTEEN

Rosie
November 22, 1909

THOUGH THE COOPER UNION'S GREAT HALL has seats for a thousand, so many arrived for tonight's meeting that four other nearby halls had to be opened to allow the overflow somewhere to wait. People pack the aisles here beneath the huge ceiling arches, and they stand so close together along the walls and even on the back of the stage that not even a pay envelope could be slipped between them.

I was lucky enough to get one of the last seats, and I sit surrounded by girls and women and a few men who look strangely out of place. The men are usually the ones on the stage doing most of the talking, not sitting in the audience among the girl workers. But most of the waist workers are girls, and so most of the members of Local 25 are girls too. And many of those girls are on strike.

I have not struck. Not yet. I almost did, so many times, started to push back my chair so I could walk triumphantly out of Leiserson's like Clara and the other strikers did back in late September, but at the last moment I stopped myself each and every time.

I am a coward. I don't want to be, but I am.

On the picket lines, at Leiserson's and at Triangle Waist Company where the union called a strike immediately after the bosses refused to allow union members to work one day, the girls are harassed by nearly everyone.

Sometimes it's the policemen, arresting them for so much as speaking to the strikebreakers Clara calls "scabs" with disgust in her voice. Sometimes it's men hired by the factory owners, who push the girls around and even punch them, and then the policemen somehow decide the girls are at fault and again arrest them. Sometimes, and this is the part that frightens me the most, fallen women and their procurers tease the girls, telling them that if they want more money they should give up selling their sewing skills and sell their bodies instead.

If it were only teasing I might be able to survive it, but those women will also sometimes attack the girls, dragging them about by their hair and kicking them, and then all the females are arrested. To be stuck in a jail cell with... with prostitutes! People would think I'm no better than them, and I can't think of anything worse.

I know I'm *supposed* to be horrified by being associated with them, I know that's why the factory owners pay them to be there. I want to be brave, as the fiery girls are, but though I hate it, I cannot find that strength within me. I am afraid of being seen with such women and afraid of being physically hurt.

Luckily, the attacks on the picket lines have been not so frequent lately, since a policeman accidentally arrested one of the rich women who have joined the strikers in solidarity. Punching and arresting a poor working girl is of no consequence, but doing the same to a woman who has social standing? Unthinkable.

But 'not so frequent' doesn't mean never, and the bosses at Triangle and Leiserson show no signs of backing down. They pay the policemen, and they hire workers from other factories, giving them lunches and dances to make them feel special and stop them noticing that they work so many hours for so little money. They hate the union.

My parents do as well. Their letter did arrive two weeks after their cable, but though they'd promised an explanation, they wrote only, "Unions are no place for a girl. We will hear nothing further of your taking part in such a disgusting organization."

And they haven't. I haven't so much as mentioned the word 'union' in my weekly letters to them.

But that doesn't mean I haven't taken part.

Though I haven't been able to make myself strike, I do help Clara sign up new girls, and I make picket signs for others to carry. I feel scared every time I walk into the union hall, knowing how my parents will react if they learn how completely I'm going against their wishes, but I still walk in because I can't believe they're right. Though nothing that's been done has made a difference yet, everyone in the union is so determined to help the workers. So how can it, and they, be disgusting?

Though it's been nearly two months now of strikes at various factories, nothing has changed. The union leaders have come to realize that it won't, since the bosses can so easily replace strikers with other girls. We need to prevent that. It's why we're here tonight: to make plans for all going out on strike together.

At least, that's what I thought we were here to do.

For the last two hours, though, man after man has spoken, and though they're all union men, or at least union supporters, they have told us to be cautious. They agree that the conditions under which we work are no good, but they want to be sure we know that a strike might last months and would be hard on us.

We do know. We would have to, with how many of them have told us and with what our striking friends have said, and also because we're not stupid.

But what is the alternative?

Samuel Gompers is speaking now. Since he's the president of the American Federation of Labor, I would think he would agree with striking, but he too is saying we shouldn't act too hastily. "If you can't get the manufacturers to give you what you want, then strike... and let the manufacturers know that you are on strike."

The crowd cheers, but I am confused. What would be the point of being on strike if they didn't know?

And we have *tried* to get them to give us what we want. For months on the picket lines at Triangle and Leiserson girls have tried, and I have seen them trying in the factory too. Only two days ago, I watched Josephine beg Mr. Rosenthal for a raise since her father was hurt in a subway-tunnel collapse and can no longer make money for the family. Our boss let his eyes run down her body then back up again, and with a smile that made me feel sick though it wasn't directed at me he said, "Well, why don't you get a friend on the side?" He was clearly willing to be that "friend", but Josephine obviously didn't like the idea any more than I did because she simply mumbled, "Thank you," and walked away.

And the next day she joined the strikers.

I don't blame her for that, and often when I'm at home in my bed, I think that I should strike too, and I think maybe I'll wake up in the morning with the strength to do it. But I never do.

Clara, I know, is disappointed in me and the other girls who aren't striking, but though she must think I'm a scab now too, she still smiles at me when she's on a picket line at Leiserson's and I walk into the factory. She's a wonderful friend, and I wish I had her nerve, her ability to stand up to men, and her belief that we girls can make a difference. I want them so much, but I just don't have them.

But she and the other girls like her, the fiery girls, have tried and tried to get us proper pay and reduced hours. They've tried everything they can in these small strikes, but it hasn't worked and I'm not sure it ever will. I don't think Mr. Gompers used the right word. It is not "if" we cannot get the bosses to treat us properly. It is "when". And the time is now. We've tried long enough. We must strike now.

As I realize this, I hear the moderator beginning to introduce yet another man's speech. Over him, though, a girl's voice calls, "I wish to speak!" and other girls shout, "Get up on the platform!" and I look to see Clara being boosted onto the stage by the eager crowd.

I would be terrified. I *am* terrified, watching my tiny friend stand there as the moderator and intended next speaker shrug and back away to give her space. Though she's twenty-three, she looks younger than me, so short and delicate. To speak to such a crowd? I could never.

But she does. She raises her chin and she speaks in Yiddish, and around me I can hear Jewish girls whispering translations to their neighbors as she says in a cool loud voice, "I am a working girl too, I have listened to all the speakers, and I have no further patience for talk as I am one of those who feels and suffers from the abuses described here. I move that we go on a general strike... now!"

The previous speakers had received cheers, but the shouting and applause that Clara's words bring almost deafen me. Men throw their hats in the air and women and girls wave their handkerchiefs, and all around me are people yelling, "Strike! Strike!"

And I am yelling it too.

Clara is right. Nothing else will work.

After letting us cheer Clara for a good few minutes, the moderator raises his hands for calm. "Is there a second to this motion?"

Again we all shout and applaud. He doesn't have *a* second, he has hundreds of them.

Once he quiets us this time, he says in a voice like one uses at a funeral, "You must think carefully about this. Those of you who do not want to strike, who have fear for hunger and cold, should not be ashamed to refuse. If you vote in favor, you are sealing a pact to struggle until the end. So, I ask you: will you strike?"

If anyone doesn't shout "Yes!", they're not sitting anywhere near me.

The moderator nods and takes Clara's right hand, raising it high. "Will you take the old Jewish oath?"

Not everyone knows it, but he says it to us in English and we all raise our right hands and repeat, Clara unafraid in front of the crowd with her eyes shining, "If I turn traitor to the cause I now pledge, may this hand wither from the arm I now raise."

So we are all on strike!

AFTER THE VOTE, A COMMITTEE OF FIFTEEN girls and women, with a man to guide it, was quickly created and sent off to the other meeting halls to let them know we approved the strike. There were more cheers when they returned to inform us that everyone else had approved it too. We were all so excited, nervous but excited to finally be doing something to save ourselves, and when we left we were united and feeling brave.

I bought a newspaper this morning on my way to work, trading my penny for the chance to see whether anything had been reported about last night's meeting, and was delighted to see a short article on the front page.

It said that we voted to strike after Samuel Gompers spoke, which isn't exactly true, but it did accurately list our demands: recognition of the union, wages increased by twenty-five to thirty percent, and a work week of only fifty-two hours. It doesn't seem that much to ask. The reporter noted that as many as forty thousand workers were expected to walk out today from about two hundred and fifty factories, and the idea of being part of that group thrilled me.

But now, I sit at my table in Leiserson's and I wonder whether I am the only one here who voted to strike. I didn't see anyone else from here at the meeting, except for Josephine and Clara and they were already on strike, and now I don't know what to do. Do I get up and walk out? Alone? Do I wait for someone to tell me to go?

Quite a few of the girls around me have their hats and coats beside them instead of hanging on the hooks in the dressing room, so they might be planning to leave too. But when? And how do we know?

"Do we go?"

We all look at the young Jewish girl who whispered those words.

"It's a general strike," another murmurs. "So..."

"Do they tell us when?"

"Who?"

"The union?"

"But they're not here," I put in. "Already walked out."

The others nod, then we hush as Mr. Rosenthal casts an angry glance in our direction.

Once he moves on we continue whispering, but nobody moves. We need a leader.

We don't have one.

After another hour or so, I can't stand it any more. I am not the leader, but I need to go. Sitting here working when I agreed to be on strike? I can almost feel my right hand withering.

Though it terrifies me, I push back my chair and get up.

Thankfully, I am not the only one. Somehow we all decided to go at the same moment, and all across the factory floor girls are pushing back their chairs and rising. Then we all take our coats and hats and walk past the shocked-silent foremen and foreladies down the stairs and out onto the street.

Policemen stand outside, glaring at us, and one snaps at a girl who walks too close to him, "If you don't behave, you'll get this on your head," while shaking his club at her.

She flinches away, and we all move down the sidewalk away from them.

Then we stop, and stand, and wonder.

What happens now?

CHAPTER SIXTEEN

Maria
December 13, 1909

"ARE YOU COMING UPSTAIRS WITH ME?"

I nod and walk toward Isabella, enjoying hearing Italian at work. We used to speak English, since most of the factory girls know at least a little no matter which country they come from, but now it's almost all Italians here at Triangle since the Jewish girls went on strike.

The bosses brought in a priest last week, who told those of us who remain that it's our duty not to strike like the Jewish girls, that we will go to Hell if we do. He made several girls cry, but he wasted his breath with me.

Margherita has been on the picket line since November because her father believes it's the right thing for her to do since she'll eventually earn more money this way. Vinnie, though, is more concerned about the money I wouldn't be earning right now if I went on strike, so he's looking for a new home for us because living with the Billotas is now uncomfortable. They speak to us only when they must, and I know they think us foolish because I'm not on strike.

Well, I feel the same way about them. Why would I strike when the bosses are treating us so well? With so many girls gone, there's plenty of work for those who remain, and I've been allowed to move from setting sleeves to making cuffs. Next week I'll begin attaching cuffs and then I'll earn an extra fifty cents a week. I am learning so much now without even needing to change factories. The strikers are fools to be out on the street, making only the one or two dollars a week the union can give them, while I learn to take over their jobs.

And as if all of that weren't enough, we also have what Isabella and I and the other eighth-floor girls are going up to ninth for.

"Welcome, girls," Mr. Harris says, a huge smile on his thin face, when we and the workers from the tenth floor arrive together through the narrow stairwell door. Mr. Blanck stands beside him, his bigger face bearing a smaller and somehow stiffer smile, which is still more of a smile than we ever saw from him before the strike, and adds, "I hope you're hungry!"

We are, as we have been every day since they started this a few weeks ago, so we collect oranges and rolls and cups of tea, all for free, from the foreladies then stand laughing and chatting as we eat.

A lot of our talk, as always, is about men. Isabella recently found a new fella so she tells us all about him, and the other girls chatter about their men too, and then Isabella says, "You're awfully quiet, Maria. Haven't you heard from that Alonzo of yours yet?"

The smile I force to my face feels as stiff as Mr. Blanck's looks. Letters from Mamma and Papà have reached Vinnie and me at least once a week since we arrived, but not even one from Alonzo.

My parents, in their last letter, talked about how glad they were that we had settled into America and especially how glad that I seemed so happy, and I know they think I no longer love Alonzo, that I don't miss him and dream of him every day.

Well, let them think that.

Since I can't ask them for news of him, I begged Vinnie until he agreed to ask a friend of his at home to find out what's happening. But I don't want to tell the girls that. "I'm sure his letters are lost in the mail," I say, reminding myself that it could be the truth. "Or maybe he's writing so many love letters that he hasn't had time to mail them all yet!"

The girls laugh, and one pulls out a letter from her fella back home and begins reading it aloud. This takes most of the attention away from me, but Isabella leans in and whispers to me, "I'm sorry, Maria. You're right, of course you'll get his letters soon."

"Assolutamente," I whisper back, and she gives my shoulder a friendly pat before turning to listen to the reading girl.

A friendly pat, but also a sympathetic one, and though I told her I absolutely would get Alonzo's letters soon, I can tell she doesn't actually believe I will.

Could she be right?

A sensation I've never felt before rises in me, like pressure building up in Mamma's sauce pot when she hasn't vented the lid: anger with Alonzo.

Too much mail *has* managed to reach us for me to believe his letters simply went astray, and I don't truly believe he's too busy writing to me to visit the post office. I've included our address in every letter I've sent to him, so he can't have lost it. Yet he's still not writing. Maybe he misses me too much to talk about it, maybe he's just not as good at finding the right words as I am, maybe—

No. The maybes do not matter. Whatever the reason, he is not acting as a fella should, and he is making the other girls feel sorry for me, and it must stop.

I've noticed that men don't always have the drive and determination of girls. It's certainly the case with Papà and Mamma, since Vinnie and I would never have come to America without Mamma's insistence, and perhaps it will be with Alonzo and me as well.

But I will handle it as Mamma would, straight-forward and without flinching. I'll find out, through Vinnie's friend, what has gone wrong, and then I'll fix it and I'll receive Alonzo's letters, and soon I'll receive Alonzo himself and we will be married.

And once that happens, I will be his wife and I'll stop working in the factories and all of this strike nonsense will be even less my concern than it is now.

A hand falls on my shoulder, startling me, and I turn to Isabella as she says, "Maria, will you be my partner?"

"Oh! I was thinking so hard I didn't even hear the music. But of course."

She smiles at me, and I smile back and push away the thoughts of why Alonzo isn't writing and what I will do about it. I have plans, and I will carry out those plans, but for now I'm here with my fellow workers and the music is too lovely to ignore.

Mr. Blanck knows our favorite music by now and he always chooses it. "Maple Leaf Rag" is our first dance, so fast it makes us pant as we do our Turkey Trot even though Mr. Harris is clearly uncomfortable with having such a modern dance in his factory. Mr. Blanck told him not to be silly when he tried to stop us the first time, so now we dance as we please. Isabella leads, since I only learned the dance a few weeks ago, guiding me through our forward and backward steps and our little jumps and elbows-out moves to make us look like turkeys, and we aren't the only pair laughing so hard at the end that we can barely breathe.

We get a chance to recover, though, because Mr. Blanck has to change the needle on the Victrola and wind it up again for the next record, so we eat and chat a little more, although I carefully steer the conversation away from fellas to what enjoyable things everyone did yesterday on our day off and what we might do next Sunday.

Once Mr. Blanck is ready for us, we change partners and sway gently in pairs to "Shine On, Harvest Moon" and then after another winding and needle change to "In My Merry Oldsmobile" before the wonderful fast song "My Wife's Gone to the Country", which we love because we dance around quickly and shout out the "hurrah, hurrah" with the husband who's so glad to be alone. We all know how husbands are, pretending they don't want their wives around, and even though I know Alonzo won't be that way with me I still shout with the rest.

The bosses smile to watch us, and clap for us, and they have even promised to start giving a prize a week to the best dancer. Nobody knows what it will be, but the fact that they're giving it is a sign that they care about us.

Us, but not the union girls, since none of them have been allowed back, not even the ones who decided to leave the strike.

Not even, I think, feeling my happiness at dancing fading away like the dying notes of a song, the girl who begged and cried at Mr. Harris's feet because she couldn't find work at as high a pay anywhere else and she had to support her four sisters. He showed her no sympathy.

Can he really care about any of—

"Maria! You're not yourself today."

I sigh. "You're right. I'm too busy thinking."

"Well, don't." Isabella catches my hand and pulls me into another dance. "Let's just have fun. We have fellas, we have work, we have dancing, so let's have fun and not worry."

I try.

I don't quite succeed.

"MARIA, I HAVE TO TELL YOU—"

"I can't talk now, Vinnie," I call over my shoulder as I hurry away down the sidewalk. "If I'm late for work, they'll think I'm striking and—"

"Wait!"

I turn back, startled by his tone, like he's seen Mount Vesuvius belching out smoke and is dreading a disaster.

When I see his face, I am dreading one too. "Vinnie, what's wrong?"

His mouth moves like he's speaking, but no sound comes out.

My hand flies up to clutch my throat, where a huge lump of fear is choking me. 'Tell me! Is it... it's not Mamma or Papà, is it?" He had a letter from them last night, same as me, and I read him everything that was in mine but perhaps he didn't do the same. He *did* seem upset at the time, but he'd insisted he was just tired from a long day of digging up pavement to put subway tunnels underneath and I'd believed him.

Did he lie?

"No, no," he says, rushing toward me. "They're fine. I promise."

Relief flashes through me then is gone because he's still so worried. "Then what?"

He looks at me, takes a breath as if to speak, then shakes his head. "Go to work. We'll talk later."

"As if I could work all day wondering what's happening. Tell me!"

"I should have kept quiet," he mutters.

"Well, you didn't. So tell me."

He studies my face for another moment then sighs and reaches into his pocket. "I'm so sorry, sorellina."

He only calls me 'little sister' when something truly horrible is coming to me, and hearing the word brings that lump of fear back to my throat. I take a step away from him, wanting to escape whatever he's about to tell me, but he pulls his hand from his pocket and holds out a small scrap torn from a newspaper.

I don't want to read it, but my eyes betray me and look down.

Alonzo Lauretti and Miss Alessandra Tortorelli of San Sebastiano al Vesuvio were made man and wife on November 20, 1909 by Father Stellino at the bride's family home.

So few words, but so unbearable to read.

My coffee and roll twist in my stomach and for a moment I think I might throw them up. I bite my lip and stare at the newspaper from home, though the words are already burned into my memory.

"I'm sorry." Though I know Vinnie's beside me, he sounds very far away. "I truly am. I asked Pasquale if he knew why Alonzo wasn't writing, as you told me to, and he asked Mamma to send this to me. I know you hoped Alonzo would—"

"When did you get this?" I raise my head slowly from the awful paper as anger fills me. "Yesterday, in your letter?"

He gives me a single nod. I can tell from his expression that he knows he should have shown me then and he's sorry, but I don't care about that.

"And you kept it from me? You're as bad as Alonzo, a lying no-good horrible—"

I can't think of anything else to call him, and I can't look at his guilty miserable face another second, so I spin around and run toward the trolley stop.

AT MY TABLE AT TRIANGLE, I sit staring so hard at my sewing that my eyes burn. I wish the fabric would catch fire and take the whole place with it.

And every man inside.

Not the girls. Girls suffer enough. Just the men. The horrible men.

I squeeze my eyes shut for a moment to moisten them and again see in my mind's angry eye the newspaper announcement.

How could Alonzo *do* this to me? He swore he would never marry Alessandra. He promised he would come to me in America, would come to me and marry me. He looked deep into my eyes, kissed my mouth, and said he loved me and we would be together forever.

He lied. Everything he ever did with me was a lie.

And my brother! He had no right to keep that news from me, even for a day. He treats me like a child.

Alonzo did too, although what we did in his parents' stable was not something to do with a child. He thought my body was a woman's, but he saw my mind and my heart as those of a child. He used me for his pleasure and he didn't care about me.

And my parents, insisting I would never marry Alonzo! They were right, as it happens, but that's not the point. Everyone acts like I am young and foolish and do not deserve to make my own decisions.

I hate it.

"Get to work, Maria," a man says into my ear, far too close, and I turn to see Mr. Saberstein smirking at me. "Be a good girl now. I'd hate to have to punish you."

I have seen this boss 'punishing' girls, pinching their bottoms and grinning at their discomfort, and I've always been afraid he will do it to me.

Now, though, I'm too angry for fear. Too angry at every man in America and beyond. *Have* to punish me? He wants to. And I will never allow it. "If you do," I say, pushing my chair back and jumping to my feet, "I will kill you with my bare hands. I hate you!"

He stares at me with his mouth hanging open, stunned that I would dare to speak to him in such a way, and that makes me even angrier. I wish I knew some swear-words in English, because I would stun him even more if I could. I would call him every bad thing in the world.

But I don't, so I show my feelings by stomping to the dressing room, past the rows of shocked-silent girls, to fetch my things then stomping back toward the stairs.

As I pass him, he shouts at me, "You'll never work here again, little girl!"

I scream back, "Good! I'd rather die!"

CHAPTER SEVENTEEN

Rosie

December 14, 1909

IN THE WEEKS SINCE WE WENT ON STRIKE, I've gotten used to the standard routine of picketing, but today is different. Moments after I arrive for my morning shift on the strike line at the Triangle Waist Company, to which I've been assigned this week, I am stunned to see a small group of strikebreakers arriving in automobiles.

They look stunned too, mostly with excitement although one looks like she might be sick onto the sidewalk, and as they climb out of the black cars, one of the three policemen near me whistles and says, "Model Ts! Wish I could get a trip in one of those."

"Maybe you should be a scab then," another replies, laughing, and they stand looking with envy at the girls entering the factory.

I'm envious too. I've never been in an automobile, and it doesn't seem right that the scabs get to experience something so special and I don't. I wonder if the bosses are actually doing this to *make* us strikers envious so we'll be scabs too.

I wouldn't be a scab again, though, for all the automobiles in America.

Even though my parents would want me to.

I have, of course, had to send them less money than I did before. The union is doing its best to give each striking girl at least a few dollars a week, but I know from Clara that it's spending money as quickly as it raises it. I'm not taking strike pay because I do have some savings, but it hurts to use them when I wanted to build them up.

The week we struck, I sent only twenty-five cents to my parents and explained that I'll be sending that much each week instead of the dollar and a half I'd built up to. I didn't tell them it was about the union, naturally; I pretended to be supporting a friend who's fallen on hard times. I haven't yet had a letter from them about this, but I know they won't approve. I'm supposed to be saving money for their passage here, not helping someone else.

Though I feel guilty at not doing what they'd want, I know I'm doing the right thing by being on strike. Even if Clara weren't my good friend, I wouldn't go against the union now. Being on the picket line each day, seeing the horrible things done to the strikers, I know their cause is worth fighting for.

Our cause, not theirs.

As Clara says, "If we stick, we will win."

She's right that all of us together can make a difference. I am determined to stick with my fellow strikers, more now than ever.

I just won't tell my parents about it.

I stamp my feet to work the chill from them, glad I need stick only another few minutes. Then the morning picketing will be over and I will go to the union hall and work there at stuffing envelopes and making signs. No point in picketing a factory once all its workers are inside for their work day and will not be coming out again for hours. Triangle is one of the factories even keeping their girls inside at lunch by giving them free food, which is of course to prevent us speaking to them and encouraging them to strike.

The policemen standing near me look almost as uncomfortable with the cold as I feel, and the fallen women who hang around to taunt us look even worse, and that makes me a little happier. With all the abuse these people have dished out to us girls, I can't help liking that they're feeling some pain now too.

"Are you going to Clara's tonight?"

I nod at Esther. It's the sixth night of Hanukkah and my first time visiting Clara's home. I'm excited to meet her parents, since I can't imagine what wild revolutionary people they must be to have a daughter like Clara, and also looking forward to eating latkes and spinning the dreidel and watching the menorah glowing with candlelight.

"Me too. Do you want to go with—"

Before Esther can finish her sentence, a voice calls, "Annie!"

I, and the other strikers including Annie, turn to see a man waving at us. "They need you back at the hall," he says to her, and she goes to pick up her pocketbook from the wall where we leave them while we carry our signs.

As she moves away, my eyes meet the man's and we both say, "You!" at once.

He chuckles and comes over. "Rosie Lehrer! A sight for sore eyes!"

"Mr. Starr," I say, then pause as we give each other an awkward hug. When he releases me, I go on with, "I didn't even know you'd come to America." He left Belostok about a year ago, and all my parents said was that he'd moved away. "You're working with the union?"

"Of course I am. But you? Your parents allow this?"

The thought of him writing to them, telling them where he saw me and what I was doing, freezes my brain so completely I can't say a word. I stare at him, feeling my cheeks getting hot, feeling like a fool.

"Ah, they don't allow it, I see! Well, I won't tell." He shakes his head. "It's brave of you, maydeleh, after what happened to Ida."

I don't like being called "little girl", but the end of his sentence wipes away my annoyance with that. "Aunt Ida? What about her?"

"Why, she—" He squeezes his eyes shut. "Oy. You don't know."

"She had a heart attack."

But even before he opens his now-sad eyes and slowly shakes his head, everything inside me seems to shift position and the truth becomes clear.

I know, I *know* that the story I've believed for months is a lie. I should have known it before. There were too many conversations between my parents quickly cut off when I entered the room, too many neighbors murmuring when we passed by. "No," I whisper. "No, she didn't. What happened?"

He take a step away from me. "You should ask your parents that."

"Please, Mr. Starr. They won't tell me, and even if they will, it'll take weeks. I need to know."

He sighs. "Forgive me, Joseph and Gussie," he murmurs, "for what I do to your daughter." Then he takes a deep breath and says, "Rosie, your aunt was killed for her union work."

"For... her..." Is it possible he's confused Aunt Ida with someone else? "No, she didn't do any union—"

"Even that you don't know?" He shakes his head. "This I can't abide. Ida deserves better. She *did* do union work, and she did it so well they killed her for it. She was the highest-ranked woman in the Bund, the Jewish Labour Bund. She gave speeches... ah, the speeches. I used to say she could charm a pickle back to being a cucumber. Such power in her words. With her passion, and that of others too, we led strikes among the Jewish workers in Belostok. It was helping too, the working conditions were improving, so a year ago we began looking beyond Belostok. That's when..." He pulls in an even deeper breath then sighs it out. "That's when the rumors started."

"Rumors?" I say, hardly able to take all this in. "Of what?"

"That we in the Bund were in danger. That's why I left, Rosie, why I came here. I wanted her to come with me, marry me and come with me. I was afraid. Afraid they'd kill us. But your aunt, never any fear in her. She always said, 'Besser tsu shtarben shtai'endik aider tsu leben oif di kni.' And that's probably true. But I'm alive, and..."

He doesn't finish his sentence, but he doesn't need to. We stand in silent memory of Aunt Ida, a woman I idolized but didn't even know, then he says, "Well. I need to take Annie here back to the hall. But we'll talk again soon, Rosie. Yes, we will."

He's already backing away from me, though, and I know we won't. I can see it in how he can't meet my eyes, hear it in how awkward he sounds. He will avoid me if he sees me again. That's all right, because I don't need anything else from him. I barely notice as he hurries away with Annie. I'm too busy thinking.

Besser tsu shtarben shtai'endik aider tsu leben oif di kni.

Better to die upright than to live on your knees.

My aunt did the first thing. Am I, a girl cowering in fear of her parents every time she so much as considers putting a toe out of place, doing the second?

"Rosie," Esther says, moving over to me from where she's been standing at a polite distance but could no doubt hear everything, "oh, Rosie, are you all right? Your aunt..."

"My parents... with every letter they—they forbid me to do union work. I didn't know why but now... it's because of Aunt Ida."

"Why wouldn't they tell you? What she did, how she died?"

I don't know. But I very much want to find out. "I have to write them a letter. I want to go home now and write."

"Of course," she says, patting my shoulder. "Of—"

Triangle's door flies open and a wild-eyed girl tumbles out. She is wearing her coat, unbuttoned, and clutching her hat and pocketbook, and she runs right into a prostitute without seeming to notice.

"Hey!" The woman grabs the girl's arm. "Watch out!"

"Don't tell me what to do!" She pulls herself away and to my shock and horror spits at her attacker then shouts something in a language I don't understand.

The woman clearly does understand, or is at least outraged by the spitting, because she shrieks and jerks the girl to the ground where she begins kicking her.

The girl squeals, and I rush forward to the nearest policeman and say, "Sir, please," in my best sweet voice. "Sir, please don't let her hurt her."

He spins around, laughing from what he's witnessing, then stops laughing and glares at me. "Why shouldn't I?"

Another policeman moves closer to me, and I want to run before they can hit me like I've seen them hit other girls, but I can hear the girl whimpering and it gives me the strength to say, "She's just a girl. She doesn't know what she's doing. It's not fair."

The moment I say the last words, I know I was wrong to choose them, because the first policeman's eyes light up. "You're right, it's not." He looks past me at the group of fallen women laughing and cheering on their friend. "One of you get over here and make this fair."

I do turn to run this time, but he grabs my coat and then a woman from the group is on me, her painted mouth stretched wide with delight. I've never been in a fight in my life, and she probably fights every day of hers, so in seconds I too am on the ground being kicked.

I curl into a ball to protect my face and my stomach, as we were told by the union, and try not to cry out because I know it will please all these horrible people to hear my pain. I've heard about this happening to other girls, and I felt sorry for them, but it's terrifying to experience it myself, to be the focus of such awful attention and to feel so many blows. I don't know how long it lasts, but I hurt everywhere when a policeman finally pulls the woman off me and says, "That's enough. Let the girl up."

The laughing woman gives me one last kick before she's dragged far enough away that she can't reach me, then I sit up and scrub the tears off my face.

I'm hauled to my feet, sharply and with no kindness, and I gasp in pain and surprise. "Let's go, girls," the policeman holding my arm says as he pulls me toward the other girl who's being held too. "Off to court with you."

Though I've seen it before, I am shocked when it's only me and the girl who are dragged down the sidewalk.

I take a breath, though it hurts my chest, but I don't waste that breath asking about the ones who actually attacked us, the ones who are now standing around flirting with the remaining policeman. Esther and the other strikers still standing shocked on the sidewalk don't waste their breath either. It's well-known that the policemen will encourage scabs and women like these to attack us and then arrest us for it, so there's no point in complaining.

The girl does not share this attitude.

She seems to have lost her reason, shouting in Italian-accented English about how horrible men are and how much she hates them. Though at first the policeman laugh, they are soon tired of her, and one of them waves his club at her and promises he will make her be quiet. She is, then, but I have a feeling she will not be for long.

I just hope she stays quiet once we get to the courthouse. If not, she'll have us both in the workhouse.

CHAPTER EIGHTEEN

Maria
December 14, 1909

THE GIRL WHO WAS ARRESTED WITH ME LOOKS WORRIED, but I know I do not. I am still furious, and I think I might stay that way for the rest of my life.

That woman who attacked me, she should never have done that. Yes, I did spit at her, but it didn't even reach her so she had no reason to hurt me. She did it because she knew she wouldn't be stopped. Those policemen thought it was funny. Funny, to watch a woman beat a girl! They're as bad as all men. I will never trust a man, or love one, again.

Vinnie's sad face when I left him floats before my eyes. How much sadder he will be when he learns I'm in a stinking crowded cell at the courthouse!

Well, what of it? I did nothing that wrong and I refuse to be ashamed. Besides, the rich women have been paying the fines of girls who are arrested, so I will be free soon and maybe Vinnie won't need to know.

A woman with her lip paint smeared across her cheek is thrown into the damp cell with us, shrieking, "He never paid me! He used me and didn't pay!" and the girl with me shrinks away into the corner.

I don't like that. I know that they put the strikers into cells with prostitutes to make them feel guilty and ashamed, and if *I* know, she certainly should since she actually is a striker.

But everyone has to survive somehow, and the prostitutes are doing what they must. I wouldn't want to do their work, but I don't think we should be horrified at being associated with them. We should be horrified with the men who hire them and mistreat them.

This girl, though, she helped me even at risk to herself. So I walk to her, carefully to make sure I don't step on any of the women sprawled everywhere, and sink onto the cold dirty floor beside her. Down here the stench of filthy bodies and fear is even stronger, but by breathing through my mouth I can survive it. "Are you all right?" I say.

She nods. "Sore, but yes. What about you?"

Her Jewish accent is strong but I can understand her. "I'll be fine," I say, studying her. She had her hat and hatpin confiscated before we were placed in this cell just as I did, and the hair falling out of her topknot is as dark as mine but her skin is paler. She could almost be my sister, and I mean it when I add, "And I'm sorry you were arrested too. I heard you trying to stop that awful woman hitting me."

"For all the good it did either of us." She tries to smile, but it's hard because her lip is swollen.

"I'm Maria Cirrito," I say.

"Rosie Lehrer. What made you race out of the building like that? Your tail on fire?"

"No, my heart." I tell her about Alonzo, how I loved him and how he lied, and finish with, "So I'll never trust a man again."

"They're not all bad," she says. "My friend Julia's fella Israel is—"

This makes me angry all over again. How can she not see the truth? I burst in with, "The bosses are! And the policemen and the judges and—"

"Shhh! You can't talk about them here!"

Though I don't want to be quiet, not now and not ever, she might be right that complaining about the judges when we are about to go before one and might be overheard is a bad idea. "Well, all the other men, then. My brother Vinnie, who thinks he can always decide everything for me, and the foremen and the bosses, and those awful men who beat the striking girls. You heard about that one girl, Clara, didn't you? They attacked her right on the street, when she wasn't even picketing."

"I know Clara," she says, her eyes brightening. "We worked together. Still do, now that we are on strike."

I am impressed. This Rosie seems like the kind of girl who always does what she's told to do, except for the one moment in which she tried to help me, but if she's working with Clara, there must be more to her than that. "Is she as wonderful a speaker as everyone says?"

Rosie nods and begins telling me about Clara, but before she can say more than a few words, a policeman appears at the door of our cell and calls us both out.

After a short walk through the hallways, during which I keep my head up high and Rosie hangs hers as if we've already been told we're guilty, we are brought into a room with a crowd of people sitting in chairs and one man in a bigger fancier chair at the front.

The policeman delivers us to stand at a wooden rail before the man, who must be the judge, and says, "Your Honor, the strikers Rosie Lehrer and Maria Cirrito," then moves to stand against the wall.

As he goes, the judge looks down at the papers on his desk then raises his head and frowns at us. "This strike is a crime against God and nature, and you girls, you attacked two innocent women. "

"We did not! They attacked us. And they weren't innocent."

He raises his eyebrows at me, and Rosie elbows me as he says, "Silence, girl. The policemen told me all." He squints. "You're the kind of girl who paints her face?"

Rosie draws a quick surprised breath at the comment, and though he told me to be silent, I have to defend myself. "I *don't* paint," I say, while dragging my finger across my cheek to show him that none of the color comes off. "It was cold in the cell."

He gives a little grunt as if he doesn't care either way, then looks past us, to the people sitting watching. "It would be perfectly futile for me to fine them," he says, sounding angry and annoyed. "Some charitable woman would pay their fines."

Rosie stiffens beside me, but I don't know why. Isn't it good if he doesn't fine us?

He gets to his feet so he looks down on us. "I have decided," he says, sounding like the voice of God Almighty, "to commit you girls to the workhouse. Five days."

Rosie sways and I feel dizzy myself. Five days of hard labor? I didn't know he could do that. Is this why Rosie has been acting so afraid and hanging her head?

"Cannot this sentence be mollified?"

The judge glares at the woman behind Rosie and me who spoke those shocked words. "It cannot."

He jerks his head toward us, and the man who brought us in leads us out again, nearly dragging us because we're both unsteady on our feet.

How will we survive five days at the workhouse when we can barely walk from fear and dread?

ROSIE AND I STAND HUDDLED TOGETHER by the railing of the ferry taking us to Blackwell's Island. We have been huddled together from the moment the policeman took us from the courthouse and pushed us into an even more crowded cell at the Tombs. I never knew, before, that the downtown jail was called that, but the policeman said rudely, "Welcome to the Tombs, girls," when he left us and I do understand the name: our cell was so cold and damp and dark that it might have been our grave.

We spent the rest of our sentencing day, and the long horrible night that followed, awake and terrified together on a bare metal bed frame while our fellow prisoners, prostitutes and opium addicts and other awful people, cried and laughed and shouted words that no decent girl could ever say or even admit to knowing. It was an awful place to be, both the cell itself and knowing what lay before us at the workhouse, and though we both tried not to cry, eventually we couldn't help it.

At least we're in the fresh air now, after being hauled in a police wagon to the ferry dock on the East River, but I know we won't be for long. So I take huge gulps of air to clean the stench of the night from my lungs and rub a few of the gently falling snowflakes into my cheeks to wash away any signs of the tears I shed last night.

Rosie is taking breaths too, but hers are shuddering and sound more like she's trying not to cry again.

I put my hand lightly on the shoulder of her now-dirty black coat, and she startles and turns to me as I say, trying to cheer her up, "I haven't been on a boat since Ellis Island. It's nice to get such a clean breeze, isn't it?"

"I..." She looks around as though she hadn't even noticed we were on a boat. "I suppose." She rubs her eyes. "I... oh, I can't believe we're here. We were nobodies, and now... we're criminals. Are we? Isn't being a nobody better than being..." She glances at the guard standing nearby. "We've been *arrested*."

I'm not sure why she's saying all of this. Of course we were arrested. Has she only just realized it? "Well, yes, I know," I say, giving her shoulder a squeeze. "But it doesn't mean we're nobodies. You know Clara, and I..." I trail off, not sure how to finish the sentence. *Am* I a nobody? I don't want to be. I refuse to be.

She shakes her head, looking frustrated. "I do, but that's not what I mean."

"Tell me."

She stares down at her dirty hands on the ferry's rail, then sighs. "I can't. I don't know how to say it."

She probably could in Yiddish but that wouldn't help us. "Well, let's talk about something else. Where were you working before the strike started?"

She tells me that easily enough, and I tell her about Bijou and Triangle, but when she again tries to explain whatever she was trying to say before, she can't find the words. Strange, since her English is as good as mine and maybe even better.

I'm about to tell her not to fret over it when the ferry reaches the dock and a guard on the gangway shouts, "Let's go, ladies!" The sneer in his voice on the last word turns my stomach; he clearly doesn't think any of us are anywhere near being a lady.

He's right, but I raise my chin and walk by him with an attitude that would perfectly suit any of the rich women living in one of the lovely expensive red-brick houses on the Row by Washington Square, and I'm pleased when he gives me a quick glance as if my calmness confuses him.

It must confuse Rosie too, because once we're on the dock she leans in and says, "You aren't scared at all, are you? How?"

She sounds near tears again, and I can understand that because the sight of the tall gray stone workhouse building looming over us like a monster from a nightmare is upsetting me too. I slip my arm through hers and admit, "Oh, I'm scared, Rosie. Very scared. But I promised myself I wouldn't let a man upset me ever again, and I won't. We can be brave together." I can feel her trembling, so I make my voice as strong as I can. "Right? It's only five days."

"Five days," she repeats, her body's trembling in her voice too, then clears her throat and says, "Yes, five days," sounding calmer. I think I've helped her, and being able to help her has helped me, so if I have to be at the workhouse I'm glad I'm not here alone.

An hour later, we both know it will be a very long five days. During that hour, after we have our clothes taken from us and replaced with heavy striped wool dresses so everyone will know what we are, we're sent with several other girls from our ferry to scrub the floors of the nearby hospital.

As we walk over together we learn that they are also striking girls, and I waste no time telling them what I think and how we need to fight back against the men who own the factories and who let prostitutes beat girls right outside their buildings.

The two Italian girls are not sure, and frustrate me by saying they need to ask their fathers and brothers, but the Jewish girl agrees with me straightaway even though we have a time of it understanding each other.

I can tell Rosie is still feeling sad and sorry for herself but she joins in our discussion to translate as needed, and she tells us all about what the union has been doing to take care of workers. She's not a great speaker, although of course we had a difficult night so that's not surprising, but even so I learn a lot. I knew they were giving strikers a small amount of money but I didn't know how hard they worked to get that money from the well-off people who support them and from speeches all over New York City and even further away. I'm impressed.

Then Rosie surprises me by saying, "Clara and the other union organizers, they aren't sure they can get the Italian girls to really be part of the union."

"And why not?" I say, annoyed.

She glances at the other two Italians, who've both just admitted they won't join without a man telling them they can, but doesn't say anything specifically about them. Instead, she says, "Jewish girls grew up with... well, some of them knew about unions back home. A lot of them did, really. Most. So now that they're here, they're comfortable joining. The Italians, though, most of them come from farming or restaurant-owning backgrounds—" She cuts herself off and turns to me. "That's true, isn't it? It's what they say at the union."

I nod, and she seems to relax.

"Oh, good. I wouldn't want to tell a lie. So the Italian girls aren't used to unions, and they're also... not... as used to..."

"They don't make their own decisions, they do what their men tell them to," I say bluntly. "Is that what you're trying to say?"

Her cheeks go pink. "Yes, but I didn't know how to say it. I... is it wrong?"

Ah, I wish it were, but when I consider my friends at home, or indeed myself before yesterday, I know she's right. "For most Italian girls, it's true," I have to admit, and the other two nod.

The Jewish girl says something I can't understand, and Rosie nods in reply then says in English to us Italians, "Because it was that way back home, she says, doesn't mean it has to be that way here."

The other Italians and I exchange glances but don't speak. She's right that it doesn't *have* to be that way. But will the men see it in that light? For that matter, will the girls?

"Hurry *up*, there's much to be done," a woman in a long black dress shouts to us from the front step of the hospital, and we stop talking as we increase our pace.

Once inside, we're each set to work on different parts of the floors so we can no longer talk. My knees ache in moments from the cold hard stone, and my ears ring with the screeches and wails of the poor patients, and as the minutes wear slowly on, the idea of doing this for nearly a week is almost unthinkable.

So I don't think of it. Instead, I think of the union. They could be right about the two Italians from our ferry, but the chance that I will get involved? It's about as high as the chance that the bosses are paying the policemen to harass strikers. When we're released, I will go straight to that union hall and offer to help in any way I can.

The Italians are still being told by priests, priests hired by the bosses, that Hell awaits any of them who strike. I can explain to them in their own language that the true Hell is sewing away our lives for horrible men who will never be fair with us.

Then we shall see what an Italian girl can do!

CHAPTER NINETEEN

Rosie
December 20, 1909

MARIA DOESN'T SPEAK TO ME as our ferry takes us back to Manhattan from Blackwell's Island and the workhouse. Since she does speak to the other girls, I think she's annoyed with me.

I understand. I'm annoyed with me too.

As we struggled to fall asleep last night in our tiny hard beds at the workhouse, I was thinking of how exhausting our five days of hard labor had been and how going back to the picket line terrified me because I might be arrested again, and before I knew it I whispered to her, "Maybe we should just be scabs. Wouldn't that be better?"

I didn't really mean it, I don't think, but before I could say anything else she snapped, "Of course it would not. We have to fight the men. Scab or no, the men don't think we matter. Remember how the bosses treat us, and how the policemen don't protect us! They think they can force us to back down and change our minds. Well, it won't work on me and it shouldn't work on you either. I'll be a union girl from now on. You be a scab if you choose." Then she rolled over so her back was to me and didn't respond when I tried to explain myself.

Not that I was able to. I couldn't find the right words last night, and I wouldn't be able to now even if I thought she wanted me to speak to her. Maria seemed shocked when I suggested that we were both nobodies and perhaps better to be so, but I know I didn't explain myself well then either. What I meant was clear in my mind, but the words wouldn't come out.

I only meant, both on the ferry heading to the workhouse and last night, that I'm not sure I have the strength to carry on. I picketed and protested, but this feels so much more personal. I am no longer just an anonymous girl on the line. Instead I've been a prisoner, arrested and sentenced, surrounded by other prisoners who have also been sentenced for their crimes. I did not feel I was doing a crime, before, but now the faces of the disgusted policemen and the angry judge swim before my eyes and I know they think I did and I know they hate me.

It is not at all how I expected to feel in America.

It is far too much like life in Russia, being watched and despised by the authorities.

And now that I know what really happened to Aunt Ida, it's even worse. I thought I could trust my parents. They've made all my decisions all my life. But they hid my aunt's entire life and her death from me, and I don't know what's true any more. I don't know who to believe, who to trust.

Maybe the judge was right. Maybe I *am* a criminal. Maybe all of us who've struck are.

I don't *think* so, but is that because I don't want it to be true?

I was beginning to feel like I was important, like my striking was helping to make a difference, but now I'm not sure that's even something to strive for. Am I better off to be a nobody?

As I promise myself to work harder on my English so I'll be better able to express myself, Maria nudges me and points toward Manhattan, saying, "Look at the crowd! It wasn't that big when we left, was it?"

I raise my head to see better past the brim of the hat that was returned to me before we boarded the ferry and squint to see the dock. "I don't think so." I smile, relieved she's speaking to me. "Maybe they're all here to welcome us back."

She gives a laugh with no amusement in it. "Lots more arrested strikers, most like."

When we reach the dock at Twenty-Sixth Street, though, nobody in the throng looks like a prisoner.

"Rosie!" I hear Clara but cannot see her since she's so short, but when she names me the people all start shouting at me and at Maria, whose name they also somehow know, and at the other girl strikers who had five-day sentences with us.

"Maria, come here and let me be the first to welcome you!"

"No," another woman snaps at the one who spoke, "let *me*!"

We girls from the ferry stare at each other, confused, then are swept up into the crowd, and in a few moments it becomes clear: while we were gone, the city fell into a rage over workhouse sentences for strikers. Now somehow we're not the evil girls they thought before.

Now we are heroines.

Men want to interview us for their newspapers, women want to have us speak to their clubs or parade us around to get attention for suffrage or another of their pet causes, and girls just want to stare at us with shining eyes and whisper, "Thank you for being so brave."

Maria was brave. She kept encouraging the rest of us to carry on, reminding us of how we need to fight the men who are against the union, and without her strong words I'm not sure we'd have made it through. I, and the others, used words mostly to complain about the lack of food and the awful pain of a day spent on your knees scrubbing. I know we weren't brave.

But these people think we were, and I can tell they would not thank us for saying otherwise. They need us to be what they think we are. We are symbols, now. The brave girl strikers, back from the workhouse.

I want to be *Rosie*, not a striking girl or a prisoner or a symbol. I want to be me, and I want 'me' to matter. But I think maybe I am more suited to always be part of a faceless crowd. Being recognized like this feels awful.

I hear a male voice shout, "Maria!" louder than everyone else, and my friend turns from the man who is interviewing her and shrieks, "Vinnie!" then runs toward her brother as he runs toward her.

When they meet, he grabs her and hugs her hard, and because he is tall I can see over her head that tears are running down his cheeks.

My throat tightens. Nobody has come to greet me. Who could? My entire family is still at home in Russia, and I have no husband or fella to hug me and cry over me. Mr. Starr probably knows where I went, but I'm still convinced he'll make sure we don't have another opportunity to speak. The girls at the immigrant home are probably worried for me, but they don't love me like Vinnie loves Maria.

Maria hugs her brother back, while I wonder why his handsome face looks familiar, then draws away and pulls him by the hand over to me. "Vinnie, this is my new friend Rosie Lehrer. Rosie, my brother Vincente, but you can call him Vinnie if you want, like I do."

That feels too forward to me, and I like Vincente much better than Vinnie anyhow so I say, "How do you do, Vincente?"

"Much better now, thank you," he says, wrapping his arm around his sister's shoulders. "I have been so worried, and so angry. To do this to you poor girls! Both of you, *all* of you. How could the judge have been such a—a—"

In his fury he cannot find a good word to describe the judge that will not offend us, and as Maria laughs and informs him that we have heard a great many unpleasant words in the last few days so he shouldn't worry, I look up at him and his anger lets me remember him.

He, and a girl who must have been Maria, were the ones Josephine collided with in the crowd at the Hudson River for that celebration back in September.

I don't think either of them is aware that we have encountered each other before, and I find myself feeling sad at that. Not that Maria doesn't remember, but that *he* doesn't. I thought of him for a long time after that day and I hoped he might have thought of me.

Of course, at the moment all his thoughts are for his sister. He pulls her closer and lets loose a stream of Italian, in which I catch only the word "Alonzo" so he must be apologizing for hiding the truth about the boy she thought loved her.

She reaches up and kisses his cheek when he says that, and for a few moments she leans against him and lets him fuss at her, but then something he says in his torrent of words makes her push back and stand alone as she says in English, "No, Vinnie, I will not go back. I would not work in a factory tomorrow for a million dollars. I will be working for the union, if they will have me."

He stares at her, his mouth opening and closing like a fish on dry land, and finally says, "You will not." His words are definite but his tone is more like he's begging her, and I think he recognizes how his sister has changed since he saw her last. He does not like the change, of that I am sure, but he does recognize it. Maria probably was one of those Italian girls accustomed to being told what to do by their brothers and fathers, but no longer.

"Sure I will," she says, as if she's agreeing to go for a walk in the park rather than announcing she will become a union girl. "I will, because they need me and because I believe in the cause now and because—" She cuts herself off, but she told me enough times while we were on Blackwell's Island that she would never let a man change the course of her life again that I know how she would have finished the sentence.

Alonzo, the boy in Italy who nearly took her innocence then lied to her so she would leave without making a fuss, has ruined her for all other men. Even, apparently, her brother.

"Rosie will go with me too," Maria says. Then she turns those brown eyes full of passion on me and adds, more firmly, "Won't you?"

As I finally fell asleep last night on my uncomfortable workhouse bed, I decided I would not. The strike will continue, the union leaders say, until the owners accept what they call a 'closed shop' where only union girls are hired. That hasn't happened yet, but some of the factories have agreed to let the union take care of all workers whether or not they're union girls. That seemed good enough for me, last night, so I decided I would find a job at one of those factories and leave my union work behind me. I never want to be arrested again, never want to be where I have been these last days.

But now, surrounded by people who support us and faced with Maria's energy and determination, I think of Aunt Ida and the strength I never knew she had, I remember taking that solemn oath at the meeting when we agreed to strike, and I feel able to say, "I will."

CHAPTER TWENTY

Maria
December 25, 1909

MR. BILLOTA FOLDS UP THE NEWSPAPER his wife buys each day for his exclusive use, annoying me because I was straining my eyes to read the small print of an article over his shoulder.

While Rosie and I were in the workhouse, a group of New York strikers and union leaders went to Philadelphia to speak to the waist workers there, and after hearing everything that has come about during the strike here, more than seven thousand of those workers went on strike too. Yesterday, the article said, five of them were placed under bail for causing disturbances around factories full of scabs. I don't know what "under bail" means, but I don't think it means being sent to the workhouse, so they were luckier than Rosie and me.

Of course, they probably aren't getting the attention that we are either. Rosie doesn't seem to like it much, but I do. The union still sees us as heroines and so do lots of regular people, and on January 2nd there'll be a big demonstration to honor us and the others who've been arrested or convicted.

I've never been so excited.

I believe in the union's cause now. Before, I didn't see how it could affect me or why I should care since I would leave factory work when Alonzo arrived. Now, though, after learning of Alonzo's unfaithfulness and being arrested and sentenced for nothing more than spitting at an immoral woman, I've grown up in only a few days. Now I know that we girls and women will never be respected unless we stand up for ourselves.

The men aren't going to do it for us, after all. Why should they give us rights when it means they'll have less power over us? We will have to *take* those rights.

So I truly am a union girl now, ready to work hard to make the world better.

But I'm also so excited to sit on the stage at Carnegie Hall, a place I've never even set foot in, wearing a placard to tell the world I was arrested. Everyone will be looking at me, admiring me, and I can't stop thinking about it. The only thing better would be giving speeches like Clara does, convincing rich people to donate money or girls to strike. Maybe one day I'll get to do that. This could be my first step.

I sit up a little straighter and look down at my chest, smoothing out my waist as if adjusting my placard. I'll need to keep my shoulders back and my head up while on the stage, because slouching with the placard won't look very—

"Are you imagining that placard again?"

I jump and turn to Margherita. "What? No, of course not."

She grins at me. She's been nicer to me since I came home because now I'm like her.

Well, not exactly like her. I'm going to be a better union girl than she ever will. She's never been arrested, after all.

"No, of course not," she echoes, laughing. "It's getting to be tiring, putting up with your airs."

"I have no airs," I say, annoyed. "I was arrested, that's all, and—"

"Oh, I know." She rolls her eyes. "We all know."

"It was even in the paper," one of the two boarders, who I can never tell apart, says.

"You're right, it was," I say, before I realize he's teasing me for having talked about that so often. The article didn't list my name, but it did say that five of us had served five days each in the workhouse and would be brought home that day by boat, and even that mention was exciting enough that I have hidden the article in the bottom of my trunk so I can take it out occasionally and read about how brave I was.

Also, because we were arrested without any proof we had done wrong, the rich ladies have begun to stand at the various picketing locations and watch, so when fights occur they will be able to provide evidence that it wasn't all the strikers' fault. Our being sent there made all of this happen. We deserve to be called heroines.

"Leave Maria alone," Mrs. Billota says, "and both of you girls need to help me with the food."

I hold back my sigh, because I know she'll give me a motherly smack with a wooden spoon if I let it out, then get up along with Margherita, leaving the men settled comfortably in the parlor.

I wonder if any man, anywhere, has ever been expected to help with the food.

Unlikely.

Once I've stirred the pasta en brodo and made sure it doesn't need any more chicken broth to keep its nice soupy consistency, I help make the salad and dress the spaghetti then work with Margherita and Mrs. Billota to arrange the roast and fishes and eel on the table along with the rest of the food for our Christmas dinner.

When we're about half done, Mr. Billota pushes himself out of his chair and says, "Vincente, I want to speak to you in the hall for a moment."

I look to see Vinnie changing his surprised expression into an agreeable one and getting to his feet. Mr. Billota hasn't spoken to Vinnie much since my brother decided we ought to find a new place to live. Now that I'm a union girl too we could probably stay here, but I do like the idea of having more space so I'm glad Vinnie has located us an apartment we will take in two days.

I can't wait to sleep on an actual mattress instead of chairs, and when Vinnie and I have earned enough money for our parents to come over, we'll all fit fine.

I wrote an awkward letter to them yesterday, explaining that I know about Alonzo and that I will now never get married and will stay focused on my union career. I know they want grandchildren, of course, but they'll have to get them from Vinnie. I don't want to be distracted.

Once all the food is set out except for the beer glasses Margherita is filling out of the bucket her brother bought earlier at the pub down the road, Mrs. Billota sends me out into the hall to collect her husband and Vinnie.

I slip out quietly, curious about what they're discussing and hoping I might be able to overhear, but the dark hallway outside the apartment is empty. Cocking my head, I listen hard and hear the rumble of Mr. Billota's low voice from the next landing down.

Luckily, I've grown to know which parts of the steep stairs creak, so I'm able to sneak halfway down without making a sound.

That's the point at which I hear Mr. Billota say, "—if he were here."

Vinnie says, "I know, he would. I'm not her father, though, and she doesn't listen to—"

"Make her." The flat statement makes me want to gasp but if they hear me they'll stop talking.

"She's been through a lot," Vinnie says, "with the workhouse and—"

Mr. Billota laughs, cold and cruel. "She got herself sent there. If you'd had proper control over her it would never have happened. This union foolishness! Fine for girls to amuse themselves with before they marry, especially since they might make more money when it's all over, but no good man will marry a girl who goes on like this. She should just work and earn money, nothing more. Maria will ruin her life if you don't take charge, Vincente. First that ridiculousness over that Alonzo boy, and now this? She runs off like a wild horse after one thing then another, changing her mind as the wind blows, and it has to stop. You have to make it stop."

I hold my breath, waiting for Vinnie to tell this awful man that I am doing the right things with my life and am nowhere close to ruining it.

Then my brother says, "I know. I will," and the breath I was holding rushes out of me as fury takes its place.

How can Vinnie agree with Mr. Billota's horrible words? A girl can go to work and make money but she can't fight for her rights? Margherita's only allowed on the picket line because *he* wants her there? A girl's not allowed to have an opinion?

And Vinnie! I'm an American girl now, a *union* girl, and yet he still thinks he can tell me what to do? He still thinks I don't know what I really want?

I will prove to him how wrong he is.

CHAPTER TWENTY-ONE

Rosie
December 31, 1909

"ONE LAST DANCE, AND THEN IT'S TIME for anyone who wants to see the ball drop in Times Square to get out there!"

We all cheer this, and Vincente gives me a little bow and says, "Will you?"

I nod and offer my arm, and he puts it through his and leads me onto the dance floor as we both pretend not to see Margherita looking annoyed. She's already danced with him at least four times, not that I was counting, and this is only my second, so I don't care a lick for what she thinks.

I smile, liking that even in my head I'm using the American slang I wouldn't have understood six months ago, and he says, "Do you like this song?"

I don't know it, but it's lovely so I nod and say, "I just hope I can keep up with it."

His arm slips around my waist and he takes my outstretched hand. "We'll make it work."

Vincente is an excellent dancer, great at leading me and making sure we don't run into anyone else on the crowded dance floor, and though the ragtime song is faster than most of what I've danced to when the girls from the home and I go out on a Saturday night, Vincente and I laugh and have a wonderful time.

At the end he says, "You didn't need to worry. You danced it beautifully."

I feel my cheeks warming, but I say, "Thank you. So did you. I don't think I've ever had a better dance partner."

He gives my hand a light squeeze then releases me as he says, "Well, thank you for that. I hated the dance lessons my mother made me take at home, but she said it'd be worth it when a pretty girl liked my dancing. Turns out she was right."

The heat in my cheeks rising until I wonder if everyone can see them glowing, I mumble another thanks. Vincente is the most handsome man I've ever danced with, and I'd like to tell him that. But I don't know how to find the words, and even if I could, I'm not sure I should. Can a good Jewish girl say such a thing to an Italian man?

He smiles at me, his own cheeks a little pinker than before, and says, "And I've been meaning to ask you a question. Were you at the Hudson-Fulton Celebration back in September?"

"I was," I say, amazed and thrilled that he does remember me after all. "But I left with several girls. And I think one might have..."

"Yelled at me?"

"Exactly. Yes, that was me. With her, I mean. Not me yelling." Will I *ever* be able to get my words to come out in order for more than a sentence or two in a row?

"I thought so," he says, and we smile at each other for a moment while I wish that moment could last forever. Then he leads me off the dance floor toward the cloakroom to join our crowd, which includes Maria, Margherita and Margherita's brother, Julia and her fella Israel, my other friends from the home, and all the girls Maria brought from her new-found union friends.

I invited Clara to join us, but she had a union meeting tonight and another early tomorrow morning to prepare for the January 2nd meeting at Carnegie Hall so she declined. If only it could somehow be her on the stage at that meeting instead of me! Maria's wildly excited about sitting up there to show the public that we girls who've been sent to the workhouse are no different from anyone else, but I'm dreading it.

My mother, who may by now have received the letter I sent the night we returned from the workhouse telling her I know the truth about my aunt's death and asking why they hid it from me, always told me not to be like Aunt Ida. But she might as well have saved her breath, because clearly I'm not. The woman Mr. Starr described would have adored being on that stage as much as Maria will. I do believe in the union, and I want to support it, but I just—

"Oh, Maria, I like that hatpin," Julia says, distracting me from my confusion. "Did you buy it in America?"

Maria shakes her head and holds out the pin to Julia. "It was my mother's, and her mother's too. Isn't it lovely? I always think those swirls at the top look like they're dancing with happiness."

We girls admire the sleek silver pin with its loops of metal at the top for a moment, while I wonder if the others all see the metal as dancing and I'm the only one with no imagination, then Vincente clears his throat and Israel says, "We don't want to miss midnight, do we?"

Julia laughs and slips on her coat. "Sorry. No, we do not."

Once we've all finished dressing for the weather, we walk out into the cold dark night and follow the flood of people up Fifth Avenue the few blocks to 42nd Street then turn left to make our way over to the Square. It's packed with people, but we're able to find a spot where we can see the huge ball of wood and iron, glowing with electric lights, atop the flagpole on the roof of the Times Building.

"So it just falls down? Like a lemon falling from a tree?"

Margherita's brother laughs at Maria, while I silently thank her for asking because I wondered the same thing. "Of course not," he says. "Why would anyone stand out here in the snow to watch that? No, it slides slowly down the post. It's fun to watch, and it means it's a brand new year. Bring on 1910, I'm done with 1909!"

The people around us cheer this, and Maria says, "I just wish the strike had ended this year." Then she raises her chin, shoots Vincente an angry look, and says, "But it will next year. With all us girls pulling together, *all* us girls, it will happen."

The other union girls and I applaud her statement, although I do wonder why she's so obviously upset with her brother, and one says, "We were so close this year. It's just the closed shop they won't accept. But next year it'll happen and then—"

Margherita's brother cuts her off. "Ladies, could we please enjoy this night and leave the shop talk, closed or otherwise, for next year?"

Maria looks annoyed, but the girl who spoke moves a little closer to the brother and says, "Only if you promise to entertain us, Giuseppe."

He smiles down at her, looking pleased. "Well, then I promise."

He launches into a story of how last year all the waiters in the many restaurants around Times Square wore top hats with 1908 in lights on them, which somehow turned to 1909 at midnight, and it fills the time until a man wielding a megaphone shouts, "It's time!" into it and we join him in yelling, "Three, two, one!"

The big lit-up ball slides slowly and majestically down its post to the roof of the tall narrow building as we were told it would, while we all cheer, then Giuseppe pulls the girl who'd requested entertainment close and gives her a big kiss on the cheek.

Blushing but giggling, she returns the favor, and we all hug and kiss each other. Vincente reaches for Maria first, then moves on to the other girls. But before he can hug me, Israel kisses Julia on the mouth and squeezes her so tight she gasps and says, "Let me go, or I'll never get to live in 1910!"

We all laugh, and Vincente says, "That would be a shame. I think 1910 will be quite the year." He leans over and kisses my right cheek. "I kissed everyone but you," he says, smiling at me. "And do you agree about 1910?"

I nod, hoping he can't tell my knees are shaking. He made a special effort to kiss me, and I like it. My parents wouldn't like it, but... "I do. I think great things will happen."

"With the union?" Maria says.

"With everything," I say firmly, cutting off Giuseppe's complaint about yet more union talk.

This causes another round of hugs and kisses, and Vincente makes sure my left cheek isn't neglected this time.

Both of his kisses seem to burn on my skin long after the lights of the ball have been extinguished.

CHAPTER TWENTY-TWO

Maria

January 2, 1910

THE THOUSANDS OF PEOPLE IN THE AUDIENCE cheer and clap as the curtains open, and I adjust the paper pinned across my chest and try to look as brave as they think we are.

Rosie takes my hand and whispers, "This is... well, I don't know what."

I squeeze her trembling hand, understanding exactly the strangeness she can't explain. Though I'd imagined myself with my placard so many times, actually being here feels like a dream.

There are twenty of us girls who were sent to the workhouse sitting before the crowd here at Carnegie Hall, a place I never thought I would be in, never mind up on the stage, wearing placards with "Workhouse Prisoner" printed on them in strong, somehow angry, letters, and hundreds more girls sit behind us wearing sashes that say "Arrested".

I never knew how many girls had been treated so, and feeling them all sitting with me, gathered close together, gives me a kind of strength I have never known before. This is what a union is all about, I think: having the support of others like you. They support me, and I support them, and together we will win.

No matter what the men say.

A lady walks onto the stage and stands waiting until silence falls, then says, "This meeting is not one of socialists or of suffragists. My friends, this is simply a group of New York citizens who are anxious for their rights. They, and we, deserve rights, and they, and we, shall have them. Let us hear from our speakers how those rights have been taken away and how we might get them back."

A man leaves the speakers' desk at the front of the audience, on which hangs a large banner that says, "The workhouse is no answer to a demand for justice", and makes his way up to the stage to stand before us with his back to us and speak to the crowd. As he does, I look around and see more banners hanging from the balconies and boxes of the great theatre, promoting the vote for women and the Socialist Women's Committee and many other things I don't know about.

I wonder if that first lady might be wrong. This *should* be about us strikers and how we deserve our rights, and that banner on the speakers' desk is, but there are people here with other interests. Will they remember us, will they work with and for us, or will they try to use us to fight their fights for them?

Speaker after speaker comes up to talk, and they do seem to remember us. They tell us that most of the arrests and all of the workhouse sentences have been illegal, and a lawyer even suggests that we girls ought to sue the judges, although I cannot imagine how we could do that if we couldn't save ourselves from being arrested. In short, they all agree we have been wronged.

But the best speech is the second-last, which comes from one of us girls. I can see her skirt shaking as she trembles with fear before the huge audience, but she speaks clearly and everyone hushes to listen as she says, "I saw my friend attacked by a man who was leading scabs into a factory, and I went with my friend to court to be her witness. But in the courtroom, the policeman and the judge accused me of attacking a scab myself. I had never seen that scab, and I had never seen the men and girls she brought as witnesses, but that didn't matter.

The policeman arrested me, and the judge sent me to the workhouse, and I had done nothing wrong. They do what they please and it's us who pay the price."

The applause and cheering she earns for this speech! I could do at least as well as her, and I want to. I want to stand on stage and be applauded and have my words reach everyone's ears. I will speak to Clara about opportunities for me to speak. I know I can do it.

The final speaker comes to the microphone and stands quite a while waiting for the cheering to die down. I'm sure he had planned a longer speech, but he says only, "You girls *are* reaching your goals, you know. Yes, things have been bad for you, and not fair, but you are reaching them. Two-thirds of your fellow waist makers are back at work in factories that have accepted all union demands. Two-thirds! It is a testament to your hard work and sacrifice. I have no doubt that soon the remaining bosses will yield and all of you will be back to work, and at closed shops too!"

We all cheer, but I do have doubt.

A few days after Christmas, the manufacturers offered us higher wages and shorter hours and promised not to prevent girls from joining the union, but they would not agree to closed shops where only union members can be hired. We rejected that with great excitement, determined to get closed shops because that's the only way we can all stick together. If some of us were union and some weren't, wouldn't the bosses simply harass the union girls until they quit?

I still think we voted the right way, but then I think of the Triangle bosses in particular and all of the uncooperative bosses in general, how they've hired men to harass us and paid policemen to ignore our assaults and brought in priests to divide us, and I wonder if the two-thirds that have settled are the easy two-thirds.

Will we ever be able to settle with the others?

This last speaker does not provide me with an answer with that, and I am quiet as I step off the stage with Rosie and go to meet Vinnie in the lobby.

Rosie has no family here, so I think it would be nice if the three of us were friends. But when I catch Rosie sneaking peeks at Vinnie's strong arms below his rolled-up shirtsleeves as we chat, I wonder if maybe Rosie would rather be my sister-in-law than my friend.

The idea of my brother with a Jewish girl shocks me, and so when she suggests we take the subway back down to the Lower East Side together, I want to refuse. I can't think of a good reason, though, so we go, and as the three of us continue our conversation on the journey I begin to think she might be good for him.

Not to marry, of course, but to be his girl for now. Vinnie is a hard worker, same as Rosie, but he never has any fun and he doesn't like me going out to have fun either. If he became Rosie's fella, he would take her to plays and concerts and other exciting things, and he would take me along too at least sometimes if I insisted.

I am now sure that I was put on this earth to do union work, but why shouldn't I enjoy myself a little along the way?

I will make it happen.

CHAPTER TWENTY-THREE

Rosie
January 16, 1910

AFTER THE CARNEGIE HALL MEETING, when we arrived back at the Lower East Side and were about to part for our respective homes, Maria said brightly, "Rosie, we must picket together, and even once the strike is over we must see each other often. Maybe we can even work together then. And we must, all three of us, go to dinner and see plays and watch the moving pictures. Won't that be fun?" and I agreed immediately because I'd been wondering if I'd ever get to see Vincente again.

To my happiness, he agreed too. So last Sunday, we spent most of the afternoon together at the nickelodeon, and now we're at the New York Aquarium before we go on to a play for which Vincente has kindly bought tickets for us all.

I've never been treated by a 'fella' before, and I think I like it.

If only my companions for the day were in better moods!

I took home a huge stack of envelopes and flyers to stuff into them yesterday and I needed to return the completed work to the union hall today.

Upon receiving it, Clara said, "Oh, Rosie, thank you. Such great work!" I was feeling a strange new pride in myself when she added, "And Maria, just the girl I need."

As my smile faded at how much happier she sounded to see Maria, she went on. "We have a meeting arranged tomorrow evening and my main girl speaker has become ill. She was going to tell us about life in a non-union shop. I don't suppose you—"

"I'd love to!" Maria burst out, over the beginning of Vincente's polite refusal on her behalf. Then she snapped her gaze toward her brother. "What do you mean, no? I'm doing it."

Vincente's face clearly said she wasn't, but he said only, "We will discuss it."

She waved him off and got all the details from Clara, then we departed for the aquarium.

On our journey down to Castle Clinton at Battery Park, Vincente and Maria barely spoke to each other. I tried, briefly, to get a conversation going, but I'm not good at that at the best of times, and a brother and sister glaring at each other didn't make me any better.

They did, fortunately, relax a little when we reached the aquarium, but only because I managed to position myself between them as we entered.

The crowd, a large one since it's quite cold outside today, flows around the aquarium looking at the tropical fish on one side of the huge round room and the less colorful fresh-water ones on the other side, and we flow in silence with it. Everyone else comments loudly on the fish we see, and the crabs and beavers and other creatures, but Maria and Vincente make about as much noise as the fish.

When we're standing before the large central pool on the ground floor and studying the five bottle-nosed porpoises within, though, Maria breaks the silence and I miss it at once. "Vinnie, I *will* do that speech. I will not change my mind for you or any man."

Vincente glances at me and replies to her in what sounds to me like Italian, and she shakes her head and says furiously in English, "First, don't use Mamma to change my mind. She's like me and she would do the speech too and you know it. Second, why not English? You don't want Rosie hearing you? She's a union girl too, you know. So tell us both why I cannot do this speech for our union. Go on, tell us!"

Vincente does turn toward me, but I can't meet his eyes. I am uncomfortable with the emotion Maria's showing, especially in public, and am still a little sad that Clara apparently never considered me as a replacement. I don't think I'd do anywhere near as good a job as Maria, but it does hurt.

Maria's so good at standing up for herself, though. No wonder Clara didn't ask me. I can't even *look* at Vincente and Maria's yelling at him in public.

"And now you've upset Rosie too. Look at her." Maria lowers her volume but not her intensity. "Are you pleased with yourself?"

I sneak a peek at him, and he does not appear to be, his eyes still angry but an embarrassed expression creeping over his face. "Maria..."

"I *will* do it."

"We will talk tonight. At home. Alone." He clears his throat and sets his shoulders back. "Can we, please, just have a good day?"

She looks like she wants to continue the argument, but she sighs and says, "Fine." Then she reaches out and links arms with me. "Shall we push him in there to swim with the porpoises?"

I laugh, more from relief than from her joke, and he laughs too and dips his finger into the pool then pulls back quickly. "It's colder than I expected. They must chill it somehow."

We move on, chatting now about the temperature the various fish must prefer and how the aquarium staff must know so much about fish, and while it's a silly conversation, at least it *is* one.

The aquarium closes at four o'clock, and we file out with all the other visitors. It's much too big a crowd to get onto the subway or El all at once, so Vincente suggests we walk down to the shore and look at the Statue of Liberty while we wait.

On our way, we pass a man telling his companions, "They used this for immigration, before Ellis Island, you know. Nearly eight million of them passed through here."

As one, the three of us turn and stare at Castle Clinton. "It's so *small*," I say quietly, not wanting the man to hear me.

"It is," Maria agrees. "I know all eight million weren't there at once, but still."

"Maybe," Vincente says while we begin walking again, "it was less frightening than Ellis Island. Do you think?"

Maria nods, but I shake my head.

"No, Rosie?" Vincente smiles at me, not looking annoyed that I disagree. "You think it would have been worse?"

"Not worse," I say, keeping my sentences short so I won't get tangled up in them. "The same. All the same questions, the same worries... just a different place."

They consider this, then Maria nods. "She's right, you know," she says as if I weren't there. "It's always scary to be an immigrant." Then she links arms with me and, after a moment's hesitation, her brother. "We're so brave, aren't we?"

We laugh and continue on our way, and are soon staring at the Statue. Though it's out across the water, it still seems huge. The night I was here for the Hudson-Fulton Celebration it was too dark to see the Statue's details, and my first day in New York I was too terrified to notice them, so now I stare out with the others.

"It's different colors," Maria observes. "Is it supposed to be green or brown?"

"The men at work, the ones who've been here more than twenty years and so saw it being built, say it's covered in copper that started out brown and is becoming green."

"Interesting," I murmur, not sure what to say.

Maria stares a moment longer then says, "No. I'm going to believe it's green turning brown. I like that better."

She sounds so definite! Even though Vincente knows men who were here when the Statue was created, she's going to believe what she wants to believe. It's like that hatpin with the dancing swirls of metal. I don't have that sort of imagination, or that sort of belief in myself.

I wonder if Aunt Ida did.

We stand in silence a few more moments, me wrestling with how dull and uninteresting I am compared to everyone else around me and the others thinking whatever they're thinking, then Vincente says, "Well. Shall we brave the subway and find ourselves some dinner before the play?"

We take the subway and walk a little to Broadway and 31st Street, and I'm glad we had our dinner just down the street from the theater, because after a huge meal of spaghetti at a little Italian restaurant I am almost too full to walk.

Maria grins at me. "I'll have to tell Mamma in my next letter that you weren't able to eat as much as me. She always says I barely eat enough to keep a bird alive. How she'll laugh that you eat even less! And this wasn't even a big meal really."

I protest, as I know she wants me to, but I don't really mind. If it cheers her up, she can tease me all night.

"Here we are, girls." Vincente looks up at the rectangular sign that stretches the width of the narrow building's second floor. "The Bijou Theatre."

Maria bursts out laughing. "I worked at the Bijou *Factory* for my first job. Isn't that funny?"

I'm not sure Vincente finds it as amusing as she does but he chuckles anyhow, probably just glad she's in a better mood. I giggle with her and wonder how their talk tonight will go. What will happen if he does forbid her to do the speech?

I push that aside, not wanting to ruin our evening, as Vincente holds out our tickets to the uniform-clad man at the front door then holds the door for us to enter. I haven't been to such an elegant place before, with green velvet seats and red leather walls, and at first I'm intimidated. But then I notice that the velvet is worn and the "leather" is actually painted burlap, and I don't feel so out of place.

After a few minutes, the lights go down and a hush falls over the audience as the curtains open. I relax into my seat and wrap my arms around myself, ready to live someone else's story for a time instead of my own.

It turns out to be a very funny story. A newspaper reporter who owes his boss money decides to earn that money, and also help sell more newspapers, by creating a lottery with himself as the prize. Thousands of women buy tickets, but while they're being sold the reporter falls in love with a girl who happens to be the daughter of his boss. He tries to cancel the lottery but can't, so instead he buys as many tickets as he can afford in the hopes he will win himself.

"And what do you think will happen?" Vincente asks us at the intermission, looking down the row at us.

"I hope some awful woman wins him," Maria says, shaking her head. "It's a foolish idea to sell tickets to yourself, and only a fool would buy them. A fool deserves a fool."

Vincente sighs. "You used to be so romantic, Maria."

"That was before—" She bites back the rest of her angry comment, but I know and of course Vincente also knows she means Alonzo. "Well, I'm not any more."

"And you, Rosie?"

I feel my cheeks go pink. I actually think it's sweet how many tickets the man is trying to buy but I don't want to hear Maria's reaction to that.

Vincente smiles at me and says, "Well, I think two of us like the play and one doesn't."

"Oh, I like it fine," Maria says. "It's funny to listen to fools."

We all chuckle and talk of other things until the lights again dim, but I wish we could talk during the play because I am shocked to hear that 300,000 tickets were sold at a dollar apiece. So much money! What the union could do with that.

I do giggle out loud when we learn that the mothers of both the girl and the reporter have also bought as many tickets as they could in the hopes of getting their children to marry, but to my surprise I have to fight back tears when the girl is revealed to have a suitcase full of tickets she bought for herself as well. Though of course I know it's not real, something about how much she loves the man, and how hard she tries to get him, touches my heart.

Once the play is over, with the actual winner given a house as a prize and the reporter and his girl off to get married, I glance at Maria to see if she might have been touched too.

"Well, I was right. Two fools ended up together," she says firmly, earning herself a glare from a sniffling woman in the row in front of us.

"Ah, Maria," Vincente says, shaking his head. "What am I going to do with you?"

I brace myself for her to say, "Let me do the speech," but though I think she considers it, she instead giggles and leans her head on his shoulder. "Take me home, I suppose. We have work tomorrow."

We all groan, even her, and the two of them escort me back to my house. On the steps Maria hugs me and whispers into my ear, "Be there tomorrow for my speech."

I nod as she pulls away, and Vincente narrows his eyes but doesn't ask what she said. Instead, he kisses my cheek and murmurs, "I'm glad you're a proper girl, not like my sister."

I'm glad he kissed me before he spoke, because heat flares into my face at his words. "I... good night."

Maria blinks twice and I cringe inside at what she'll say, but she just smiles and says, "Good night, Rosie."

I nod, flustered, and hurry inside where I lean my back against the door and let my fingers touch where he kissed me.

A proper girl. Am I? Is Maria not?

Do I even *want* to be proper?

And if not, why do I feel so overjoyed?

CHAPTER TWENTY-FOUR

Maria
January 17, 1910

"Are you nervous?"

I turn to Clara, surprised. "Not at all. Why, are you?"

She chuckles. "Well, a tiny bit. I always am a bit. But I'm glad you're not. You feel ready, though?"

I don't say anything, I just grin at her.

"Well, good," Clara says, grinning back. "Because it's almost time." Her smile fades, and she adds, "No more trouble with your brother?"

I shake my head, then admit, "Well, he did try to forbid me."

She rolls her eyes. "But you didn't let him."

"I told him he couldn't stop me unless he chained me to the kitchen table."

Clara bursts out in a giggle. "Which he didn't do."

"I'm here, aren't I?" I say, giggling with her. I don't think Vinnie really thought he could forbid me, and when I told him I'd drag the whole table out of our new apartment if I had to, he backed down. It was foolish of him to try at all.

"You certainly—"

A man sticks his head out of the room where the meeting has been set up and says, "Come on in."

Clara nods and sweeps forward, and I follow her into the room and up onto the small stage to sit beside her. Only about a hundred people make up the audience, and I do wish it were more, but then this *is* only my first speech.

My eyes land on Vinnie, at the back of the room, and he gives me a gruff nod. Rosie, sitting beside him, looks terrified, and I want to laugh. What is *she* afraid of? I'm the one who should be afraid, and I'm not. I'm as peaceful and unconcerned as one of those fish floating about in a tank at the aquarium.

I sit like a queen on her throne and listen to the man drone on with "we appreciate your attention" and "we welcome donations to help the cause" and "unions do so much good", and I don't feel even a lick of fear. I can do better than his boring words.

He introduces Clara, and she walks at a steady but not rushed pace to the microphone, where she speaks for a few minutes about how important we union girls are to the cause, ending with, "And I have one of the newest of those girls here today, Maria Cirrito. She has worked at Triangle and I know you'll enjoy what she has to say. Maria?"

Everyone claps, and I rise to my feet as easily as Clara did.

Then I almost fall over.

My heart is instantly pounding like I ran up all ten floors of Triangle's building with my corset laced too tightly, and little black spots appear before my eyes. Everything I thought I would say has gone from my mind, and I'm not even sure I can take a single step, never mind make it to the microphone.

Clara turns to face me, and gives me an encouraging smile. "Maria?"

My eyes locked to hers, I make myself take one step. I have so wanted to do this, and if I give up here, I'll never get another chance. If I faint, well, I faint.

When I don't, I manage to take another step, then another, and with each one a little more of my fear falls away. Clara squeezes my arm as she passes me on her way back to her seat, and that helps too.

At the microphone my nerves rise again, but I look out at the audience and think, "Why, they're just people." I knew that, of course, but I've always been able to talk to a person or a few people. This is simply a bigger group. I was right not to be afraid before.

"Ladies and gentlemen, thank you for being here tonight," I begin, the words I'd planned returning to me in a rush. "I was employed at Triangle during the early stages of the strike, and I'm happy to speak to you of what it was like."

My rehearsed words would next have me explaining how the door is locked at night so they can search us before we leave, but as I take a breath to say so, it occurs to me that that didn't only happen during the strike. "At lunch time," I say instead, "they played music for us, and provided oranges and tea and rolls. We felt..." For a moment the right words won't come in English, and an echo of my earlier fear returns, but then I say, "We felt cared for. They *wanted* us to feel that way. Because you can't strike against someone who cares for you, can you? But they didn't care. Of course they didn't. And they still don't."

A murmur of agreement spreads through the audience, and a glow of pure satisfaction spreads through me, and I speak for the rest of my allotted five minutes and could have gone on for five hours.

When I am finished, I smile and nod at the applause I receive and wish I had a way of knowing whether it's more than what Clara got. I think it might be. I hope it is.

The man who brought us in wraps up the meeting by inviting the audience to donate to our cause, and I follow Clara off the stage to Vinnie and Rosie

"She did quite well, your girl," Clara tells them.

Quite well? I nudge her. "Is that all?"

She laughs and shakes her head. "All right, fine, you were wonderful. Is that what you want to hear?"

"It is," I say, then hug her.

"You recovered so well," she whispers. "We will certainly have you speak again."

"And next time I won't need to recover," I whisper back.

She squeezes me a little tighter then lets me go. "I ought to go help with the collection, but you stay here, Maria. Thank you again. You *were* wonderful, truly."

As she leaves, Rosie catches my hand. "Oh, I was so afraid for you. I can't imagine—weren't you terrified?"

"Not at all," I say. "I knew I would do well and I did."

"Non bisogna mai vantarsi, Maria," Vinnie murmurs, and my cheeks warm. He's right, I shouldn't brag, especially when...

"Oh, all right," I say, moving closer to them both. "I *was* terrified. But just for a few seconds. Once I started speaking, that all went away. The words seemed to rise up in my mind and fall out of my mouth, even when they weren't the speech I had planned."

Rosie shakes her head. "And they sounded beautiful, like the lines in that play last night. I could never."

Vinnie gives me a look that I know means, "Reassure her," but instead I hug her.

Because I think she's right.

She couldn't.

But I can.

And I hope I'll get to do it again very soon.

CHAPTER TWENTY-FIVE

Rosie
February 8, 1910

MARIA TAKES HER PICKET SIGN INTO HER LEFT HAND, wriggles the fingers of her right to relax them, then moves the sign back. "Somehow this gets heavier and heavier every day."

I nod and smile but don't say anything. There isn't anything to say. She's right.

It's been over five weeks since the Carnegie Hall meeting at which we were told we would win soon, and here we are not having won. Leiserson did settle with the union two weeks ago and will now only hire union workers at both of his factories, but none of the remaining big factories, like Triangle outside which we are standing, have given in, and none of them seem likely to either.

Only about a thousand of us are still out picketing of the original tens of thousands. The rest have gone to the shops that have settled, are scabs at the others, or have found work at factories that make other things. The newspapers don't talk much about the strike any more, but when they do they report that there's not much enthusiasm left for the strike among the girls, and in that they have the right of it. We were so sure we'd win, but we haven't and it's hard to see how we will.

Especially because, even with so few of us picketing, the union can barely afford to give us three dollars a week to keep body and soul together. The immigrant home has been good to me, only charging half the usual fee, but most girls don't live in such kind places. Maria, if it weren't for Vincente's wages, would have had to go back to work weeks ago.

Although perhaps that's not what would have happened. My friend is a few months younger than me, and shorter and thinner, but the passion in her eyes every day rivals anything I've seen from Clara or the other most fiery union girls. She might well have starved rather than give up on her beliefs.

That first speech she gave! I didn't even see the moment of fear she admitted to: what I saw was a younger Clara. Maria's done two more speeches since, and I know the union has plans for her to do even more. It's been so easy for her to step into that role, and I don't understand why it seems impossible for me.

Especially with the same blood as Aunt Ida running through my veins. She was clearly a 'fiery girl' herself, from what Mr. Starr told me, so why am I so different from her? My parents have sent me two letters since I discovered the truth, and in neither of them did they even mention Ida, so when I wrote to them yesterday I didn't bother asking again.

I feel angry still that they didn't tell me what really happened to her, but also strangely like I won because they haven't mentioned her or my union work again. That means I don't have to mention it either and I can just keep doing what I believe is right and not telling them about it.

But Maria tells everyone what she believes. Perhaps without Vincente her drive would indeed have kept her on the picket line, but her life without him would not have been anywhere near as good or easy.

Mine would also not have been as good.

Although my father would never accept Vincente as my husband and so I am not considering that at all, I like the man. He's kind and funny.

And handsome. So handsome.

The men I knew at home, like my father and brother, are thin and weedy, pale from always being inside reading Torah and their other books, and that has always been my ideal of how men look.

Vincente, though, has visible muscles in his arms from digging subway tunnels and moving away the rubble, and though I shouldn't think of this, I suspect he has visible muscles everywhere. His skin is ruddy and his eyes bright from the effort he puts in every workday, and I like his height and his smile and the way he rolls up his shirtsleeves so I can see his arms. He's not rolling them up for me, of course, but I like it anyhow.

He kisses my cheek now every time we part after a Sunday together, but he hasn't called me a "proper girl" again. I know he still doesn't like Maria's union work, though, especially not the speeches. My way of helping, quietly stuffing envelopes or making signs, seems to suit him more. I so wish I could change the minds of an audience like Maria does, and his dislike of that is more proof, as if I need it, that Vincente and I can never be anything more than good friends. But I look forward to his kiss each week and the touch of his lips against my skin always makes me feel—

"What's got you so happy?"

I turn to Maria, feeling my cheeks getting hot and trying to calm myself. "Nothing. Why?"

"You look all..." She wrinkles her forehead, looking for a word, then makes a ridiculous love-sick dreamy face while batting her eyelashes at me. "Like that."

"I'm not, not at all. I just—"

I hear excited voices growing louder and turn in relief, since I didn't know what to say, to see Clara and a few of the other union organizers running along Washington Place toward us, holding up their skirts to avoid the slush on the sidewalk being spattered up by their frantic feet.

"What on earth—"

"We won!" Clara reaches us and hugs Maria then me as she says again, "We won! It's back to work tomorrow for us!"

We all hug each other, ecstatic, then Maria says, "Everyone agreed to the closed shop? Even..." She jerks her head up toward the Triangle's sign at the top of its building.

Clara and her organizers exchange glances. "Well," she says, "no, not them. There were a few others that didn't too. But we did get nearly everything. Let me tell you what they all did accept, girls. We have our fifty-two-hour work week now, four holidays with pay each year, and no discrimination against union girls. Not only that, but we don't have to pay for our needles and thread any more in any shops, and in the slack season the bosses will divide work equally instead of only giving it to their favorite girls."

The strikers, not strikers any more, who have been around long enough to experience not having any work during the slow winter times have complained about this enough that I understand what a big concession it is, so I cheer with the others and we all hug again.

As we depart, though, Maria holds me back from the others and when we're alone says fiercely, "Well, what of it? No closed shop means they can take all that away again."

"But they agreed."

She looks at me with such disappointment I find myself squirming.

Then she says, "Rosie, don't be dizzy," and we burst out laughing at the memory of the old woman at the workhouse who called everyone who didn't immediately understand their tasks dizzy.

"But," I say when we've calmed, "really, they *did* agree. Isn't that enough?"

Maria shrugs and links her arm in mine. As we walk on she says, "Well, it's not what I want. I think we should have held out for closed shops. But we have twenty thousand union members now, when we had only a hundred before the strike started, and that's something. Isn't it?"

"It is," I said, seeing her commitment yet again in the way she says 'we' had a hundred members when I know she was anti-union when the strike began.

"So I'm happy for that. I am." She nods, as if trying to convince herself. "But I won't be leaving the union and I won't stop working on its behalf. Or who knows where we'll be next year?"

Part Two

CHAPTER TWENTY-SIX

Maria
March 4, 1911

ROSIE TURNS AWAY FROM THE BUILDING across the street and faces me. "Are you sure?"

"After all this time they won't remember me, and they need another union girl here. Two union girls."

She smiles. "You count for two or even three of those all by yourself, you know. The union wouldn't be the same without you."

I pretend to be modest, but she's right. In the year since the strike ended, I have become the most visible Italian girl in the union.

I was so foolishly proud of myself back in early 1910 for sitting on that Carnegie Hall stage wearing a placard, I so foolishly thought I was the best union girl there ever was, but now I know better. There's ever so much more to being a strong union girl than getting arrested then sitting silent on a stage. I translate speeches and posters and am interviewed whenever the Italian-language papers are interested in strikes, and I've spoken many times at union meetings and for fundraising. I've even traveled to other cities to talk to Italian girls there.

But there's more to it even than that. Other girls get the attention instead of me sometimes, when the union leaders think that necessary, and I accept it now as I could not have back then. I do like being up front, being noticed and applauded, but for the good of the union I will gladly be behind the scenes too. It's about the union, not me, and I have matured enough to be able to handle that.

At first I swore I would never go back to a sewing job, but last June, Clara suggested I move from factory to factory every month or two to quietly encourage girls to join the union. Clara herself can no longer do this sort of work, because the anti-union bosses all recognize her and won't hire her, but most of my speeches have been to union supporters or young girls so none of the bosses know me.

Rosie, who is not known either since she has never done so much as a tiny speech, has gone with me to each of those factories. She watches and listens for girls who seem like they might be open to hearing about the union and then I convince them to join. She's nearly always right when she directs me to a particular girl, even when I see no signs of that girl's interest, and with her help I've brought in many new members.

In the process I've also managed to learn all aspects of waist making, and so Rosie, who already knew those aspects, and I are now ready to take our union message to the most challenging shop of all.

I look all the way up to the Triangle building's tenth floor. "During the strike they played music at lunch for us to dance to, and I thought that meant they cared," I say, shaking my head at my own earlier foolishness. I was such a child back then, so focused on my ridiculous dreams of Alonzo that I couldn't understand what was truly happening around me. "It only meant they thought a little dancing and a cup of bad tea would be enough to keep us quiet."

Rosie gives my arm a squeeze. "Well, it wasn't, was it? Not for long, anyhow. And now look at how things stand. Not just for waist makers either."

I nod, knowing she's talking about how the cloakmakers, mostly men, went on strike last summer. Their employers, remembering all too well how our strike slowed waist production nearly to a standstill, settled with them in September by signing the Protocol of Peace document. Those workers ran their own strike, of course, but our success made theirs possible.

Now Rosie and I are going to try to extend our success even further. In the year since our strike ended we have kept most of what we gained, but not all. Employers, especially Triangle, still choose non-union girls when they can, and though we are not supposed to work more than fifty-two hours a week, it still happens often. I will not rest until all of us have the fair treatment we deserve.

"Let's go," I say, and we join the crowd of girls heading into the big front door of Triangle. Rosie hasn't been in here before, but I know where we're going and I know what'll happen when our freight elevator reaches our floor.

The doors open at eighth, and we slowly trickle out as the operator says, "Keep moving, girls. I have to get back down."

"There's no room and you know it," a girl ahead of me shouts back. "A body can't go anywhere."

"Why not?" Rosie asks me. "We were moving fine before, when we came into the building. Why so slow now?"

"It's the partition," I answer. "It only lets one girl onto the factory floor at a time."

She frowns at me. "Whatever for?"

"It's more there for letting us *out*," a Jewish girl beside her says. "We have to line up after work so they can search our pocketbooks as we leave. In case we stole lace or thread or even a waist."

Rosie stares at me, her eyes huge. We have talked at union meetings about how the bosses don't respect us, but this must be the first time she has seen it so directly. I'd forgotten about this, myself, since at the time it didn't seem to matter.

It does now.

I told Rosie nobody here would remember me but I'm nervous as we finally get through the gap in the partition, because if they *do* remember me, remember how I stormed out, I'm not likely to get a job here and neither is Rosie.

I didn't understand this before, but now I know that I wasn't working for Mr. Harris and Mr. Blanck, the owners, directly back then. Instead, I worked for a man who worked for them. He would arrange with them what he'd be paid for a bundle of completed waists then hire girls to do the work for him. Whatever he didn't pay us, he got to keep. No wonder he and the others like him charged us for thread and needles and paid us as little as they could.

That system, the subcontractor system, was abolished by the Protocol of Peace but that doesn't apply to our union, so I'm not surprised to see a man I know is a subcontractor talking with a girl on the other side of the factory floor. I'm glad, though, to see a different man closer to us, one I haven't seen before who can't know me, and I lead Rosie over to him.

"Sir," I say, making sure my voice holds no hint of my union-speech-giving strength, "are you hiring girls?"

He nods. "I'm Mr. Bernstein. Have you any experience?"

I nod too. "My friend Rosie here and I, I'm Maria, we make waists, and we are very good."

He looks from me to her and back again. "The whole waist? Both of you?"

I have never made a whole waist on my own, but I do not hesitate. "Yes. Both of us." He begins to speak, but I add, "And we need ten dollars a week each." At our last job Rosie earned nine and I eight, so this is a large raise, but I know Triangle is in its busy season and I know he needs us.

He doesn't look pleased, but he says, "Well, you'd better be great workers then, but all right. If you aren't, you'll be out on your ear at the end of the day, both of you, and no pay either."

"Of course," we both say, and I can tell Rosie is trying as hard as me to sound sweet and innocent.

He narrows his eyes, and I wonder if we tried too hard, then he smiles. "All right, girls. We work only until quarter to five today, as it's Saturday, so you don't have much time to prove yourselves. Go tell

Lena the forelady, that's her right there, I said to give you bundles of waists."

We do this, while I feel relief that I've never seen Lena before so she can't know anything about me, and are soon set up at machines. We aren't close enough to talk, but when nobody is looking we smile at each other, and we smile even more when at the end of the day Mr. Bernstein and Lena inspect our work and he agrees he will give us the ten dollars I asked for.

As we join the line to be searched at the exit, Rosie grabs my arm, her smile gone. "Do you smell smoke?"

We are all terrified of fire since December's awful events in Newark, where twenty-five night-gown-making girls were burned alive or forced to jump to their deaths from their fourth-floor shop when a gas-lamp factory below them caught on fire. This building is known to be fireproof, but it's still an awful thing to imagine.

I sniff, sure this is just her fear and not an actual fire, then frown and sniff again. "I do."

We look around for the source, then I find it and say, "Look, there. The cutter."

She rolls her eyes at the sight of the man holding the lapel of his jacket over his mouth so he can blow the smoke from the cigarette he's not allowed to smoke at work out through it. "He thinks that stops it. I guess it doesn't."

"It doesn't *show* any more, but it's still in the air. Well, at least it's him and not actually a—"

"Don't even think it!"

"I won't. Don't you either."

We smile at each other, while the cutter hides his crime by crushing out his cigarette against the wooden side of the cutting table then slipping it through the open space between the table's top and side panel where he stores fabric scraps after cutting out pieces of waists, then we move forward with the other girls in the line.

"Mr. Bernstein might even have given us eleven dollars," Rosie says once we have punched our time cards and opened our pocketbooks to be searched and are walking down the street. "We should have asked for more."

"After a month or two we can insist," I say, tucking my arm into hers. "Or we will quit and go somewhere else."

She chuckles. "I agree. Oh, and I hate to say this because it's *Triangle*, enemy of the union, but I do like that big room to work in. Those huge windows make it bright. It's so loud, though!"

I nod. "Hard not to be, I guess, with a few hundred girls at machines. So, what are your plans now?"

"I have to send a letter to my parents," she says, then grins at me. "With another three dollars in it, which will more than pay off my ticket over here. Now what I send them will go toward bringing them and my brother and sisters over."

"Well done!" I say. "We should celebrate. We could go to a vaudeville show or something, since we didn't get to do that last Sunday. But at least you're coming to my speech tomorrow."

Rosie used to spend nearly every Sunday with me and my brother, but since the beginning of January, she's had a different excuse every time why she's not available. I really want to know what she's doing instead, but she never answers my hinted questions about it, and she's only coming to my speech because I begged her.

This time again, she doesn't explain. She just says, "I'd like that," and then her cheeks pinken and she adds, "Do you know Vincente's plans tonight?"

He suggested to me this morning that I should see if Rosie would come out with us soon, but I know he wouldn't want me to tell her that. Their... is it a courtship? No, it can't be that. Anyhow, whatever it is, it's not progressing quickly if at all, but that does make sense. They're from very different worlds. I do know, though, that one of the other subway workers tried to get Vinnie to take his daughter out and my brother said no, and he also never tried to see Margherita again after we moved into our own apartment. So he must like Rosie.

And her blush says she likes him too.

And I am happy with that.

Everything is going our way, at last.

THE NEXT AFTERNOON, CLARA STANDS CALMLY waiting for the applause at the end of her speech to die down, then says, "And now, we will hear from Maria Cirrito, one of the girls sent to the workhouse back in December of 1909. She will let you know how that experience affected her and how you can help make sure such things never happen again. Maria?"

Clara and I exchange smiles as I pass her to take her place at the podium, but I let mine fade away as I study the crowd.

In the time since the strike ended, I have learned a lot about how to understand an audience and how to know what they need to see and hear from me so they'll support us. When I go to other cities to see groups of Italian girls, our meetings are full of laughter and tears and hugs and arguments, and I love convincing other girls to follow their own hearts and minds in our usual passionate way. I rarely lack a smile at those meetings, because seeing the girls, who are so like I used to be, realizing that they can choose their own paths in life is wonderful.

Today, though, our audience is largely union men, with a few girls and women here and there, and I know from my past speeches that audiences of men tend to think us girls are so dizzy that we can't tell them anything. So that means I need to be dignified and serious and prove them wrong. I need to be strong.

Fortunately, I am.

I raise my chin, take a deep breath and say, "Good afternoon. Thank you for taking time on your Sunday afternoon to listen to us. It's so important that what happened during our strike is not forgotten. We made great changes happen, but we will lose those changes if we do not remember, and that will hurt everyone no matter where they work. Picture how many girls work together to make a waist, each with their role. A union is like a garment: we all have a role to play in creating and maintaining it. Every girl, woman, and man."

Someone in the front row gives a grunt that tells me he doesn't agree, and I turn my head to look at him. For an instant I think it's Alonzo, and fury fills me at the idea he would dare to come to America after what he did to me, but this man's a few years too old to be him.

Handsome, though.

But I am not here to find a fella, so I look calmly away from him and address the entire room. Speaking slowly enough that nobody will be confused by my accent but not so slowly that they'll be bored, a balance I learned to achieve in my past speeches, I explain how I was arrested and sent to the workhouse and how it only increased my desire to make sure that no other girls suffered the same treatment.

Sometimes when I speak I must explain how a union works, since the rich ladies we often stand before have no idea, but with this audience I don't need to. Instead, I say, "We won our fifty-two hour work week, and we won no discrimination against union girls. But now that work week is stretching out again, and nobody refuses union girls work to their faces but the second they can replace us without being obvious, they do. And getting jobs as a union girl, as a known union girl, is difficult and for some girls impossible. The bosses say they treat us fairly, but they do not."

I pause as several girls in the audience call out their agreement, then I explain how we will use their donations to continue fighting against the bosses. As I speak, I look over the audience and make eye contact with various people. Clara taught me to do this, to make sure that they do not see me as nervous or weak, and I am good at it.

I don't look at Rosie and Vinnie, in the second row, because I don't need to impress them, but I can see out of the corner of my eye that they're watching me intently. I only look once at the man in the front row who grunted, as I near the end of my speech, and seeing he now looks impressed makes me even more sure I've done well.

Pleased with myself, I launch into my final words. "So, we all need to be in this together. Our strike made the cloakmakers' strike faster and easier, and theirs in turn will make another one easier in the future. We cannot fight as individuals."

Happy I easily got out the long English word, with which I struggled in my practice, I finally send a smile out to the audience. "No, we cannot. One person alone can do nothing. One girl alone cannot make a waist. She needs someone to make the fabric and someone to cut it and people to sell the finished garment too. They all work together, and we must too. Together, all the workers of America together, we will win. As Clara said during our strike, 'If we stick, we will win.' We did stick, and we won, and I hope you will all give what you can today to support us, to stick with us, as we continue to fight for ourselves and you and every worker in America!"

The audience bursts into applause, and I stand before them and find myself wondering whether it might be even louder applause than what they gave to Clara. I'm not sure, but it's definitely not less.

When I was younger I would have been happy only if I knew for certain it was louder. Now, though, I'm happy purely because I know I have reached the audience. I know it even before people begin waving dollar bills in the air and stuffing them into the baskets being carried around by my fellow union girls.

I am so good at this, I'm doing such a good job.

If I had married Alonzo, as I so desperately wanted to before, none of this would have happened.

Marrying him would have been un destino peggiore della morte.

A fate worse than death.

The union man who brought us in to speak says a few closing remarks as the money collection continues, and then I am free to leave the stage and join Rosie and Vinnie who are shuffling out toward the end of their row to get into the aisle.

When I am in the aisle too and only a row away from them, though, the man from the front row steps in front of me, blocking my path. "Miss Cirrito, that was quite the speech," he says, his voice deep and his accent American. "I admit I wasn't convinced a girl could make a difference in the union, but you've changed my mind and I'd very much like to hear more from you. Might I take you out for coffee and a chat?"

Over his shoulder I see Vinnie pulling himself up to his full height and moving toward us, but I don't wait for him. I don't need him. This isn't the first time a man has tried to see me after a speech, and I have never once succumbed. "Thank you, but no. I have union work to do."

"Right now?" He smiles at me, and I can tell he thinks himself too handsome to resist. "Surely you have some time to have fun."

I raise my chin and take a deep breath so I can make my voice as firm and unyielding as the rocks Vinnie digs out in the subway tunnels. I'm not angry, now that I know he's not Alonzo, but I don't care a lick about him either and I want him to know it. He listened to my speech and didn't think of anything but being my fella, and I don't appreciate that. "I don't need a man to have fun. Don't want one either. I'm a union girl and that's what I am."

He stares, and before he can answer I say, "Excuse me," and brush past him to join Vinnie and Rosie.

Vinnie glares over my head in the direction of the man, and I grab my brother's hand and say, "What did you think of my speech?"

"He's leaving," Vinnie mutters, dragging his eyes back to my face, "and che liberazione."

Rosie raises her eyebrows, and I say, "I know what that means, but not in English."

"It means, 'good riddance'," Vinnie supplies, and Rosie smiles and says, "Ah. Yes, it definitely is good. You stunned that man, Maria."

"I should have helped," Vinnie says. "A girl shouldn't have to deal with that alone."

"But I didn't need your help," I say, choosing not to tell him I've dealt with such things before. He doesn't need to know.

He sighs. "No, you didn't. My little sister's become quite the speaker but this might have been your best yet. You did a wonderful job, Maria."

I smile and thank him. I know he's still not happy with my union work but he's come to accept it, and I'm touched that he'd say such a thing instead of teasing me.

"You really did," Rosie says, but she sounds sad.

I glance at her, wondering why, and she straightens her shoulders and says, "We should celebrate. A nice sandwich at Katz's?"

"Where?"

Vinnie and I spoke in unison, and Rosie looks appalled. "You've never been to Katz's Deli? Really?"

When she accepts that we haven't, she says, "Well, then we must go," and soon we are down in the Lower East Side eating delicious sandwiches stuffed with meat and mustard.

"A true Jewish meal," Rosie says, offering me yet another pickle. "I can't believe you've never been here before. I can't believe I didn't bring you before."

I can, because most of our outings together have been to theaters and other things that don't happen to be near this restaurant, but before I can say anything Vinnie belches, then covers his mouth with his hand as his face goes red. "Excuse me," he says, as I elbow him for his rudeness in front of Rosie. "Please consider it a compliment to the food. This is wonderful."

"Where do we go now?" I lick pickle juice from my fingers. "Is there anything else around here that we might not have seen?"

It turns out there are many things. Vendors along the roads sell clothing and jewelry and eye-glasses and all sorts of interesting items, and we stroll along together admiring all the wares until a gold-colored ring set with a piece of deep blue glass catches my eye.

I slip it onto my right ring finger and hold my hand before my face to admire it, while the wrinkled old woman at the cart tells me in broken English, "So pretty. You buy, yes?"

I reach for my pocketbook, and Vinnie laughs and says, "I seem to remember some girl making a speech today about giving all our money to the union."

"Never said *all*." I peer at my coins, then to the woman I add, "How much?"

"Fifty cents," she says.

Rosie laughs. "I thought you said 'fifty', but that can't be," she says, "because that can't be right for this shlok."

I don't know what that word means, but the woman does because she raises her eyebrows at Rosie and says, "Shlok? Never. You've bought from me before, you know my wares." She heaves a huge sigh. "Well, my son won't eat tonight, but thirty?"

I don't want her son to be hungry, but Rosie calmly says, "Yes, thirty will do," and when she turns to me and adds, "If you want the useless little thing, that is," her eyes are dancing and happy so I realize this is just how haggling works in the Jewish area. We Italians tend to yell a lot more.

I was willing to take the ring for fifty cents but thirty is even better, so I shrug and say, "I suppose," so as not to encourage the woman to raise the price again, and return to looking for my coins. I know I have a quarter somewhere but I can't seem to find it.

Rosie says, "And I'll take this hatpin," while picking up a silver one with a pearl atop twists of wire. It's not real silver like my one from my Mamma, of course, but it is pretty. "Fifteen cents?"

The woman shakes her head. "Twenty-five."

Rosie looks down at the pin, wrinkling her nose. "Twenty. You should be able to feed your *son* from that, right?"

The woman gives a cough as if something suddenly choked her. "Twenty," she agrees, looking annoyed but also like she's holding back a smile.

"Girls, please let me," Vinnie says, holding out two quarters on his palm toward the woman.

Rosie sucks in a quick breath and says, "You don't have to—"

"I want to," Vinnie says, in that tone of his that means he doesn't want to be argued with. I still often argue with him, of course, even when he uses that tone, but Rosie doesn't. She just smiles at him and lowers her head, but not before I realize she's blushing.

The woman checks the coins, then smiles at Vinnie. "Thank you, sir," she says, then turns to smile and thank me too. Then she turns to Rosie and smiles. "And my *son* thanks you too."

Rosie bursts out laughing, and so does the peddler, and we move off.

"What was that about?"

Rosie slips her arm through mine, still giggling. "The first time I bought from her, not long after I got here, it was a daughter she had and couldn't feed. She must change it from time to time to sound more..." She blinks a few times. "More like she needs money."

"Sympathetic?" Vinnie suggests, while I think how like Rosie it is to remember what a peddler said more than five minutes ago.

"Yes, that." Then she clears her throat and says shyly, "Thank you, Vincente. For the word, and for buying me... that was very kind of you."

"After you saved us twenty cents on Maria's ring, it only seemed right to buy you a little gift."

Perhaps, but buying a hatpin for a girl is the kind of thing her fella would do.

I hold my hand out to again admire my ring, happy both with it and with Vinnie's action. I love Rosie, and I love my brother too, and the only thing that would make me happier than seeing them together would be having Rosie up on the stage giving speeches with me. Then we'd really be sisters, in all ways.

A few stalls later I spot a beautiful blue skirt, darker but the same kind of blue as my ring, and Rosie helps me get a good price for it. As

Vinnie finds the money, I see my chance and say to Rosie, "Wasn't today wonderful, with the speeches? We should ask Clara to let you do speeches too. I don't know why she hasn't thought of it yet."

She blushes a deep ugly red. "I don't know," she says, not looking at me. "I don't know if I could do it."

"Of course you could," I say, surprised. "Why not?"

She shrugs. "Maybe I'm better doing the mailings and that sort of thing. Not on the stage."

"Don't be dizzy," I say. "The speeches are what matter. They can get any girl to do the other work. We'll talk to Clara and—"

"I'll think about it. Don't talk to her yet."

I smile, glad she's considering it. Rosie's a smart girl and so sweet, but I think she might need a little encouragement. I can give her that encouragement, and then she can be a fiery girl like me.

CHAPTER TWENTY-SEVEN

Rosie
March 12, 1911

HOLDING HANDS TO MAKE SURE WE'RE NOT SEPARATED by the crowd of people arriving from Manhattan to find their newly-immigrated loved ones, Julia and I step off the small ferry at Ellis Island, as we've been doing together nearly every Sunday since January.

"Is that a new hat? From Israel, perhaps?" I say as we use our free hands to raise our skirts enough that we can easily hurry over the newly-fallen snow to get inside and out of the cold.

Julia laughs. "It is, but as a joke. I got him a new hat last week since I hated his old one."

I laugh too. "Is that how it works? Give your fella a gift to fix something about him you don't like?"

"Why not?" She gives me a sly look. "And what have you bought for Vincente? Or is he perfect already?"

I feel my cheeks getting warm but raise my chin and say, "Nothing. Why would I?"

She raises her eyebrows at me. "He's as good as your fella, isn't he?"

Is he? I love dancing with him, and going to movies or shows with him, and he treats me nearly every time we go anywhere. I touch my hatpin, the one he gave me. "He's a good man, but..."

"But what?" Julia says when I don't continue.

"He's Italian," I say, feeling awkward. "So... my father... I wouldn't be able to..."

Her eyes widen. "I didn't mean he should be your *husband* or anything, of course. No, just..." She tips her head to one side. "Wait. That hatpin... that's new, right? I love that pearl."

My face gets even hotter but I nod.

She gives my hand a squeeze. "From Vincente?" There's laughter in her voice. "From the man who isn't your fella?"

I nod, dropping my skirt and pressing my cold hand to my face to soothe it, then say, "And what about you?" so we won't talk about me any more. "Israel's been your fella for almost two years, and—"

"Closer to one and a half, thank you."

"But still. When will you put the poor man out of his misery and marry him?"

"Oh, you sound like everyone," she says, tossing her head. "Why would I marry him?"

We pass through the doors into the main building as she says this, and I catch her arm and draw her off to the side to stop her. "Why? I thought you loved him, that's why."

"I do," she admits, sounding like it's somehow shameful. "I truly do. But..." She waves her hand, taking in our surroundings. "He doesn't want me to work. Not at the home, not here, not anywhere. Only at taking care of his house and raising his children. Once we marry, everything else will stop, and I... Rosie, I'm having too much fun and enjoying my work too much to want that to happen."

I squeeze her arm. "I understand. He really wouldn't let you work?"

She shakes her head. "He's uncomfortable with this anyhow. Not the home, so much, but here. But it matters. *We* matter, being here."

Though I wonder sometimes whether we really do, especially against the public work Maria and Clara are doing for the union, I know she doesn't want to hear that so I say, "Yes, we do."

She nods, then hugs me. "I'm so glad you agreed to this," she says into my ear, and I say, "So am I," and for right now I mean it.

We go to the room reserved for the National Council of Jewish Women and hang up our heavy black woolen coats, then we separate and go to our work assignments for the day. Julia is downstairs where I met her the Sunday I arrived in America, where she'll help new immigrants exchange their money and take them to the immigrant home if they're girls alone just as she helped me, and I am upstairs serving as an interpreter as Cecilia did for me.

The day passes quickly, although it's tiring. I am called forward whenever a Yiddish-speaking immigrant arrives, and I must translate what the inspector and the immigrant say as accurately as I can. My English is more than good enough for this now, but some of the immigrants are so tired from their journey that they can barely speak, and some give answers that I know will make the inspector frown. I hate translating those, so I do sometimes change the answer a little to improve the immigrant's chance of being admitted. Only a little, though: I am not allowed to lie.

Cecilia told me that rule when she invited me to work with her back in December. Another worker had quit, finding it too draining, and Julia thought perhaps I'd be good at it, but after my first meeting with Cecilia I nearly said no. Her stern words about always being honest and never letting in or banning an immigrant unfairly had frightened me. It felt like a lot of responsibility, being the voice of a new immigrant.

With Julia's encouragement I'd tried anyhow, though, starting the Sunday after New Year's Eve, and to my surprise I *am* good at it. It's nothing like the work Maria does with the union, loud and passionate, but these immigrants need me and I'm able to help.

I haven't told Maria what I am doing, and I know she wonders why I can no longer see her and Vincente on our Sundays away from our factory work and his subway digging. I miss those long relaxing days with them, when we'd meet after they attended church and spend the rest of the day having so much fun and staying up so late dancing that we could barely stagger into work on Monday. But after what she said about speeches being the only way to achieve anything, I'm afraid she'll think my work here is a no-good waste of time and I don't want to hear—

"Miss Lehrer!"

Startled, I hurry over to stand beside the same inspector who allowed me into America. I've interpreted for him several times but I don't think he remembers that he interviewed me on my arrival.

But whether I am memorable isn't what matters right now, so I pull myself together and smile at the young man who stands trembling before me. "Good morning, I'm Rosie Lehrer," I say in Yiddish. "I will translate for you. May I ask your name?"

"Jacob Schpunt," he says, his eyes lighting up at the sound of our shared language. "Oh, Miss Lehrer, my wife! I haven't seen her and I don't know if she passed her inspection. I must know. How can I—"

"What's he saying?"

I turn to the inspector. "He's looking for his wife."

"Ask him the questions and then he can go find her."

I nod. The inspector is as abrupt as he was when I stood before him as a terrified immigrant, but I understand him better now. He sees so many people a day, over a hundred on his busiest days, spending at most five minutes inspecting them before deciding whether they will enter America or be sent home. He isn't a bad man; he's serious about his work, and he should be.

But I can't bear Mr. Schpunt's fear, so I say in Yiddish, "I am going to ask you the questions now, but with each I will also ask about your wife. Keep your answers short." If he doesn't, the inspector will know I am doing something unusual. "Are you ready?"

He nods so quickly the payot strands of hair on each side of his head bounce. My father and brother also wear their hair with these curls down past their ears, of course, as all good Jewish men do, and seeing them on this man makes me feel his pain even more. He could easily be my brother, and it's hard to see him suffer.

"What is your occupation, and what is your wife's name?"

"I'm a tailor, and she is Frieda."

I nod and continue asking both the questions I'm required to ask and the ones that might help me help him find Frieda.

His descriptions of her clothing and height don't help me, but when I ask about her face and he mentions the scar on her cheek from a childhood fall, I see her in my mind's eye. I didn't interpret for her myself, but she was at the desk next to mine and I heard her earnestly explaining that the scar was not a sign of disease, and I remember her result.

"Oh! She made it through, not too long ago. She'll be waiting for you downstairs."

He murmurs something in Yiddish I cannot hear, but the relief and joy in his face make it clear what he must have said and they also bring tears to my eyes. Will I ever be loved as much as he loves his wife?

"Thank you, Miss Lehrer, thank you. May I go to her?"

I am still supposed to ask him whether he has been in a prison or an almshouse or an insane asylum, but I'm certain the answer to all three will be no and I cannot make him wait any longer. I turn to the inspector and say, "He has answered well."

The inspector studies me for a moment, making me wonder if he somehow knows I left out that last question even though he wouldn't understand my Yiddish. But as I'm about to admit my wrongdoing, he says, "Very good. Let him through."

I nod then return my attention to the immigrant. "Congratulations, Mr. Schpunt," I say. "Welcome to America."

He thanks me profusely, then thanks the inspector in halting but clear English.

"You're welcome," the inspector says, and as I begin to lead Mr. Schpunt toward the stairs the inspector adds in a quiet voice, "I hope he finds his wife soon."

I stare at him, surprised he cares, and he turns sharply away to deal with the next immigrant, but I notice his ears turning red.

It must be hard for the inspectors, I realize, to so quickly make decisions that will change the course of immigrants' lives. Clara and Maria and Vincente and Julia and so many of the people I know here passed through this building; if any of them had been denied, my life would be so different now. I'm glad to know that at least this inspector knows and cares how important his work is, and about the people whose lives he holds in his hands.

I lead Mr. Schpunt downstairs, chattering away to him about where he and his wife plan to stay and how they will find jobs. I know my words are probably a little overwhelming for him, as Cecilia's were for me when I arrived, but hers calmed me and I know from my encounters with other immigrants that mine help too. They won't all be remembered, but my saying them gives the immigrant something to focus on and in a small way makes things seem more normal.

Mr. Schpunt answers my questions, but he's looking back and forth as we descend the stairs and move through the crowded lower level, and then he catches one quick breath and bolts away from me to a short thin young woman with frizzy light brown hair beneath a battered black hat.

She throws herself into his arms, and they cling together in silence as if the rest of us have all vanished and they are alone in the world.

I stand awkwardly, not wanting to leave without saying goodbye but unable to bring myself to interrupt them, for a few seconds, and just as I decide that I will have to walk away Mr. Schpunt pulls back and leads the woman by the hand to me.

"This wonderful girl is Miss Lehrer," he says to her in Yiddish. "She remembered you, of all the immigrants she sees, and told me you would be here for me. The fear she saved me, you would not believe it."

Mrs. Schpunt gives me a shy smile and wipes tears of happiness from her cheeks. "Thank you," she whispers, her wet eyes glowing, and though she's not loud, her words ring through me and touch my heart.

"You're so welcome," I respond, blinking back my own tears. "May I help in any other way or are you—"

"We will get through it together," Mr. Schpunt says, giving his wife's hand a squeeze. "You've done so much already and there are so many others for you to help. A sheynem dank." He clears his throat then adds the translation in English, "Thank you very much."

"Mitn grestn koved," I murmur. I don't follow it with English; the closest would be "you're welcome" but that doesn't go far enough. It *is* my great honor to have helped them, and I don't want to take away from those Yiddish words with an English approximation.

They both smile at me, and we nod to each other, then I turn to go back upstairs and leave them to fend for themselves in America. I hope they will do well. I think they will. And I have helped.

Feeling good about that, I climb the stairs only to meet at the halfway point a woman attempting to carry two shrieking babies down. Cecilia told me not to get caught up in helping people on the stairs, instead leaving them to make it down on their own as she did the day I arrived, because I could spend all day escorting people up and down and get nothing else done. I understand, but I'm uncomfortable every time I leave someone to struggle and I simply can't do it this time. "May I—"

She shouts past me in a language I don't know, and a boy and a girl emerge from the crowd and each take a baby. As they depart with their wriggling siblings, the woman gives me an exhausted smile.

I smile back and continue on my way, hoping her day gets better.

The rest of my day continues in its usual way, and eventually it's time to meet Julia back in the cloakroom and return home together.

When I arrive there, she's waiting with a girl I don't know. "Ah, here's Rosie. Now, this is—"

"Are you really friends with that Maria?" The girl interrupts Julia in English with a strong Italian accent, her brown eyes wide with excitement. "I can't imagine. I went to that meeting last Sunday instead of coming here, brought three girls with me who weren't in

America during the strike, and all three joined the union right after her speech and they've even tried to recruit other girls this week all on the strength of what she said. I've never heard a speaker like her. She's simply wonderful."

"She is," I say, trying not to sound bitter. I don't want to be bitter. Maria *is* wonderful. But...

We three board the ferry, the girl still chattering on about Maria, and my happiness from my work with Mr. Schpunt seems to sink to the bottom of the Hudson River and vanish.

Yes, I helped him and other people today, but so few. Maria has spoken in front of groups of four hundred or more girls who were hostile to unions and convinced most of them to change their mind and join. This girl's friends are even recruiting other friends to join from hearing Maria speak for a few minutes. Against that, what is bringing twenty or thirty more immigrants into America?

Julia's refusal to marry Israel because he would insist she stop working comes to my mind. If she didn't work here, or at the home, those immigrants would not be helped. *I* would not have been helped. Doesn't that mean this matters?

But someone else would have helped. Cecilia would find someone else to work for her if Julia left, as she found me to replace the other girl who left, as she'd find someone else to replace me if I left. Training me to do this work took only an hour or two, but replacing a speaker like Maria is nearly impossible.

It's a drop in the bucket, what we are doing, compared to the flood of immigrants.

Our work is a tiny bit of water, while Maria and Clara light fires in people's hearts.

I so want to be a fiery girl too, but I seem fated to be nothing but a water drop.

CHAPTER TWENTY-EIGHT

Maria
March 25, 1911

I SIGH AND FINISH MY STORY with, "Then at the end of the day yesterday, Mr. Bernstein told me that from now on I work on ninth. Right next to the windows."

The other girls shake their heads and Esther says, "So far down the aisles, it'll take you at least an extra ten minutes to leave each night! How cruel, just for missing one day of work."

"One day for doing *union* work," someone points out, and the others nod. She's right, he's punishing me for that.

"Well, I knew he'd probably do something unkind, but I'm still glad I went," I say. "That meeting in Philadelphia on Thursday went so well. We raised $1000 for the union and signed up a lot of new girls too. So I don't care a lick for what Mr.—"

"Wait," Rosie interrupts, looking at Esther. "What did I just see?"

Annoyed, I say, "How would I know what you—"

Rosie doesn't let me finish. Instead, she picks up Esther's left hand. "And when did you get *this*?"

Esther laughs, says, "Last night," and holds out her hand to show us her engagement ring. The diamond is small, of course, but it flashes prettily in the sunshine, almost as bright and glowing as Esther herself.

I don't know how I didn't notice it but Rosie did. "When were you going to tell us?"

"Whenever you stopped talking," Esther responds, nudging me with her elbow.

The other girls clamor to see and I try to push away my aggravation. I *have* been talking a lot at this lunch break in Washington Square Park, but even so I haven't told them the most important news.

"You'll get tired of doing that," Rosie warns teasingly as Esther shows her ring to each girl in turn. "When my cousin back home got engaged she said people never looked at her face anymore, just her hand."

"I'll never get tired." Esther waves her hand in Rosie's face. "Never never never. Joseph and I are getting married in April and we'll be married for a hundred years and I'll show off this ring every day of those years."

"A hundred!" I roll my eyes, smiling, and put my arm around her shoulders. Esther was Rosie's friend first, they picketed together, but now she and I are great friends too as we give speeches and work together at the union. "You'd have to get tired of him after that long."

She leans into me. "I'd as soon get tired of breathing. He's wonderful." Then she says, "So, when are you all getting married?"

I pretend to be exasperated. "Always this way, isn't it, girls? The second she gets a ring on her finger, she's trying to drag the rest of us into it too."

The others laugh, and Esther says, "If it's evil to want my friends to be this happy, then I am evil and glad to be so. Well? How about you, Rosie? Got a special man?"

Rosie's cheeks pinken, and I laugh and say, "I think she's working on getting my brother."

The Jewish Esther and Beckie look taken aback at the idea of Rosie with an Italian, and she looks even more embarrassed, but Isabella claps her hands and says, "Oh, he's so handsome. If you don't want him as your fella, Rosie, let me know. I'm sure I could make him very happy."

To my delight, Rosie looks jealous at the thought of the pretty Isabella pleasing Vinnie. She forces her face into a smile quickly, but I saw the jealousy anyhow and I like it. Vinnie should have lots of girls fighting for him.

"He'd make his girl happy, and no mistake," I say. "Listen to this, though. My parents are coming over from Italy. They're leaving tomorrow, and Vinnie saved enough money, along with some of mine, to bring them." I pause, then deliver the best part. "Third class."

"Ooh," Isabella says, clearly impressed, as she should be, that they aren't traveling in steerage. "He *has* done well. Are they coming to stay? Or take you home?"

"Neither. They'll be here a few months to see America and have a good time, then they're going home. Vinnie and I will quit work while they're here, and... um..."

I stumble, remembering what he said last night when we were discussing our parents' journey, about how he was looking forward to a little time away so he didn't need to hear about sick friends.

Taking a deep breath, I push away the thought of silicosis. Too many of Vinnie's coworkers have developed that terrible lung disease from breathing in all the dust from their digging underground. They had so much trouble with the horrible cough and shortness of breath that they eventually had to quit for jobs that paid less, and two of them have actually died gasping for air. Thankfully, Vinnie is young and strong and doesn't have it and probably won't get it. And thankfully for me, the worst thing I'm likely to face at work is a needle piercing my finger if I'm not careful.

"And we'll go back to work once they leave," I say, pulling myself together, "and then we're supposed to go home for good in 1913, after four years here."

The others comment on how glad I must be to know I'll see my parents soon, but Rosie says, "Supposed to go?"

That girl always seems to notice the little details. I nod. "That was the plan. Go back and marry a nice young man and live as my mother did and her mother before her and— but now... oh, girls, I want to stay. Be a union girl, give speeches that make a difference. Going home with money for another restaurant... I don't care anymore. I told my parents in a letter, and they said I would change my mind, but I will not. I know I won't. Vinnie can go home but I want to stay *here*."

As I spoke my voice got louder and more excited, but the girls don't tease me as they usually do when that happens. Instead, Isabella gives my arm a gentle squeeze and Rosie says, "Well, you're staying for now. And who knows, maybe we'll all stay right here."

"Right here in the park?" Esther chuckles. "Not sure that's allowed."

"Oh, you know what I mean," Rosie says, her cheeks going pinker than they already were in the fresh March air. "Staying in America. I just didn't say it right."

"Yes, we know, don't worry," Esther says, slipping her arm around Rosie's shoulder. Then she giggles and waves her ring in front of Rosie's nose again. "Did I show you this?"

"Several times," Rosie says, pretending to be annoyed.

"Much as I'd love to sit looking at that pretty thing all day, we'd better get back, girls," Beckie says, and we all groan. "I know," she says, "it's too beautiful out here to want to be cooped up inside. But at least we only work until four forty-five today." She nudges me. "Thanks to our fiery union girls like this one."

We are all union girls, but she's right that the others aren't as fiery as me. Even Rosie still works only at stuffing envelopes and making signs. As far as I know, she's never spoken to Clara about doing speeches, and when I suggested it again she refused to let me ask for her. With her every Sunday spent away from me doing who knows what, she's turned her attention to something else, and since I don't know what it is, I hope it somehow involves dreaming of Vinnie. I'll make sure she meets my parents while they're here; I don't think they'll want Vinnie marrying a Jewish girl, but if I'm wrong maybe Rosie and I will end up sisters.

"Will you be able to get any work done with that big ring holding your hand down?" I ask Esther with fake concern.

We all giggle as we walk out of the park and back toward the factory, and she says, "I will admit I spent a lot of time this morning staring at it and not quite as much time working. But I'll get used to it."

"You'll have to," Isabella puts in, "if you're going to be married for a hundred years."

We keep talking and laughing until we reach the building and I look up, all the way up to the ninth floor where I'm now forced to work. "They aren't supposed to punish me for union work," I say, shaking my head, "and yet they have."

"But we'll keep working for the union," Beckie says, "and we *will* make that stop. We'll make a difference. Even at this factory. We will."

We all nod silently, then join the line for the elevator which soon hauls us upward to the eighth floor where Rosie and Beckie and Isabella leave us.

Though I told the girls I didn't care, I am actually angry to not be working on their floor anymore. I told Vinnie I wanted to quit, to find another factory where I wouldn't have the worst seat, but he reminded me that ten dollars a week was good money and convinced me to stay. Maybe I'll be able to convince Mr. Bernstein to move me back to eighth in a few days, as Vinnie convinced me to stay at Triangle. If not, Rosie and I will only stay a few more weeks at the most anyhow before finding a new place and new girls to bring to the union.

"See you after work," Rosie calls to us as she and the others begin shuffling toward the narrow door in the partition.

"See you," we call back, and I remember how shocked Rosie was the day we started working at Triangle when she first learned about the daily searches of workers.

It *is* shocking. We should all be shocked at being treated like thieves when we have done nothing wrong.

I will not rest until all workers are treated fairly.

CHAPTER TWENTY-NINE

Rosie
March 25, 1911

"ROSIE!"

I look up from my machine, startled, to see Dinah the office manager holding out my pay envelope. "Maybe you don't want this?"

"Of course I do," I say, smiling and taking it from her. "Sorry, I was thinking."

"As long as you sew at the same time, you can think all you want."

She smiles back and keeps working her way down the crowded aisle. There's barely enough space between the rows of machines for her to pass, but since we're all pulled right up to our tables, she can squeeze through. When we get up at the end of the day, we push our chairs in, but even so it takes ages for the girls who sit at the very back by the windows to make their way to the dressing room.

Poor Maria is now right by those windows, up on the ninth floor, and I feel terrible about that. She's paying that price for her union work, and I'm not sure I'd be willing to pay it myself. But I should be.

To distract myself from thinking about it all, I get back to sewing, but the thoughts keep coming into my mind. I *am* in the union, despite my parents' opinion, but the mere idea of giving a speech turns my stomach. Maria is so much more use to the union than I could ever hope to be. Why am I risking upsetting my parents when I can't even do more than stuff envelopes or pick out girls for Maria to talk to? I believe in the union, but I don't believe in my worth to it. A thousand girls could do what I do.

After about half an hour of working and thinking and trying not to think because I have no answers, the bell rings and the machinists turn off our machine axles so all the sewing machines stop at once. The sudden quiet is almost painful after getting used to the noise, but the usual clatter of girls talking and laughing as they move toward the dressing room fills in the space.

"Fire!"

I spin round with the others at this most unusual sound to see a red glow beneath one of the cutting tables, in the scrap bin. A girl near me gasps, and I feel my heart leap in my chest, but someone else says, "Look, it's all right, they're getting water."

Three men are indeed grabbing pails of water from shelves on the wall. The first throws his water, somehow managing to get most of it through the gap of only a few inches between the tabletop and the bin, but to my horror, flames burst out from the other side as if running away from the splash.

That man shouts, "More!" and the others throw their water too, but the tables are tall enough for the men to work standing and the bin underneath holds all their scraps of light fabric, so the little water they've got isn't enough to douse the fire. With each bucket, the flames leap out again, climbing up from under the table and creeping along it devouring the piles of fabric lying there, and the smoke grows thicker.

"Get the hose!" Mr. Bernstein yells, and he and a cutter fight through the crowd of shocked girls to the stairwell then fight their way back dragging a fire hose behind them. They point it at the fire, but nothing happens.

"Help me fix it!"

They try, Mr. Bernstein fiddling with the hose itself while the cutter runs back to the stairwell, but they can't. No water appears, not even a drop.

Then, horribly, the growing flames shoot up to the wire above the tables where the cutters hang the metal-edged thin paper patterns when they're not using them, and the fire races along the wire, lighting the patterns and dropping pieces of them down onto each fabric-covered table it passes.

The cutters race too, trying to rip the patterns off the wire before the fire reaches them, but the flames are too fast, and in moments glowing bits of fabric and paper are flying around igniting everything they touch.

It's only been a few minutes, but the room is ablaze.

"Call ninth and tenth," Mr. Bernstein shouts at Dinah, who stands shocked with the rest of us. She stares for another moment, then rushes to the table where the telephone sits. "Get them out! Girls, don't just stand there, go down the stairs!" He coughs with the smoke. "Hurry! And you—" He points at a young cutter whose name I don't know, then at the wall. "Open the fire escape and get them out that way. Now!"

I didn't even know the building had a fire escape.

As the cutter fumbles with a window, I want to move to him but my feet seem a million miles away and I can't control them.

Nothing seems real. Our normal day, where did it go? Burned to nothing. Will I also be—

That thought feels like a slap across my cheek, and a voice like Aunt Ida's in my head says, "Don't you die here."

This time when I try to move, my feet cooperate, but a girl stands between me and the now-opened window, screaming and clutching at her chest.

"Go," I yell at her, trying to push her forward. "Go!"

She doesn't budge with my first push, and with my second she turns and runs away. I want to get her to come with me but I can't see her any longer through the smoke, so instead I let the cutter help me step over the sill that's about the height of my knees and am the second girl out the window.

The metal fire escape is wobbling already with only two of us, and as more follow and we make our way down single-file because there's only room for that, I begin to be afraid it won't hold us.

When we pass the seventh-floor window, I am certain that it won't, and as we approach the sixth floor, I hear a terrible groan as if it's pulling away from the building.

I scream to the girl ahead of me, "Can we go in there?"

"But the building's on fire!"

"This isn't going to hold!"

We're both right.

She rushes ahead, making the fire escape rock even more, and I help her fight with the huge metal shutters outside the window to lift their heavy fastening pins and open them then we kick the glass until it shatters.

I follow her inside, holding up my skirt so I don't trip and being careful not to cut myself on the leftover glass in the frame, then turn to help the next girl into the building. Every instinct says I should run to the door and run down the stairs and run as far from the building as I can, but I can't leave the other girls to—

Maria!

She's on ninth. At the back, by the windows. Not these windows, the other side. Is there a fire escape over there, a better one? Will she get out?

I start to go back out the window, somehow imagining I will race up the stairs against the crowd of terrified girls and go in at ninth and get my friend, but the first girl hauls me back and shrieks, "No! Let them in!"

I do, and more and more of us pour into this unknown darkened factory, some crying, some stunned silent, and some screaming. I'm silent, but in my head I am begging Maria to find her way out.

As the young cutter steps one foot into the window, the fire escape makes an awful sound like it's screaming too and begins to pull away from the building.

The girl and I grab the man's arms and pull him inside, then I shriek with her as the fire escape rips entirely off the building and tumbles to the ground six floors below.

Carrying with it I don't know how many girls.

Their screams of terror are horrible, but the awful thumps when they land are worse, and the silence after that is worse of all.

"What do we do?" a girl whimpers. "We have to get out."

We all stand frozen for a moment, shocked by how quickly our world went from usual to disastrous, then a small group of us move as one to the door of the factory in which we've found ourselves.

It is locked.

Bolted.

From the outside.

We try everything to open the door, while the others collapse to the floor behind us and sob, but it doesn't budge. The fire's not here with us yet, but it will be. With the blaze on eighth so huge already, I can't imagine it won't reach us here soon. And then how will we survive?

CHAPTER THIRTY

Maria
March 25, 1911

THE BELL ENDING OUR WORK DAY rang nearly ten minutes ago, so Esther and I have finally got our turn in the small dressing room to get our hats and coats then join the line of girls waiting to be searched before they leave.

We aren't doing that, though; she's giggling and showing off her engagement ring to a few girls who haven't seen it yet and I'm admiring it again right along with them.

"You're so lucky," one of the girls says, shaking her head. "I can't get Hank to even talk about getting married never mind buy me a ring."

Esther pats the girl's arm. "You'll get there, I'm sure of it. And if he won't marry you the men will line up for you, a pretty fun one like you."

The girl sighs. "I hope you're right."

"Of course she is, she's about to be an old married woman. They're always right," I say, and we all laugh.

Someone is singing a song from a musical she saw last week, while two other girls dance though there's hardly any room for it, and as I look around I feel so lucky to work with such sweet people. So lucky to be an American.

Then we leave the dressing room and walk into Hell.

Flames are bursting through broken windows all around the floor and leaping onto the cutting tables piled high with fabric, and thick black smoke is darkening the room.

"What on—what happened?" Esther asks a girl standing frozen near us.

"It just... showed up," the girl says, her words coming slow and strangely calm. "A moment ago. Nothing, then everywhere."

"We have to get out of here," I say, gasping for air and trying not to let my mind go to those poor girls who died in that factory fire in Newark. "We have to."

The closest exit to us is the stairs down to Washington Place so we race over there, dragging the stunned girl with us, and pull on the door.

It doesn't open.

"Locked," Esther says in despair. "Just like always." She's right. They lock it about an hour before quitting time to make sure we all go out through the partition door to be searched. That's probably not locked, but it's on the other side of the factory. The other side of the fire.

The girl sinks to the floor. "We're lost, we're lost."

Ignoring her, I say, "Try it again." What else can we do?

We pull and tug and kick and beg the door, everything we can imagine, and more girls join us and do the same, crying and shouting and desperate, but nothing works.

"Step aside!" A man's commanding voice makes us move even in our terror, and he raises a metal piece of one of the sewing machines and begins pounding at the glass window above the door. "We need air!"

With a few vicious blows, he does shatter the glass. But instead of air, more flames rush in. We all recoil, and he drops the metal and runs away, to where I don't know.

Esther says, her face streaming with the same tears my smoke-filled eyes are shedding, "We have to find another way out."

We turn around, the crowd of us, to realize there are two right near us. The doors to the passenger elevators, which we aren't normally allowed to use, are open and girls are cramming themselves inside. Even as we see them, one elevator car drops down out of sight.

There's no room in the remaining one, though. The operator can't even close the door with all the girls inside, and the elevator is sinking down under all the weight.

Then it speeds up. He must have yanked the cable inside and sent it down to the ground. Taking those girls to safety. Leaving us here.

One of the girls with us gives a desperate cry and leaps onto the heads of those inside when the elevator's lowered enough that she can. New shrieks of fear and pain come from the elevator as she lands on top of the girls there, and she herself screams as her feet hit the floor hard when the elevator drops even further and out of sight.

We all stand staring for a moment, shocked and not knowing what to do next, then the stunned girl seems to wake and runs toward the empty elevator doorway. We scream at her not to, but she doesn't so much as slow down before she leaps into the open space.

Despite the ferocious crackle of the fire and the screams and sobbing all around us, we still hear the thud as she lands on the roof of the metal elevator car.

What do we do? What *can* we do? Was she right to jump? How else can we escape? Did Rosie get out? I have so many questions but no answers, and my heart is racing so fast I feel I might faint. Several fainted girls lie on the floor around me, and more scream and cry where they stand, and a few even run back and forth in panic with their hair ablaze. I want to help them all, but I can't even help myself.

The smoke is thickening so that we're all near-choking now, but Esther manages to say to me, "It'll be back. He'll come back. If not, we'll..."

She doesn't finish her sentence, and I know why. We don't have any options if he doesn't come back. The door near us is locked, and the elevator cars are gone. Other than the dressing room, which offers no escape, I can't see anything but the fire, so high and angry that though I know where our usual exit is, I can't see it at all.

All I can see is fire, like a red demon. Blazing over the tables, racing across the floor soaked with oil from the machines, eating the piles of fabric and our wooden chairs and the wicker baskets in which we keep our work.

Pouring in through the broken windows.

Those windows are the only exit I can see.

CHAPTER THIRTY-ONE

Rosie
March 25, 1911

THOUGH THE FLAMES HAVEN'T YET REACHED US on the sixth floor, I've never been so terrified. The fire grew so fast it must be everywhere on eighth by now, so how much time do we have before it gets to us here? The fire escape is gone so we can't go back. All we can do is wait and pray.

I am doing that, plus worrying about Maria, when the young man leaps forward and begins pounding his fists on the exit door again. "Help! We're trapped in here!" To us, he yells, "I think I heard someone!"

We rush over and kick and hit whatever part of the door or wall we can reach, screaming with what breath we can find, then a deep voice shouts from outside, "Get away from the door!"

We do, in time for it to be hit from outside by something huge and heavy. A few more hits, then the door splinters at the lock and it's pushed open by a policeman holding his club high. "Go down the stairs," he says, pointing. "And quickly!"

We don't move.

"Run!"

The young man says, "But the fire... is it safe?"

"It's upstairs, not down. Go!"

He rushes up the stairs, and we all rush down before the fire can reach us here.

In the lobby, a policeman is blocking the doorway to the street. When we try to get past him, he pushes us back then grabs the young man's arm and says loudly and firmly, "Don't let the girls out, son, it's not safe. None of you can go yet. They're..." He swallows hard, and I realize with horror that this burly man is trying not to cry. Then he says, whispers really, "They're jumping from the top floors."

Several of the girls with me scream and one faints. I stand frozen. All I can see in my mind's eye is Maria, my lovely little friend, jumping from the ninth floor.

She can't. She won't. She has to have gotten out. When I left, Dinah was calling the other floors on the telephone so they would know and get out. That has to be what happened. Maria must be on the street already waiting for me.

The policeman steps cautiously outside and looks up then shouts over his shoulder to us, "Now!"

We rush out as fast as we can, and people on the sidewalk across the street scream at us, "Over here! Hurry!"

Water sprays up from our feet as we run, but we're not fast enough. I hear a cry and a thump, and look back over my shoulder to see that the last of us has been hit by a falling body. She lies half beneath the other girl, whose hair and clothing are ablaze, and neither of them is moving.

Someone grabs me and pulls me off the street onto the sidewalk, and I look up, dazed, to see a policeman. His face is blackened with smoke, tear streaks cutting white paths down his cheeks, but I know him.

He's the one who arrested me.

He's sorry, now, I can tell, sorry that the girls he harassed are dying, but I can't spare a moment for him. I pull away and turn to look up at the building, trying to keep my eyes from the still forms on the sidewalk.

Flames fill the windows of all three Triangle floors. The eighth floor windows hold only flames, and the tenth too, but the ninth...

Oh, the girls stand in the windows of the ninth.

The flames are behind them, and I can hardly breathe at the sight. Dinah was calling them! Why didn't they get out?

"Don't jump!" The crowd, policemen and firemen and people whose clothes say they must have been relaxing in the park, shouts up at the girls. "Don't jump! Wait for the ladders!"

The fire trucks are arriving and their ladders are going up, and relief fills those of us waiting.

Then horror.

Everyone seems to realize at once that the ladders have stopped at the sixth floor, that they can't go any higher, that the girls are left three floors above unable to escape. Firemen are spraying water up to them, while others try to get their hoses into the building, but it's barely a trickle. It might cool the workers down, a little, but it can't save them.

A girl climbs out onto the window ledge, clutching the frame tightly. When she's fully outside, I realize her skirt is burning. She slaps at it, but can't put it out, then looks down at the top edge of the ladder three floors below.

Realizing what she's considering, I scream, "No!"

But it's too late. Even if she heard me and the others shouting over the roar of the fire, which I doubt, it's too late. She leaps into space, her hands flailing for the ladder. She misses, tumbles to the ground, lands with a horrible thud, and lies still.

As I stare at her body, so horrified I can barely stay standing at seeing someone's life end like that, the wetness of the pavement around her begins to soak into her white shirtwaist.

I shouldn't be able to see it, the water.

But I can.

Because yes, it's the firemen's water.

But it's also the blood of the girls who jumped before her.

Seeing their blood in the water, running down the sidewalk and into the gutters, makes my knees give way so I sink into a pile on the curb.

"Here!" A man shouts up to a girl in the window. "Here, to the net!"

She stares down at the net the firemen and passers-by are holding, and for a moment everyone freezes. Then she jumps, landing in the middle of the net with an awful jolt.

She gets out and staggers slowly toward us, making the crowd cheer, but those cheers become screams when she collapses after only a few steps and does not move again.

Three more girls come down, holding hands to keep themselves together. They tear the net when they hit it and shatter through the glass deadlights set into that part of the sidewalk, and I clap my hand over my mouth as their bodies fall from sight.

Even after that, people keep holding out nets and picnic blankets and coats and whatever they can find, and girls keep jumping.

None of it, none of it, works.

The girls come down alone or huddled together, and none of them can be caught or saved. The men try, every time, to catch them, but their nets and blankets and coats are torn from their soon-bleeding hands and the girls either rip through or simply land on the sidewalk atop the fabric the men could not hold.

More and more girls climb to the window ledge, and each watches the previous one, her eyes on her all the way to the ground, before jumping herself. I don't know how they can do it, how they find the courage.

Some of them fall straight to the sidewalk, landing feet first then crumpling backward or sideways.

Some of them hit the wall of the building and tumble down to land in a heap.

None of them rise again, no matter how they fall.

Their bodies are landing on the firemen's hoses, still burning, so the firemen have to turn the stream of water on them to put out the flames. Other men pull their poor burnt corpses off the hoses to let the firemen work, and some of those men lead the fire horses away because the animals are rearing and panicking at the sight and smell and sound of the bodies falling all around them.

I see more than one man crying as he works, and many in the crowd are sobbing too, but I am not. I don't know why, but I'm not. All I can find it in me to do is to sit on the curb and stare up at the building and pray with all my heart that Maria somehow made it out ahead of me and isn't a corpse on the sidewalk or a brave girl about to jump.

A young man steps out onto the window ledge, then brings a girl to stand beside him. They cling together for a moment, and I have just enough time to wonder if he is talking to her, encouraging her, before he holds her out away from the building and lets her drop.

He draws out another girl, as the crowd shouts at him not to though it knows he can't save the girls from the fire any other way, then he releases her too and brings out a third and my stomach feels like I myself have been dropped from a great height.

Maria.

That new blue skirt of which she was so proud has flames at its hem, but she doesn't look down at those. Her face is turned up to the young man, and I hope that if he *is* talking he's telling her something that will help, that will make her last moments something other than this nightmare.

I don't want them to be her last moments at all, but there's nothing I can do but watch as he holds my friend, my best friend, out from the building.

Then he lets her go.

I shut my eyes at once. I cannot let her falling to her death be my last picture of her.

I open them in time to see the young man jump too, in a halo of flames, and crumple to the sidewalk next to a still body in a new blue skirt.

Then I begin to get up, because I have to go find Vincente, but the thought of telling him what's happened makes the world go black around me and I slump back to the curb and know no more.

CHAPTER THIRTY-TWO

Rosie
March 25, 1911

I WAKE TO FIND A MAN IN A WHITE COAT crouched in front of me. "I'm fine," I say, confused for a moment as to where I am and why he's there, then everything returns to me in a rush that makes me gasp.

He pats my shoulder, his face grave. "You've had a shock, my dear, but you're one of the lucky ones." He gets to his feet and holds out his hand to me. "Let's see if you can stand."

Once with his help I do, he releases me and says, "I have other girls to attend to. Are you all right?"

I try a nod, and it doesn't make me feel faint again so I say, "I am."

He gives me a smile that moves only the corners of his mouth. "I'm glad. Now go home to your family. You don't need to see this any longer."

Though I know I'll regret it, I can't help looking past him to the scene on the sidewalk across the street. The shattered bodies of my friends and fellow workers still lie there, drenched with firemen's water and the blood of all of them mingled together. Several doctors work, each bending over an unmoving person then rising and shaking his head before moving on to the next one, and behind them men lay white sheets over the bodies in which no life could be found.

Maria's is one of those bodies.

"Look away, my dear," the doctor with me says urgently. "Turn around and look away."

I do as he says, though it feels disrespectful to show those poor dead people on the sidewalk my back, and that's how I discover that a huge crowd has gathered and is being held a block away on all sides of the factory by policemen. So many policemen. There must be hundreds on foot and another hundred on horses. On the ground near me is a long line of wooden coffins, empty for now. How did all of this get here so fast? How long was my faint? "Sir, what time is it, do you know?"

He pulls out his pocket watch. "Five-fifteen," he says, putting it away.

Our work day ended at four forty-five. How can that be? How can everything have changed in a mere half hour?

"You go on home now to your family. You *do* have family here, don't you?"

"I—" It occurs to me that if I tell him I don't he might try to send me somewhere, and I can't let that happen. I must find Vincente. "I do, of course, and I will go to them."

He smiles, relieved. "Good. Take care, my dear."

"You too, sir," I say, then turn and walk along Washington Place, into the crowd and away from Washington Square Park and away from Triangle.

I don't go far, though. I stop where the crowd is a little thinner but I can still see the burning building, because here I will also be able to see Vincente when he arrives. If I leave and go to his home I might miss him, and I cannot bear to have him find out from someone else. With all these people here news must be spreading, so he will hear about the fire somehow and he will come here. I will wait and I will see him and I will tell him though it will break both our hearts.

Where I stand, I can see both the Washington Place and Greene Street faces of the building, both sidewalks full of corpses. Men load the white-covered bodies into coffins, which are then hauled away by an ambulance or patrol wagon or any other vehicle that can carry them, while firemen drag more hoses through the building's doors and up the stairs to fight the flames that still leap in the windows where the girls no longer stand.

I think of Mr. Bernstein trying to use the hose in the building, and I wonder: did he survive, and why didn't that hose work? If it had, if he'd been able to put out the fire right away, none of this would have happened.

Here and there around me people are crying, but it is largely a silent vigil we keep. At least, it is until the policemen and firemen begin searching where the fire escape fell.

Though we can't see because that side of the building is blocked from us by other buildings, somehow the word spreads through the waiting crowd that not only did those metal stairs reach only to several floors above the ground but where they ended was above a spiked fence. We could never have used the fire escape to get out safely, and when it collapsed, it threw its load of terrified workers everywhere and some even ended up impaled on that fence.

As the news, and the outrage about it, spreads through the crowd, the silence is taken over by muttering. "That Mr. Asch what owns the building, he did this to them." "A fire escape ending over a fence, what's the sense in such a thing?" "It's not right. Rich men don't care."

Then a woman screams, "They killed my daughter! I need to see her!" and a man shouts, "My daughter *and* my son", and then everyone is screaming and shouting and pushing forward. Though I don't want to be, I am caught up and pushed forward too.

The policemen rush toward us, their clubs held high, yelling, "Back! Back! You can't go to them. Stay back!"

I shrink away from the clubs, knowing how a beating feels from the day I met Maria, and enough other people do too that the policemen are able to get us controlled again.

"We are taking the bodies," one shouts, "to Misery Lane, to the Charities Pier on the East River at the end of Twenty-Sixth Street."

The ferry that took Maria and me to and from the workhouse has its dock at Charities Pier. That's where Vincente and I met for the first time, where he and Maria celebrated their reunion after our five days away. I can't imagine how I will return him to a place that was briefly so happy for him and Maria on this awful day.

"If you think your family member has died, go there," the policeman continues. "Do not wait here. You will be needed there, to identify them. The walk will take you about forty minutes, or trolleys and subways can get you a little closer. Go now."

Some leave, but most do not, and the policemen have to stop the crowd rushing forward again and again. I want so badly to leave, to run away and hide and somehow forget all that has happened, but I still believe Vincente will come here and I must wait for him. I look down the street for him and then back at the factory and then down the street again, and I do my best to keep my mind focused on those two actions. I don't want to think about anything else.

After a while, I can't tell how long, the flames no longer light up the factory's windows. The sun is beginning to set and the last light sparkles on the water dripping from the sills. It might almost be pretty, if I didn't know why it's there.

"Fire's out," a fireman who has just returned to the sidewalk reports to his chief, and the news is passed through the crowd as he murmurs something else we can't hear.

Soon we can guess what it was, as firemen set up equipment on the corners of the building and lower a black-tarpaulin-wrapped bundle to the ground while a man stands in each window guiding the bundle down so it doesn't bounce against the building.

When it's down, another man carefully places it in a coffin. When the waiting people realize it's a body, of someone who burned to death inside, yet again fury and grief carry the crowd forward until we are forced back by the policemen.

Three more bodies in black tarpaulins have come down and been taken away when I see Vincente, running with his hat gone and his face pale with dread. I break from the crowd and run toward him, and he shouts, "Maria! Where is she?"

While I was waiting I should have thought of how to tell him, but I didn't and now I can't find the words. I stare at him, then manage to whisper, "I'm so sorry."

He stops as if he's run into an invisible wall. "You mean... are you sure? No, you can't be. *It* can't be."

I see, in my mind, Maria beginning to fall to the ground. I am sure.

Though I still can't speak, he must see it in my face because he doesn't ask me again. He stares at me, then stumbles forward and falls into me.

I hold him tight, not caring if anyone is watching, and he clings to me like I'm the only thing keeping him alive, and for the first time I cry for Maria and the other girls and the men too who've lost their lives today. I don't know why I was saved and they weren't, and the pain of being here without them shreds my heart like their bodies shredded the nets.

Vincente and I stand together for a long time, without a word, and then he gently takes my shoulders and eases me back from him. His tear-stained face makes my tears fall faster, and he takes a deep shuddering breath and says, "I must go to her. Do you know... where did they..."

I take my own shuddering breath, wipe my eyes, and say, "Twenty-Sixth at the East River. We would be best to walk."

"We?"

"Yes. I am coming with you."

He wants to tell me no, I can see, tell me it's not the place for a girl. But Triangle, today, wasn't the place for a girl either, and I have already seen horrors beyond imagining, so he pulls my arm through his and says, "Thank you."

These are the last words we say to each other until nearly midnight.

After walking in silence to the Charities Pier, we wait in silence in the short Misery Lane before it, which is well-named today, standing close together in our grief. More and more people join us, until the crowd grows too huge and the policemen have to push us back a block to First Avenue where they move us into two lines, one each side of Twenty-Sixth Street.

Some of those who arrive are also Triangle workers, and I hug them and we cry together at the fear of how many of us are lying in this makeshift morgue waiting to be identified and at the realization that we are lucky enough to be alive.

One of these escaped from the ninth floor, and she said they received no telephone call, no warning, even though I saw Dinah reaching for the telephone. The flames simply burst through the windows and appeared in an instant. This girl happened to be beside the Greene Street partition door and was the first out. Maria was not so lucky.

Others who appear are workers from other factories, worried about their friends and fellow union girls. Some are relatives of Triangle workers, asking questions of everyone they see.

"Have you seen a girl with a hat with a red ribbon?"

"A young man with a silver ring on his right hand?"

"An older woman with a scarred cheek?"

These sorts of people have a right to be here.

But the others, the ones who arrive later in the evening wearing fancy clothes? The ones who laugh and joke with each other and seem to be treating this disaster as an entertainment put on for their amusement?

Well, I should like to put them all in the Triangle and set it on fire anew and see how amusing they find it then.

How can they be so cold and horrible? There were hundreds of people on the three floors of the factory, and I haven't seen more than twenty survivors here. Did all of the rest die? Even if only the people I saw lying shattered on the sidewalk died, that is still something so awful that nobody should laugh. How can they find this exciting? Is it because we're mostly immigrants? Mostly girls? Why does this death and horror entertain them?

As those of us who belong here wait, watching the wagons arrive with the dead and wondering if the person we love is among them, a policeman walks up and down the growing line, alternating telling us that the doors will open at midnight with shouting questions at the crowd. "Who seeks a woman with a cameo necklace?" "A man with the name of Adler on his pay envelope?" "Who seeks a girl with a ring bearing the initials F.R.?"

At this last, a woman a few people ahead of us screams and rushes toward the policeman. He grabs her arms and holds her up as she sways, then says, "I'll take you inside to see her."

They go together, the woman sobbing so loudly I can hear her long after I can't see her anymore, and disappear into the morgue. She doesn't return when the policeman does, so I assume the girl was who she needed to find. I don't know whether to be happy she found her or sad for her loss. Both, I suppose.

The policeman doesn't ask any questions that would seem to have Maria as an answer. Vincente does ask whether he has seen a girl in a blue skirt and white waist but he simply says, "Quite a few, sir. You'll have to wait, I'm afraid," and so we do.

Moments before the doors are to open at midnight, Vincente turns to me and says, "I don't know if I should let... you shouldn't have to see..."

His voice is rough and I can hear the tears he's trying not to let out in it, and I know he's probably right. But I also know he doesn't want to have to see his dead sister alone. So I say, "I need to do this. For Maria."

"For Maria," he echoes in a whisper, and I reach out and take his arm both to hold myself up and to give him something to do beside think about his sister.

He lays his other hand on my arm and I put my other hand atop his and we stand shivering in the cold night until the huge iron doors of the building they've made into a temporary morgue slowly open.

Nobody moves. We wanted to go inside, but now that we can...

A policeman shouts, "Come along now!" and an old woman at the front of the line moves forward. About twenty people follow her in, including Vincente and me, before the policeman makes the rest wait their turn.

In the strange swinging light of the policemen's lanterns, I see two long rows of wooden coffins. The floor around them is wet with what I hope is only water, and the air reeks of smoke and death. In each of those coffins, arranged as if holding themselves up on their elbows, lies one of my lost fellow workers. I could almost believe they're sleeping, except for their pale faces and the wrongness of their shapes beneath the white sheets that cover them.

My knees shaking and my heart racing, I keep pace with the crowd, then a girl in front of me faints. A policeman catches her and eases her to the floor out of the way, where he calls for someone to bring her hot coffee. I feel like I might faint again myself, but I tell myself I cannot. I have to be strong for Vincente.

The old woman who led us inside leans down to peer at a body in the third coffin then screams, and I press my hand to my heart because the sound of her agony hurts more than I can bear.

Vincente says something to her in Italian, and she throws herself on him and sobs against his chest until the waiting policeman says gently, "Tell me who she is." I don't know the girl she names through her tears, and I wish I did. All of the victims, I should know them. We all worked together, after all. But there were hundreds of us.

Are there hundreds of bodies here?

The policeman covers the coffin, hiding the pretty pale face from view, and writes on a card which he tacks to the lid. "Come with me," he says to the woman, and leads her away.

One identified.

We keep moving forward, all of us both afraid and hopeful to find those who matter most to us, and as we go I realize that the more damaged ones have been placed further from the door. They don't look like they're sleeping anymore. Now they're burned or badly broken, or burned *and* badly broken, and I know I will be seeing them in my nightmares for the rest of my life.

I still recognize some, though, despite their condition. Here is Isabella, who just this morning joked about wanting to please Vincente, one side of her face burned almost black. Here is a different Maria, a woman who started work near me only a few days ago, excited about having such a good job to support her five children. How will they survive now? Here is the girl who sat beside me working all day today. I never knew her name, and now I never will.

And here...

Oh.

Though several people are studying this body, trying to convince themselves she is theirs, I know immediately she's ours.

Our Maria, with her head misshapen from her fall but her face still recognizable, and a bit of her blue skirt peeking out at her hip from the white sheet covering her. Her eyes are closed, her whitened face is still with none of her usual excitement and energy, her wet hair straggles limply down over the edge of her coffin. She is here, and she is gone, and sadness catches my chest in its cold clammy hands and squeezes the breath from me.

Vincente sees her too, and he drops to his knees with a groan that brings tears to my eyes and goosebumps to my body.

I can't speak, but I step in front of him, to protect him from the awful sight, and take hold of his shoulders.

He presses his face into my belly, wrapping his arms around my waist, and I can feel his body shaking as I hold him against me. It's not proper to have him near me like this, and ordinarily I would be shocked, but this isn't an ordinary day and I'm not sure we'll ever have one again.

As Vincente clutches me, a nearby policeman says softly, "Her name, please."

"Maria Cirrito," I say. "His sister, and my friend." I want to say more, about how wonderful Maria was and how committed to the union, but my throat's too tight to continue and I doubt he cares anyhow. None of them cared before.

The policeman nods at my identification, and covers Maria's coffin. After writing her name on a card and tacking it to the lid, he writes on another piece of paper and says, "Take this, and him, to the desk over there. They have her things and can arrange to release her to him."

I accept the paper, and my eyes lock with his. He takes a breath as if he wants to say something else, then nods and turns away to deal with the next grieving relative. And the next and the next.

I hate the policemen for how they handled the strike, but I pity this one now. How can he do this? How can all of this be happening? How will any of us survive?

I lean down and say into Vincente's ear, "Did you hear him?"

He nods against me.

"Are you ready to go?"

He shakes his head.

So we stay there, beside his sister, for another long moment before he releases me and gets to his feet. He doesn't look in my direction but blindly reaches out his hand toward me, and I grip it as we take our first steps away from Maria together. With my other hand, I smooth the front of my skirt and I feel wetness there. Vincente's tears.

I squeeze his hand hard, wanting to say so much but not knowing how, then turn at the sound of another man weeping.

With his shaking back to me he's crouched beside a coffin, holding a poor burned hand in his. In the flickering lamplight the diamond ring on that hand, the ring Esther showed off so proudly only hours ago, still sparkles.

Rosie
March 26, 1911

VINCENTE AND I REACH THE DESK WE WERE SENT TO, and I hand the policeman there the paper I was given without speaking because I can't think of anything to say. He nods and looks through a box on the floor, then brings out a large brown envelope from which he places three things on the desk before us.

Maria's gold ring with the blue glass stone which the three of us bought together.

The silver hatpin she always wore, which had belonged to her mother, the one she said had its metal dancing with happiness.

Her battered black leather pocketbook, which she must have been clutching when she jumped.

This is all that's left of my beautiful friend?

"Pay envelope is in the pocketbook," the policeman says quietly. "Contains ten dollars. You can..." He clears his throat. "You can have a funeral home claim her body for burial sometime this week." He takes a piece of paper from a stack, fills in a few blanks on it, and holds it out to Vincente. "Give them this permit. They'll know what to do."

The man doesn't tell him, and Vincente doesn't ask, how he is supposed to afford a funeral, or how to plan one so quickly when there will be so very many. Vincente simply gives a single nod and reaches out his free hand to take the permit from the policeman and put it into his pocket. Then he tucks Maria's jewelry away with the permit and settles her pocketbook under his arm, and we leave without a word, still holding hands.

"Let me walk you home," he says once we're past the crowd waiting outside the morgue. "Please."

He sounds exhausted, and I want to say no to save him the effort, but I don't want to be alone and I don't think he does either so I nod then add, "Thank you."

We don't speak again as we walk, and I both want and fear to know what he's thinking. For myself, I am trying not to think of anything. I can feel his warm hand in mine, and my feet in my shoes and my hat on my head and the depth of my tiredness, and I want all of that to be all that's in my mind.

When we arrive at my home, I reach for the front door but it's yanked open and a half-laughing-half-sobbing Julia stands in the doorway. "Rosie! Oh, Rosie, when you didn't come back I thought... I thought..."

I hug her hard, barely able to hold back my tears. "It was awful," I whisper into her shoulder. "I can't even tell you. Oh, Julia."

"But you're alive. It's all right now."

It will never be all right.

She squeezes me tight, then lets me go when Vincente clears his throat. I turn to him and see in his eyes how badly he wishes he and Maria could have had this sort of reunion.

"I'm sorry," I murmur to him, and Julia does the same, and he gives us both a nod as his jaw tightens.

"When will—"

"May I—"

We exchange tiny sad smiles at having spoken over each other and he says, "May I see you tomorrow? Well, later today, I suppose. I need to decide on... arrangements."

I agree at once, glad he isn't going to be alone in his sadness but also unsure of how I can help him, and we settle on a late lunch at a little Italian restaurant not far from Triangle.

The fact that Maria won't join us, can never join us again, hangs in the air between us but neither of us acknowledges it, and he leaves with another nod but nothing else said.

Julia hugs me again. "I can't imagine. Your... friend, he lost someone?"

"His sister, my dear friend," I say, then am suddenly so tired I can hardly stay standing. "Julia, I... can I sleep? Please?"

"Of course," she says, and she takes me up to my room and flutters around as she did my first night in New York, straightening my blanket and plumping up my pillow and doing everything she can to fix what cannot be fixed.

Once she reluctantly leaves me alone, I sit on the edge of the bed and stare at my lamp and remember my first night here when I nearly set the room on fire burning my father's letter. I believed, then, that life in America could only be good. I believed what everyone said, that here "they" wouldn't let you burn. Well, everyone was wrong. They let us.

And it's hard to imagine that life will ever again be good.

CHAPTER THIRTY-FOUR

Rosie
March 26, 1911

I BARELY SLEEP, OF COURSE, DESPITE MY EXHAUSTION, and when I wake early in the morning I don't know what to do with myself. Eventually I dress in a black waist and skirt, wondering as I do whether the stink of smoke will ever wash out of yesterday's clothes. I would throw them away unwashed but I don't have enough clothing to spare.

After listening carefully to see if any of the girls are in the hallway, I slip out of the house, managing to avoid seeing anyone. I don't want to talk to them. I have nothing to say.

I should be going to Ellis Island, but I left a note for Julia that I can't. How can I welcome immigrants to America when I know they might die at their work?

A newsboy stands on the corner, and when he sees me he tips his flat cap and says, "Read about the big fire, miss? Only five cents."

I don't know whether I want to, especially whether I want to pay so much for the Sunday paper instead of the usual one cent during the week, but I can't help wondering how the newspapers that often ignored our strike have reported on the fire. So I fish a nickel from my pocketbook and accept the paper the boy hands me. Seward Park isn't far from where we are, so I walk there then sit on a bench and read the first few pages.

I'm too angry to read beyond that.

The front page bears a huge picture of girls lying dead on the sidewalk while men lean over them, and the print below the picture calls them "the unfortunates who jumped from the windows". As if they had a choice! To stay inside amid the flames and smoke, that wasn't a choice.

Inside, articles talk about how we girls all panicked, and claim that those inside the building would have been saved if they had kept their heads and waited on the window ledges for the firemen to catch them. I know that's not true, and anyone else who was there and saw the nets ripped from the firemen's hands by the weight of a falling body would know it too.

So were these reporters not there, or do they just want the public to believe the girls were that foolish?

They might want that, actually, because they don't seem to know who else to blame.

In various articles I see Fire Chief Croker criticizing the building's lack of proper fire escapes, the assistant superintendent of buildings blaming how few staircases were inside, and Mr. Croker again suggesting that the doors on the Washington Place side might have been locked.

Might have been! They certainly were, they always were at the end of the day. If the men don't know that, then it's no wonder they don't know who to blame.

And so why *not* blame the girls? Blaming the workers instead of the bosses seems to be the way of the newspapers. And the world.

I throw the horrible paper into a trash can, feeling even more sad and angry than before, then begin to walk. I don't have a plan for where I'm going, at first, but as I listen to the sobbing and wailing that I can hear on every block as people mourn their dead, I know where I should be. I turn toward Triangle and walk directly there.

I am not the only one who's had this idea. The policemen have prevented the crowd from getting to the factory itself, for a few blocks in all directions, but on the edges of that secured space there are thousands of people.

Some are weeping, or simply walking with their heads down in a way that shows their sorrow.

Some stand and stare up at the building, and I imagine them trying not to picture how their friend or sister or wife died there. Trying, and failing.

But again, there are those who are here simply for the spectacle, and as the day wears on more and more of those appear. Buses even arrive, full of people in bright and happy clothing who point and chatter as if visiting the Menagerie in Central Park or the Botanical Garden, and pushcart vendors sell them hot jellied apples and other treats.

Most horribly, I see men carrying trays walking among the crowd, shouting, "Souvenirs of the fire! Buy a dead girl's earrings! Wear a dead girl's bracelet!" Did they really pick up the girls' jewelry from the sidewalks or are they selling new things instead? It doesn't even matter, I don't think. It's awful either way.

And people are buying the jewelry!

None of these people care about the fire, or about those who died. They're the same people who thought us silly for striking.

I hate them, more than I've ever hated anyone before.

The crowd keeps walking in a huge square around the factory, and though I don't know why or how it started, I join in and somehow it feels a little better than standing still. We can't get any closer to Triangle, and we can't see the whole building because it's surrounded by others, but as we travel from West Fourth Street to Mercer Street then up to Waverly Place and along to the edge of Washington Square Park and back down to West Fourth, we can get glimpses of everything there is to see.

The Washington Place side of the building, from which poor Maria jumped.

The Greene Street side, with the partition and the exit door she would have been able to take if only she'd had enough warning.

The ruined sidewalk glass panes where girls broke through.

Other buildings block our view of the fire escape, but I remember the feel of it beneath my feet and the sound of it pulling away from the wall and I am not sorry not to see its remains.

Around and around we go, and eventually I feel a hand on my arm and realize Vincente has joined me. I tuck my arm through his, and he draws me a little closer, and we make one full circuit and a bit of another in silence before he pulls me out of the flow and stops me where we face the corner of the building.

He looks up at it, his face raised to the sky that seems too blue and clear for the day after such a tragedy, and says quietly, "Where did... she..."

I swallow hard, not wanting to tell him because that will make it all too real. Then I realize that nothing I say will make it any more real or horrible than it already is, so I look up at the ninth floor, count the windows until I see the one from which Maria stepped, and say, "Second floor down from the top, third window from the corner, on Washington Place."

His head moves in that direction with three small jerks, then he holds still and stares at the window.

I stare too, wondering what he's thinking and so glad he didn't have to see his sister and the others jumping because they had no other choice but to burn, and it isn't until he tightens his hold on my arm and says, "You're shivering," that I realize I am.

"It's... hard to look at it," I admit.

"I should never have made you stand here," he says, sounding disgusted.

"No, no, I didn't mean it was your fault," I say quickly, not wanting him to feel bad for me on top of everything else. "It's just... hard."

"I'm not ever coming back," he says. "I don't want to remember her here. This is how she... died, but it's not how she lived. But I had to see it, once."

"I under—"

"I made her keep her job here," he says as if he didn't notice I'd started to speak. "When she was moved to the ninth floor after her union trip to Philadelphia, she wanted to quit. I told her ten dollars a week was nothing to pass up and I insisted she keep working." A shudder goes through him. "I killed her."

That shudder moves from him to me. He shouldn't say such things. "Never think that, never," I say as I turn to him. "She *was* earning good money, and if she'd told *me* she wanted to quit, I'd have said the same thing you did. Plus, she didn't really want to leave. I know it. She loved the girls here and working to get them all into the union, and the big windows and—"

I cut myself off, horrified that I mentioned the windows as a good thing after how the fire ripped through them shattering glass and lives, and he winces but says, "She did love them? The girls, I mean?"

"She did," I say, knowing I'm right and putting as much sincerity as I can into my voice. "She was so happy talking to us all at lunch yesterday. She was."

"And... do you think she suffered, much?"

I remember the flames blazing in the windows, so close behind her that the heat must have been unbearable, and the fire devouring the fabric of her skirt. I try, and fail, to imagine how hard it must have been to breathe with the smoke all around her, or how much fear she felt when the young man released her and she dropped toward our dead fellow workers on the sidewalk. "No," I say, trying to keep that sincerity in my voice. "No, I do not."

Vincente wraps his arms around me and pulls me against his chest. "Thank you," he whispers, "for being here. And for lying to me."

AFTER OUR LUNCH, which we pass mostly in awkward silence, Vincente and I are walking back to my home when we near the headquarters of the union. The red brick building is draped in black fabric from its roof right to the ground, and seeing it in mourning makes me think of how often Maria and I stood in front of it and talked of how much good the union would do.

It doesn't seem to have done much, in the end.

Vincente sighs. "She spent so much time here. I hardly saw her once she got involved. I should have taken better care of her."

I tighten my grip on his arm. "You couldn't have done anything more. She loved you so—"

I'm interrupted by a cry of, "Rosie!" and spin around to see Clara racing toward me. "Oh, I'm *so* glad to see you," she says in Yiddish as we hug. "We're still figuring out who we've lost and I didn't know about you."

I squeeze her tight and murmur, "Maria, though... she's gone."

She sighs. "I know, I heard. It's such a loss to the union, never mind the tragedy of her dying at all. She worked so hard for us. I don't know how we'll replace her."

I realize that I haven't thought at all yet about what I will do now. Clara and her fellow union leaders are no doubt making plans, and I have done nothing but cry and be angry.

Clara releases me and clears her throat. "I'm so sorry, Vincente," she says to him in English, "about your sister. So very sorry. She was a wonderful girl."

"Thank you," he says quietly.

She nods, then says to us both, "We had a protest meeting earlier today, with representatives from many unions," tripping a little over the long word in English. "We're determined to never let another disaster like this happen again. Rosie, will you stop by the union some night this week? I'd love to talk to you about it all."

I nod. I do believe in the union, of course, and I am certainly in agreement that we have to prevent another fire. But she may want to set me on the path to replace Maria, and much as I want to follow that path, the path of Aunt Ida, I don't know if I'm capable of it. That makes me sad. Sadder.

"I must go in," Clara says, then shakes hands with Vincente and hugs me again. She's only taken two steps toward the building, though, when a female voice calls her name.

We all turn to look and she says, "Ah, Jennie," and holds out her arms to the arriving girl.

They look quite a bit alike, so I'm not surprised when Clara says after their hug, "Jennie is my cousin. She worked at Triangle too, and I spent most of this morning at Misery Lane looking for her. We were lucky, though, and she wasn't there." She shivers. "I couldn't imagine how I'd tell her parents."

"No, it would be so hard," I say, trying to imagine how even a wonderful speaker like Clara could find the words to do that.

She nods, then she and Jennie hurry off into the building.

Vincente begins to walk away. I go with him, but he doesn't offer me his arm so I feel strange about trying to take it.

When we're at the building next to mine he makes a strange sound, as if he's choking, and I look up at him.

The single tear rolling down his cheek makes my heart hurt. "I'm so sorry." I wrap my hand around his upper arm. "I wish I could help."

He swipes at his eyes with his free hand. "I just..." He sighs. "Clara mentioning parents... mine are on the ship on their way here. I'm going to have to meet them when they arrive and tell them Maria's..." He swallows hard and shakes his head. "How am I going to tell them?"

People are looking at us, at him, and I don't like it for him, so I draw him into a nearby alley. "I don't know," I say helplessly.

"They'll be looking for us at Ellis Island. They'll see me and look past me for her, and then somehow I'll have to find the words to..."

He squeezes his eyes shut tight and shakes his head, and I reach up and put my arms around his neck and pull him close to me. "I know," I say softly as his arms wind around my waist. "I'm so sorry."

We hold each other for a long time without speaking, then he tightens his arms around me. "Will you come with me?"

"To meet your parents?" I say, sure that can't be what he means. Why would he want that?

He nods. "They'll be so sad about Maria, of course, but getting to meet you will help at least a bit."

"It will?"

His hold on me loosens and he moves his hands to my shoulders. "Of course. They've heard so much about you."

"I... don't understand. Why?"

"Well, Maria spoke of you often, of course." I notice his ears turning red. "And... I might have mentioned you too."

"Oh," I say, feeling heat flooding my face. Why would he have? Maria joked about me trying to catch Vincente; has he been trying to catch me and I didn't even know?

Of course not. His parents no doubt worried about Maria and so he told them about me as Maria's friend. Traditional Italian parents wouldn't want me as a daughter-in-law any more than my parents would want Vincente as their son-in-law.

I can't imagine what I could say to his parents, but he's looking at me so hopefully, and I can't say no and send him to break such awful news alone. "If it will help, then of course I'll go with you."

He squeezes my shoulders then releases them and walks me to my front door. "Thank you. Thank you so much, Rosie."

"You're welcome," I say, wishing I could do more.

"I'll see you at..." He clears his throat. "Wednesday morning."

I nod, not sure what to say. Maria's funeral. He had already arranged it when we met for lunch, but I would have gone no matter when it was.

He nods too, we exchange sad smiles, and he departs.

I go inside, trying not to cry, then am startled by squeals of laughter from the girls crowded in the front room.

"What has happened?" I say, surprised to hear such delight so soon after the fire but also glad to be in the midst of pleasure.

Several girls push Julia over to me, and she gives me a huge hug then pulls back so she can wave her left hand in front of my eyes.

I catch it to hold it still so I can see the gold ring on her hand and its small diamond with a smaller sapphire and diamond on each side. "It's beautiful," I say, then I realize what it means. "Israel... you're getting married?"

The girls all cheer again and Julia says, "I am! We are, I mean. Soon. Next week."

"So romantic," someone says behind me, and the other girls agree, but I have to ask, "Why so quickly?"

As I say it, I realize what could be the reason for the rush and my eyes lower to her stomach.

"No," she says, blushing. "I'm not... no, it's just that we want to be married right away. It..." She sighs. "Ah, didn't we all just learn that life is so short? I love him and he loves me, so why not?"

Our eyes lock, and I know she remembers our conversation on Ellis Island about how Israel didn't want his wife working, but I can't ask her about it and make her sad.

Another girl, though, says, "You'll keep working here, right? He wouldn't make you leave us?"

Before she can answer, several others chime in to beg her to stay with us, and I see her blink back tears before saying, "Well, actually, I will stop." She raises her ringed hand to calm the outcry. "But I'll visit you every week, and naturally you're all invited to the wedding on Sunday afternoon. We'll have a party!"

I join in the clapping and cheers at this with the others, but I don't truly share their happiness. I know Julia loves her work, and now she's losing it to keep the man she also loves.

It's hard to be happy knowing poor Julia was forced to make such a difficult choice.

CHAPTER THIRTY-FIVE

Rosie
March 29, 1911

"READY?"

Vincente nods in response to the man who will drive Maria's hearse to the cemetery, then climbs up onto the first wagon behind the hearse.

The family with whom Vincente and Maria lived in their first days in America is already seated on the wagon's wooden benches with me. Mrs. Billota and her daughter Margherita are sobbing freely into their handkerchiefs, and Mr. Billota and his son look like they're struggling to keep from doing the same. Margherita works in waist factories too, so they must all be thinking how lucky she is to be alive even as they mourn with Vincente.

Vincente's friends are all at work or at home ill and so can't support him through the funeral, but Clara and other union girls who were good friends with Maria fill the remaining room in this wagon and also a second. More girls would have joined us, since Maria was so popular and well-known in the union, but there are so many other funerals happening now.

I learned of the others Monday morning when I went back to the Triangle, drawn by some impulse I didn't understand to again bear witness to what happened. I wasn't the only one: a group of survivors stood at the front door, let through the blocked-off roads by the same policemen who had harassed us and who had tried to save the other girls. We cried together and talked about those who had died and when they would be buried. Then those of us here alone went together to the bank and sent cables home to our parents to let them know we survived, crying again at how lucky we are and how unlucky our dear friends.

Esther's funeral is also happening now, and Isabella's is in an hour, and Beckie's is this afternoon along with several others. All week long, there will be funerals. I will attend as many as I can, and I'm sorry to miss any, but I need to be here for Maria.

And for Vincente, whose skin has a pale sickly cast and whose eyes are red. I can't imagine how much he's cried, alone in the apartment he shared with Maria, but I have no doubt that he has, and my heart bleeds for him. I know, too, that he wishes the funeral could wait until his parents arrive. They are still more than a week away, though, so he had to go ahead. It must have been so hard to decide on such an important matter on his own.

Our wagon lurches forward, and I stare at the slow-moving hearse before us. The curtains are drawn all around it so I cannot see inside, but I watched earlier as Vincente and Mr. Billota and several union men carried Maria's coffin from the union hall, where the undertakers brought it earlier this morning, out to the hearse. My best friend in the world is in that rough wooden box, and it all hurts so much I can hardly breathe.

Vincente reaches over and takes my hand. I glance at him, surprised at this public display of affection, then realize he isn't doing it for affection. His lips are folded so tightly together that they and the skin around them have whitened, and he's blinking repeatedly.

I squeeze his hand hard and lean into him, in a desperate hope it'll comfort him.

As we ride slowly along Grand Street and then onto Delancey to make our five-mile journey across the Williamsburg Bridge to the Catholic cemetery in Brooklyn, people on the street break off their conversations. The pushcart vendors stop doing business too, the one who sold us Maria's ring and my hatpin giving me an especially sympathetic look, and old ladies wipe tears from their wrinkled cheeks and call, "Rest in peace, poor girl," after us. Everyone here knows someone who died at Triangle, and we all share each other's grief.

As the horses carry us across the bridge I see Vincente's lips moving, I think in prayer, and though Maria was Catholic I run through the Jewish prayers for the dead in my mind. However it comes, she deserves to rest in peace as those women said.

After another half hour or so we reach the cemetery, but there is no peace to be found there, at least not for us. Another Triangle girl's funeral is happening a few rows of graves away, and the sound of women wailing feels like it will tear me apart.

Our service is over quickly. A few words from the clergyman Vincente brought from his church, a moment of silence, a prayer I've never heard before that starts with "Our father who art in Heaven", and then the clergyman says, "Ashes to ashes, dust to dust," and Vincente moves forward to place the first shovelful of dirt onto his sister's coffin.

I have brought a rose for the same purpose, and I kiss its white petals and tell Maria silently that I love her then drop the flower into the gaping hole in the ground.

As it falls, I say something else to Maria. I promise her, in my head but no less sincerely for being silent, that I will make sure this never happens again.

I will not falter, I cannot let myself falter, even though I'm not at all the speaker she was.

Somehow, I will help the union protect workers.

CHAPTER THIRTY-SIX

Rosie
March 29, 1911

THAT EVENING, I AM ON A STAGE for the second time in my life, and remembering being on one the first time with Maria makes me miss her even more. Thousands of people, mostly girls and women, sit facing me and the other Triangle survivors here in the Grand Central Palace's huge exhibition room, and everyone in the audience and on the stage looks as sad and exhausted as I feel.

Getting here after Beckie's funeral this afternoon and also finding myself a new job was challenging, but the trip up to Forty-Sixth Street and Lexington wasn't enough to keep me from attending this memorial meeting. A trip ten times longer wouldn't have managed that.

I didn't want to find a job, especially not another one sewing waists, but I want to bring my family to me now more than ever so I can't afford to accept only the little the union could pay me. I found the job easily, at a smaller factory not far from home, and the boss said that if my trial from tomorrow until the end of the week goes well, he will pay me the ten dollars a week I asked for.

He didn't ask where I'd worked before, and I didn't tell him. As the sign in his window said, he simply wants "hands". I've seen that sign many times before and it's never bothered me, but this time it makes me think he and the other bosses don't care about the girls to whom those hands are attached.

Still, a job is a job, and with the energy of my success in finding one giving me strength, I told Clara before this meeting began that I want to take over at least some of Maria's work. She studied me for a moment with her eyebrows raised, then nodded and said, "Of course. We'll talk later." Her obvious surprise worried me then and still worries me, but when she added, "I know you'll do your best," I thought maybe she thought I could handle it.

I hope I can. I have to.

A man moves to the front of the stage and shouts for silence, and after a few repeated calls and shushing noises through the audience he gets it. "I am Abraham Cahan," he announces, "the editor of the 'Jewish Daily Forward'."

A murmur goes through the crowd, a murmur that somehow has a Yiddish inflection. We all know his newspaper as a wonderful source of information for how to be Jewish in this new country.

"We are gathered here to honor the victims of the Triangle fire," he continues, "and I want to thank those who have donated money to the relief fund for the survivors and the victims' families. And of course, I must thank the man who heads the fund, Mayor Gaynor."

The girl beside me hisses at the mention of that name, and she's not the only one. Throughout the audience there are more hisses, and cries of "Shame!" and outright boos. I don't make any noise, but I understand. The union hall has been full of talk about how none of the departments of New York's government will accept any responsibility for the fire. The building department blames the fire department, fire blames the labor department, and labor blames the building department.

And Mayor Gaynor is the boss of them all.

Mr. Cahan tries to calm the crowd by talking about how wonderful the lost girls were, and it's working. But then he seems to think he has us all under his control, because he starts a story about a young man who came into his office raging about the fire and saying he wanted to make someone pay. "He told me," Mr. Cahan says, shaking his head as if disgusted by the young man's foolishness, "that the only way to bring redress to the workers would be to place a few bombs in the camp of the capitalists."

I don't know how he thought the crowd would react, but when shouts erupt of "Throw a bomb under City Hall!" and "Blow the place up!" he flinches back in shock. I don't shout, but I understand why others do. *Something* must be done.

The chairman sends him a look that says, "You fool!" so clearly I can almost hear him speaking the words, then begins rapping his gavel on the table before him and calling, "Order! I will have order!"

He doesn't get it, not entirely, but the crowd quiets enough that he can say, "Let us have a moment of silent prayer in memory of our dead."

The last shouts and complaints blur down into a strange quiet sigh of sadness, then for a moment all is entirely silent.

For one moment.

A girl in the front row of the audience bursts into loud tears then, and one behind her follows, and many in the rows further back. The girl beside me whimpers, and I can't hold back a sob myself. We have all lost so much, and thousands of us are feeling the same thing at the same moment. It spreads through the crowd like the rage did earlier, a tide of terrible sorrow sweeping everyone up in its wake.

Then a woman near the back screams, "Emma!" and the tide swamps us all. Everywhere girls and women are calling the names of the ones they lost, or just screaming in pain, and wailing men and women leap to their feet and shout and sob.

The chairman is banging his gavel, and shouting too, but I can't hear him over the noise of the crowd and my fellow survivors on stage crying and calling out names. Over my own noise too. Shouting Maria's name can't bring her back, but joining in the agony of the others by adding her name to the tumult somehow releases a little of my pain. Vincente is out there somewhere, in the crowd, and I hope he's shouting along with them. He needs his pain released too.

All around women and girls are fainting, collapsing into their seats or into the aisles, and the frenzy grows until policemen begin moving down those same aisles. People flinch away, afraid of what they'll do, but the men only pick up and remove those who have fainted and speak calmly to the others, and the crowd begins to quiet.

Wisely, Mr. Cahan does not attempt to speak again. Instead, one of the founders of the Women's Trade Union League, Leonora O'Reilly, moves forward. I know Leonora from the strike and know her long face usually bears a smile, but there's no trace of one now. She speaks slowly and solemnly, and when she talks of "the martyrs who died that we might live" the crowd's pain rises again but the policemen quickly calm it.

Her word sticks in my head, though. We must make sure these girls truly are the last martyrs to industry. If the union doesn't, if *I* don't, ensure Maria's work is completed and workers are protected in the future, she and the others will have died in vain.

I cannot allow that.

After Leonora, the rest of the speakers take care to keep their speeches at a level that will not stir up the crowd, but one catches my attention nonetheless. He is another newspaper editor, from Chicago, and he speaks of how important it is for the workers to take care of their own safety.

"We have the votes," he says. "Why do we not have the power?"

He goes on to encourage us all to participate in our union so that it can turn things in our direction, but I can't get past the word "votes".

"We", the girls and women, do not have the votes. Men do, of course, but do men care about our safety? The Triangle owners didn't seem to.

Is this speaker wrong? Is the right path not working for the union but instead participating in suffrage so women have the vote and can use it to guarantee their own safety without relying on men?

I AM STILL PONDERING THAT when I go to a rally Friday evening at the Cooper Union. This is where we decided to go on strike back in 1909, and being back here makes me think: we struck for reduced hours and higher wages, but we didn't even ask for better and safer working conditions. We didn't ask, and they didn't offer. Did none of us realize we needed them? Maybe not at the time of the strike, but after the factory fire in December that killed those night-gown workers? How did none of us see this need? Is the union only for questions of money and time, not for our very lives?

The banner across the platform makes me wonder if attempting to gain suffrage is the path we ought to have taken.

"Votes for women," it says. "Locked doors, overcrowding, inadequate fire escapes. The women could not, the voters did not, alter these conditions. We demand for all women the right to protect themselves."

Maria deserved that right. So did all the others who died, at least 140 of them and maybe more depending on the fate of those still fighting for their lives in hospital, and the many more with injuries that did not kill them but have still left them in pain and not easily able to work. Even those of us who survived without physical injury now face the misery of living without our loved ones. Nobody protected us, and we could not protect ourselves.

I listen to Dr. Anna Shaw, president of the National American Woman Suffrage Association, talk about how the men are responsible for the fire. "As voters, it was your business," she proclaims. I've heard she's a preacher, and seeing her eyes alight with passion and her hands held high as if calling on the heavens, I can imagine her shouting the word of her god to all. Here, though, she's preaching about votes. "It was your business and you should have been about your business. If you are incompetent, then in the name of Heaven, stand aside and let us try!"

The women and girls in the audience applaud this. A few men do too, but most sit still, looking uncomfortable at the thought that women voters might have done a better job.

But isn't it true? How could we have done worse?

The suffragists believe women should have the right to vote, and I can't see an earthly reason why they're wrong. The anti-suffragists, though, say that since most women are married they will either vote with their husband or cancel his vote out, so what difference does it make either way? I don't have an answer to that so maybe they're right, but something inside me tells me they're not. I believe having the vote would make a difference. It has to.

Something has to.

Dr. Shaw's strong clear voice is now reminding us that at one time women in America worked at home and could at least to some degree control their own conditions and their own hours, as my mother does still back in Russia, but that a female factory worker no longer has that power.

"She has been driven into the market with no voice in the laws and powerless to defend herself. The most cowardly thing that men ever did was when they tied woman's hands and left her to be food for the flames."

The crowd cheers again, and I do too but I also shiver. I know she doesn't literally mean women were tied up and left in the fire, but the image she's created is so strong that it almost feels true.

Clara has the ability to create images like that as she speaks. Maria did too, and Aunt Ida likely also. I don't know if I do. I've seen no sign of it so far. How can I be a true union girl, or a suffragist for that matter, when I can't rouse a crowd like they do?

Dr. Shaw finishes her speech, by announcing that if the constitution doesn't permit protecting the lives of workers then we need to smash the constitution and get a new one, and takes her seat amid applause and cheers. I watch her settle herself and adjust her skirt, and I realize that she never once looked nervous. Was she? Clara told me before the meeting that she'd like me to do a speech with her in a few weeks since the union has lost so many of its speakers, and I'm already terrified. Does that mean I'm not meant to do it?

But I have to. I want to. I will practice and practice and practice again and I will make it work, for Maria and all the others who died. I have to push past who I was raised to be and become a fiery girl. I owe that to my fallen friends.

The next speaker only strengthens my conviction. The man, a lawyer named Morris Hilquit, talks about the strike and how we were trying to change our work conditions, then wonders if the judges who sent picketers to jail realize that if they hadn't done that, our strike might have been completely successful and the Triangle workers might have been safe because they'd have been gone from the factory hours before the fire began.

He tells us that over a thousand workers a week die in industrial accidents in America. I look around and realize there are probably that many people here listening to him. If all of us died at once, would anyone notice?

He doesn't answer that question directly, but he clearly doesn't think the Triangle bosses would be too concerned. "Mr. Harris and Mr. Blanck were there at the time the fire broke out," he says, a sneer in his voice. "They escaped. We congratulate them." He pauses to let the audience hiss and boo, then goes on with, "My friends, what a tremendous difference between the captains of ships and the captains of industry!"

We all laugh and cheer his mockery, and I wonder for the first time whether the bosses even thought of us. I read in the newspaper that they scrambled up to the roof and climbed across to another building then went safely down that building's staircase. As they did that, did they question how few of their workers were there with them?

At the union hall, I learned that the Triangle's telephone system connected the eighth floor to the tenth, and the ninth to tenth, because the bosses worked on tenth, but it did not directly connect the eighth and ninth. Dinah managed to reach tenth when she made her call that day, but the girl who answered hurried off to inform the bosses and didn't relay the information on to ninth, which is why so many of them didn't escape.

With their earlier notice, those on the tenth floor all survived, except for one poor girl who panicked and jumped to her death long before the flames reached her. But the tenth floor didn't have nearly as many girls as eighth and ninth since so much of it was taken up by the bosses' offices, so they must have known most of their workers were still trapped.

Did they care? At all?

They escaped, and I don't remember seeing them on the street afterward. They must have run away like cowards. If they cared about us at all, it wasn't enough for them to stay and help.

It makes me so angry, thinking of it, that I don't even notice the end of the lawyer's speech. I do notice, though, when the crowd boos and hisses, and I look up to see Meyer London, a lawyer who worked with the union during the strike, holding a sheet of paper high.

"Don't you want me to read it?" He looks across the crowd. "Don't you care what Fire Chief Croker has to say?"

The continued angry response suggests we don't, but he says, "Well, he sent it, because he's so busy with official business that he couldn't join us today, so I think we should hear it."

It's not easy to hear it because of the hissing throughout, but in the end we all know that the fire chief blames the girls for their deaths.

"Girls should 'refuse to work when they find the doors locked'," a girl beside me fumes. "Easy for him to say. And then where do we work? How do we eat?"

Unanswerable questions. Mr. Croker didn't even try to answer them. He wrote that the owners will refuse to follow the fire department rules because they can't afford to, and the builders won't put in fire escapes or build wider stairwells because they can't afford to either, and when his letter ends with "it comes right down to dollars and cents against human lives" it's clear that he thinks it's up to those human lives, the girls who make the cents, to somehow fight back against the men who earn the dollars and have all the power.

I'm furious, but I don't know where to direct my rage. I have to do *something*, but the union didn't prevent this and suffrage might not protect us in the future, and frustration makes me start to rise from my seat so I can leave. Fresh air might calm me.

I sit back down, though, when Mr. London begins talking about the strike. Since he's one of the union's lawyers he knows it well, and he is completely on our side. He talks beautifully of the Triangle girls and how hard they fought and how their earlier striking helped to bring out the others, and I'm not the only girl in tears at memories of a lost friend by the time he's done.

"But now, my friends?" He shakes his head. "Now we will get an investigation by a committee that will report in 1913, and by 1915 a law will be passed, and after that? It won't even be enforced."

He pauses as if expecting applause or boos, but all he gets is a tired silence. We know he's right. Fire Chief Croker said so, with his 'dollars and cents against human lives' speech.

All we've had since the fire is meetings. Words upon words, outrage and anger and sadness, but none of it looks to me like it is leading to anything that will prevent another fire. How will a committee do anything that those meetings have not?

How will we ever make a real change?

CHAPTER THIRTY-SEVEN

Rosie
April 1, 1911

WORD HAS SPREAD that Triangle survivors are to go to Mr. Harris and Mr. Blanck's other factory on University Place today to pick up our final pay envelopes, since we're always paid a week behind. Though I would like to never go near anything related to those men again, I also don't want them to keep the money that is rightfully mine.

Vincente feels the same as me, on both parts, so we're not exactly cheerful when we meet in Washington Square Park after my factory closes at noon to walk together to University Place. He has left his own work early, for which they'll no doubt dock his pay, but if he didn't, he wouldn't get Maria's money.

Our route doesn't take us past Triangle, but we both know it's only a block away, and when I glance in its direction my grip on his arm tightens at the mere thought of the place. It's been a week, and it feels both like yesterday and like an eternity ago.

"I know," he says, laying his hand over mine and giving me a squeeze. "I don't know how you managed to go back there on Monday. I meant what I said, I never will again."

"I won't either now." I sigh. "I can't imagine they'll ever use it for a factory again. Who could ever work there after what happened?"

He shrugs, then pulls me to the side to avoid a pushcart man who isn't watching where he's going.

Then to my surprise he pulls me even farther to the side, into the entrance of an alley. I look at him, confused, and see him reaching into his pocket.

"I have something for you," he says quietly, then holds out his hand. On his palm sits Maria's ring with the blue glass.

Receiving this from Vincente feels wrong. I wouldn't have accepted a gift of a ring from him if he'd bought a new one for me, so is this something I should permit?

"I think Maria—" He clears his throat. "No, I *know* she would have wanted you to have it. And so I do too. I'm giving that silver hatpin back to my mother, but this..." He reaches his hand further toward me and doesn't finish the sentence.

I look at the ring for another moment then decide he's probably right that Maria would like it to go to me. It's nothing valuable, not like the hatpin, but she loved it, and whenever I look at it, I'll remember buying it with her and how my recognizing the peddler helped us get a better price. It'll be a lovely memory for me instead of the ones of her in the window and at the morgue.

Swallowing hard to loosen my suddenly-tight throat, I reach out and pluck it from his hand then slip it onto my right ring finger, the same place Maria wore it.

We both study the ring on my hand, then he says, "Right. Good. Ready?"

I nod, and we walk on in silence for the few moments until we reach 9 University Place and climb the stairs to the sixth-floor factory.

Inside, a forelady I recognize sits at a table piled with pay envelopes, a line of girls facing her. Four policemen stand behind her, arms folded and faces set in expressions of blankness, two on each side of Mr. Harris. He is watching intently as the forelady speaks to the next girl in line then gathers money from the box on the table and puts it in an envelope for her, and I feel like he resents having to pay us.

Well, I've been resenting him and Mr. Blanck since I learned they fled the fire and left their workers to burn, so he's welcome to resent us a little.

Vincente and I attach ourselves to the end of the line, and after a few minutes of waiting I jump as someone grabs me and spins me around.

"Oh, Rosie, I'm so glad to see you," she says, pulling me into a hug. "I was worried about you!"

We used to sit a few seats apart at Triangle, so I can't admit that I don't know her name. I'm sure she told me once, but I don't remember. I *did* think of her, though, on Monday when I didn't see her at Triangle with the other survivors. "You too," I say, returning the hug, delighted she survived.

"Will you be in the parade Wednesday?"

I nod. I'm not looking forward to it, but I will. When the city announced it would bury the seven bodies that still haven't been identified in a joint funeral, the union decided to hold a funeral parade the same day for those seven victims and all the others too. It's at one o'clock, when we should all be working, but I haven't heard of any boss announcing that he won't let his girls go. Perhaps they realize how much the public is against them at the moment.

"Me as well. And are you busy after this?" She pulls a leaflet from the bag on her shoulder and shows it to me. "I need help handing these out on the street. We've got thousands of them."

I don't recognize it, so it's probably not something the union put together. In English, Yiddish, and Italian, it invites the reader to join the parade as a way of "rendering a last sad tribute of sympathy and affection" to those who died in Triangle.

I fear handing out leaflets less than I fear speaking in public, so I say, "Of course I will." Handing out thousands, if she really meant that, will take a long time, and it's too bad because I was planning to read through some suffragist literature tonight to decide whether I'd rather go in that direction. There simply isn't enough time to do everything I want to do in the way I want to do it.

Though none of the paths open to me feel right, I need to pick one. I cannot be a fiery union girl and a suffragist at once, not if I want to truly make a difference. I need to focus. I need to be as driven and passionate as Clara and Maria.

Somehow.

Unaware of the confusion in my mind, the girl gives me another hug and starts to head to the end of the line. After a step or two, though, she turns back and hugs me yet again.

I'm surprised, but only for a moment before she uses our closeness to begin whispering to me. "You do know what happened here, right? What the bosses did?"

I shake my head.

"They blocked the fire escapes. With sewing machines and tables. So they could fit more girls in."

My heart skips a beat. "Really?"

"They didn't do it at Triangle because the machines fit better in a different way but they've been doing it for years here. Apparently a newspaper reporter saw it yesterday and said he'd report on it and so just this morning they moved everything so the fire escapes can be used. But can you believe it?"

She doesn't wait for an answer before releasing me and following the line back to its end, but I'm sure she knows how I'd respond.

I look around at the large room we're in, feeling sick. The Asch Building was called fireproof, and indeed it was. The building itself didn't burn. Only the things in it. The tables and chairs, and the wicker work baskets, and all the fabric and waists. And the people.

Even after such a horrible fire the bosses didn't bother changing things here so their workers would not be trapped if another fire broke out? After all the deaths and pain, after girls leaping in flames to the sidewalk, they didn't see the need?

They really don't care about us at all.

Vincente and I eventually reach the front of the line, and I am so stirred up with fury that I barely speak to the forelady when I take my envelope from her. She looks surprised, and hurt, but I can't make myself regret that. She works for them still, after everything that happened, and I can't smile and be friendly to someone like that. I understand that we all need to earn money so I should have compassion for her, but I simply can't.

I can't even more when she's unsure about giving Maria's envelope to Vincente. I assure her he's Maria's brother, and so do several girls in line behind us, but in the end the poor man has to show her Maria's death certificate to convince her to release the ten dollars to him. Maria alive and well. Ten dollars. I know which one Vincente would rather see before him.

Mr. Harris stands silent through all of this, and when I sneak a quick peek at him I see he looks bored.

I would like to bite him.

I do not, of course, and Vincente and I move toward the door. As we pass the line, the girl who spoke to me earlier says, "Wait for me outside?"

I nod and she smiles.

When we reach the street Vincente says, "You aren't really going to hand out those leaflets, are you?"

"Of course I am. Why wouldn't I?"

"I thought maybe I could buy you a jellied apple and we could sit in the park."

The memory of an apple vendor feeding the people who didn't care about the fire as I walked around Triangle with the thousands of other mourners snaps through me, infuriating me. "I hate those apples. And yes, I am handing out the leaflets. I'll hand them out for hours, all night long if I have to."

Vincente frowns. "Even if I don't want you to?"

"Even then." Why would he think that would matter? He's not my father or brother or husband, not even my fella.

We glare at each other for a moment, and as I am about to turn and leave him, he gives me a single nod. "I understand. Will you meet me tomorrow?"

I take a sharp breath to answer, still annoyed with him for telling me what to do, and he speaks quickly. "*Not* for an apple, if you don't want one. Just... maybe a walk."

I do want to spend more time with him, and since his parents will arrive in a little over a week I should take my chance. By tomorrow I will probably not be so annoyed with him. "I haven't been to Central Park for a while."

He smiles and gives my upper arm a squeeze. "I will meet you there, at the entrance to the Menagerie. Two o'clock?"

"I can't. There's the meeting at the opera house, and then afterwards is Julia's wedding."

"Oh, yes, that's right." He's not coming to the meeting with me but he is taking me to Julia's wedding dance. "Ten, perhaps?"

I nod, and he smiles again then leaves.

In the end it *does* take us hours to hand out all the leaflets. I'm exhausted afterward, but at least I've done something to help honor the victims of the fire.

Still, though, what I've done is so very tiny. Nobody will remember or know that I did it. I want it to be enough that *I* know, but somehow it's not. I know I should be content with what little bit of help I can be. I shouldn't need everyone's attention.

And I don't, not really. It's more that I want to make a difference, and giving out leaflets isn't a real difference. There has to be something bigger and more important for me to do.

Why else was I saved from the fire?

THE NEXT AFTERNOON, I SIT in one of the Metropolitan Opera House's high-up balconies with many other workers, all of us looking down at the rich people in their fine clothes. Feathers and furs and silks, things I'll never own, on people who probably see operas every week of their lives. I've never been in here before, and I doubt most of the others in the balcony with me have either, but for this afternoon we are all together in remembering the Triangle victims.

New York's Governor Dix was supposed to run the meeting, but he has instead gone to a funeral. A fire tore through the State Capitol building five days ago, destroying thousands of books and artifacts and killing a watchman. Mr. Dix apparently thinks a funeral for one man is more important than a memorial for the 146 people who have died in and after Triangle. Surely that can't be because most of our victims were girls and women?

I don't like being so bitter and cynical but I also can't help it, and I feel even more that way when Clara passes me an article torn from today's newspaper and I realize that my friend at the factory yesterday was right. Mr. Harris and Mr. Blanck *did* block access to that factory's windows and fire escape, they blocked it for years, and they only changed it because a newspaper man saw it and said it was dangerous.

Mr. Harris clearly didn't think so, though, and he didn't even think the layout of the Triangle factory had been dangerous because he claimed in the article that "if one could get out all could get out". He insisted the door wasn't locked, and he said the only reason anyone died was because the girls were "steric".

Of course they were hysterical! How could they not be, as the fire trapped them before a door we all know was locked despite Mr. Harris claiming it wasn't? The newspaper says that bodies were piled before that door, so it was indeed locked. Some girls, like me, were lucky enough to be on another floor and near the fire escape, and our managing to get out doesn't mean the girls on ninth did something wrong. He's blaming Maria for her death and I can't stand it. He's a liar, and reading his words makes me wish I did bite him yesterday.

I tell this to Clara, and she laughs and says, "I wish you did too. You'd be the heroine of the union for it, no question."

I wonder what Vincente would think if I took to biting people. We didn't enjoy our time at Central Park as much as I think we were both hoping to, because Maria's absence was so painful. He delivered me here but didn't stay for the meeting because his parents should be arriving this week and he wanted to make sure his apartment was ready for them.

Will they be ready for me? He still wants me to meet them, but I don't know what they'll think of the Jewish girl their son's been treating. If that's even what he's been doing.

Fortunately, the meeting begins before I can worry too much about this.

Unfortunately, it's even more frustrating than the worrying would have been.

Speaker after speaker tells us how the laws should be followed, and how we shouldn't let government put us off with complaints about having no money, and how the responsibility and guilt of the fire is on everyone's head, and it seems as though they'll talk forever. Talk and talk and talk, and nothing will ever change for the workers.

Some call for adopting a resolution that there should be a Bureau of Fire Inspection and that there should be more fire inspectors and some form of compensation for injured workers. Other speakers suggest committees and careful thought and taking the time to decide what to do.

The wealthy people sitting close to the stage applaud politely, clearly in support of all suggestions that involve committees and discussions. Probably because they tend to be the ones who are asked to join the committees and speak during the discussions.

But we workers sitting high up in the balconies mutter, and many of us boo and hiss outright as the meeting continues and we see that nothing much will come from it. Another speech, another suggestion, another proposition to a government that clearly doesn't care, and the longer it takes the more of us will die.

A girl beside me sighs and says, "What good will more talking do?"

I nod at her words, as does Clara and many others around us, but then it strikes me that a lot of union work involves talking. Suffragist work too. Am I wrong to be aiming myself in either of those directions? Is there something else that will truly make a difference?

But what? My Ellis Island work? I haven't been back since the fire; through Julia I told Cecilia I needed a few weeks to recover and Cecilia gave me those weeks. I may not go back at all, because it doesn't feel useful. Nothing does.

Mr. London said at Friday's meeting that there would be a committee and it would be useless. The people today clearly think their planned committees will help. So who is right? Either way, I won't be asked to be on one. Girls like me never are. So what am I going to—

All around the hall, people are suddenly shushing each other, and I peer down at the stage and realize Rose Schneiderman is standing ready to speak. Though short and thin, she was a force in the strike. She was working at Triangle the day of the fire, and though I don't know how she escaped, I'm glad she did.

"I would be a traitor to these poor burned bodies if I came here to talk good fellowship."

A gasp goes through the room. Others have mentioned the deaths, of course, but Rose's quiet but carrying voice is the first to so clearly spell out how they were lost to us.

"We have tried you good people of the public," she continues, "and we have found you wanting. The old Inquisition had its rack and its thumbscrews and its instruments of torture with iron teeth. We know what these things are today; the iron teeth are our necessities, the thumbscrews are the high-powered and swift machinery close to which we must work, and the rack is here in the firetrap structures that will destroy us the minute they catch on fire."

I'm not sure what she means by "necessities" but it doesn't matter because the rest of her words have burrowed into my heart and soul. We *are* being tortured. We are victims.

Helplessness sweeps me as she goes on to talk about how often girls are burned alive and how often we die or are maimed through work, and how property is held so much more sacred than our lives. How can we ever change that? What's the use in even trying?

Then shame takes my helplessness's place, as she tells us exactly how we can change it and what we need to do in a calm clear way I know I could never copy.

"I know from my experience," she says, still quiet but with passion in her voice, "it is up to the working people to save themselves. The only way they can save themselves is by a strong working-class movement."

Nobody cheers this. Nobody applauds. Nobody so much as whispers a response.

But as she turns and goes back to her seat, I know I am not the only one in the balconies who is now utterly convinced that the union is the path to safety and peace. Suffrage is important, but it's for all women. Unions are for the working-class, and we need them.

I am weak, where Rose and Clara and the others are strong. But I will learn to speak like them, with words and phrases that lock onto people and refuse to let them go, and I will finally do something that matters and make my mark on the world.

As a fiery union girl.

For an instant I feel the strength that Maria and Clara and the others must feel.

But only for an instant. Then I remember all the times I've tried and failed to speak my mind, and I wonder if I can truly change that.

Well, I will try, anyhow.

I must do something.

CHAPTER THIRTY-EIGHT

Rosie
April 5, 1911

I PULL MY DRIPPING COAT MORE TIGHTLY AROUND ME, hoping the parade will begin soon. We've been waiting for an hour, getting colder and wetter in the steadily falling rain, but nobody has uttered a complaint. The first thousand or so of us are past Triangle employees, and the thousands more behind are our friends and family and supporters, so kvetshing about a bit of bad weather, when so many of our dear ones died in the fire, would be unthinkable.

Despite the chill deep in my body, I am glad that I chose not to wear a hat or overshoes, not to carry an umbrella. Most of those around me also made that choice, and somehow our discomfort as we prepare to march through the city seems to be another way of honoring our dead. While the weather is unpleasant, I'm glad it's not a bright sunny day. That would seem wrong. Now it feels as though the sky is crying with us.

I wish Vincente were here with me as he'd intended to be. But he stopped by my home last night to tell me that the newspaper says his parents' ship will be arriving tomorrow, so he's working today to earn one last bit of money before he quits his job for the duration of their stay.

I'm so nervous about meeting them, about what I can possibly say to help them get over Maria's death. But he insisted they'll love me, and the way his neck flushed when he said it makes me think he might be starting to... care about me himself.

I definitely enjoyed dancing with him at Julia's wedding on Sunday, but I saw how Julia looked both happy and sad and I didn't know whether I'd be able to make the bargain she's made. I believe I'm meant to make something important of myself, and from everything I saw back in Russia, becoming a wife is the end of all that. But I do like him, and—

A deep sigh goes up from the crowd and I look ahead to see that the hearse at the front of the line is now moving. The fire victims who haven't been identified are being buried in Brooklyn this afternoon so our hearse is empty, but it symbolizes those seven unknown victims and all the others who've died.

We follow the hearse out of Seward Park and onto East Broadway, heading away from Triangle so we can pass the union hall, and I wonder if the uptown section of the parade, leaving from Twenty-Third Street and marching down toward us, is also headed by a hearse.

I had thought, before, that we should all walk together to Washington Square and then to file past the Triangle instead of beginning in two groups, but the downtown group nearly filled the park ourselves so it was probably a wise decision to break into two. I don't know who made the decision. Maria probably would have known, but I am not high up enough in the union yet to be involved in such important details.

I wipe rain from my cheeks and push aside my feelings about my lack of union ranking. This is not the time for that. It's time to honor our dead and be together in our pain.

I would have expected, had I thought about it, that with so many girls in one place there would be talking and chattering as the parade progressed, but there is none. Other than sobs, we move like a single silent swarm, all in black, along the street. Those on the sides watching us, wearing black clothes and holding black umbrellas over their heads, also do not speak. Many of the buildings are draped with black mourning fabric, so it feels like the very structures of the city grieve in silence with us.

We turn onto Clinton Street and file past the union hall, still fully draped in black, then follow Broome Street along toward Triangle, and even through my sadness I'm amazed and touched at all of the support we're receiving.

Both sides of every street we take are completely packed with observers, and tenement windows along the route are filled with people waving handkerchiefs at us. As they see the hearse pass, many cry out in pain and sadness, and I look back and realize that many of those watchers are coming down out of their buildings and leaving their sidewalks and joining our march.

Seeing how many people are walking to honor the lost workers makes me think perhaps there is hope after all. If this many people believe that what has happened is wrong, if this many people choose to show their solidarity with us, surely there will be a way to make sure it never happens again.

After about an hour, the girls in front of me stop walking, and I look past them to realize nobody there is moving either.

"Fire," people murmur, sending the information back through the crowd. "A tenement's on fire."

I stand in the rain, hoping that this fire will not be as destructive as the one at Triangle, feeling the coldness of the weather and the misery of those around me sinking deep into me, for what seems like forever until the parade begins moving again.

When I pass the corner of Broome and Mott Streets, I see people sitting on the curb staring up in shock at the tenement with smoke stains around its fourth-floor windows, but since nobody is weeping, I assume they all survived the fire. I hope. I've never wondered before how many fires happen daily in New York, but I'm wondering now.

After about two hours of walking, we finally reach the southern edge of Washington Square Park, where we are stopped by stone-faced policemen. We were supposed to march through the park and join the uptown group at its north-east corner and then march down to Washington Place and past Triangle together, but when the policemen allow us to get moving again, we file through the park and under the Washington Square Arch to meet the others at Fifth Avenue to head north instead.

The two groups merge together as we make our way back uptown, and from the whispers in the crowd I learn that the policemen were afraid of how we might react to seeing the tragic building again. This annoys me since we have been nothing but orderly in our parade, but I suppose they fear a sudden release of our emotions and our outrage.

Well, maybe they should.

Maybe all of the workers releasing our outrage together in one loud scream is the only way anything will change.

CHAPTER THIRTY-NINE

Rosie
April 6, 1911

MY FEET STILL SORE FROM YESTERDAY'S MARCH, I stand with Vincente on Ellis Island, by the Kissing Post where people meet their fresh-off-the-boat family members. He hasn't kissed me, of course; we've done a little nervous chatting as we await his parents but mostly we've been standing in silence because we're not getting along all that well.

He doesn't seem to understand how thrilled I am that so many people joined the parade. The newspapers say that we started making our way through the Washington Square Arch at a little after three o'clock and that it wasn't until six that the last marchers reached the end point at Madison Square. They say 400,000 people saw the parade and about a third that many actually walked in it.

I never dreamed that so many people would participate and support us, and I am delighted and humbled by it. Though we marched in silence, we made everyone take notice.

Vincente, though, wasn't there, and while he hasn't come out and said he doesn't believe the attendance was so high, it's clear he doesn't, and that frustrates me.

Of course, he may just be worried about seeing his parents.

When I think that, a wave of sympathy hits me. He *must* be worried. How is he supposed to tell his parents that their only daughter is dead and buried?

He startles and takes a few steps forward, waving and shouting, "Papà! Mamma!"

A man, as tall as Vincente but with white hair and wrinkles, and a short round woman, with an old-fashioned black hat and a mouth like a straight line, wave back and hurry down the stairs toward their waiting son.

I hang back as Vincente hugs them both, but I am near enough to see the woman look past him and hear her say, "Maria?"

Vincente lays one hand on each parent's shoulder and speaks haltingly in Italian, and though I don't understand the words, I can hear the misery in his voice and I wish I could hug him as he gives his parents the worst news they could ever receive.

His mother sinks to her knees on the hardwood floor, ignoring the crowds of people rushing past them, and wails in agony, and his father hugs his only surviving child, his face over Vincente's shoulder contorted.

I clench my hands together, not knowing how to help and desperately wishing I had the right words. *Are* there right words? Would even Clara know what to say? Nothing anyone could say would bring Maria back, after all.

No, but the right words could provide at least a little comfort.

The men attempt to raise the grieving mother to her feet, but she'll have none of it. In fact, she begins beating the floor with her fists, sobbing and shouting out words in Italian. Vincente and his father try to calm her, but if anything, they anger her more.

Most of the people around watch, as I do, without understanding, but a few people who I think are likely Italian gasp in horror and hurry away from the scene. Whatever she's saying, they don't like it.

After at least a minute, Vincente comes to me, his face red. "She's upset," he says unnecessarily.

"I can tell. Why?" I feel a fool. "I mean, about Maria obviously, but is it just—"

"It was her idea for us to come here. To America, to earn money. What happened to Maria... she's blaming herself."

He rubs his forehead, and I notice a cut, not too deep but jagged, on the back of his hand. He didn't have it the last time I saw him, so he was probably hurt at work. We workers are injured, and killed, so often. Did Vincente's boss care any more than the Triangle bosses?

Vincente reaches that hand toward me, and I push away my thoughts as he says, "Would you come meet them now? I think it might calm her."

We haven't held hands since Maria's funeral so I don't take his now, but I do move forward with him to stand before his parents. They don't see us arrive, as his mother is still doubled over on the floor and his father crouches next to her.

Vincente leans down and says a few quiet words, from which I pick out Mamma and Rosie, and I assume he's telling her I'm here and asking her to meet me.

At first she doesn't respond other than stopping her wailing, but after a moment she takes a deep breath, so deep she throws her head back as she does it, and nods. The men gently ease the grieving mother to her feet and all three turn to look at me.

I smile and nod, wishing I'd thought to ask Vincente how to greet them in Italian.

It might not have mattered, though, because as Vincente takes a breath to speak his mother begins shouting again, directly at me this time.

Neither man tries to calm her; instead they both stare at her as if they've never seen her before.

Then she drops to the floor again, shouting even louder than before.

Vincente grabs his father's arm and snaps something at him over the din, but though I can't hear his answer and wouldn't understand it if I did, his face makes it clear he has no idea what has upset his wife so.

One of the other Jewish girls who work with Cecilia to help immigrants rushes over. "Rosie, what on earth is going on?"

"I have no idea." To Vincente I call, "What is it?"

He comes to us, looking nearly as stunned as he did when I told him Maria had died. "She..."

He clears his throat. "She thought..."

He takes a long breath and blows it out slowly, while the girl and I wait impatiently, then he takes another breath. As I notice his ears and neck turning bright red, he says, his words rushing together, "She thought we were going to get married."

The girl says, "You are?" but I don't answer her. I'm now as shocked as Vincente and I say to him, "Why?"

He shakes his head. "Maria told her a lot about you, and I mentioned you too," he says, his blush getting worse, "but neither of us said you were Jewish. Why would we? So she thought you were... Rosie could be an Italian name too, and..."

And she thought Vincente and I were in love. So she came here to meet the Italian girl her son would marry.

Vincente squares his shoulders and finishes his sentence, but not the way I had finished it in my head. "And she came here to take all three of us home to Italy where we'd get married and all of us would be happy."

"Home? Italy? But I'm Jewish!"

The girl with me gives one burst of shocked laughter then pulls herself together and says, "Sorry. But... what do you do now?"

The first thing has to be making Vincente's mother stop shouting. She's also now pointing at me, and whatever she's saying about me is making other Italians duck their heads and rush away.

But after that, I have no idea.

The girl squeezes my shoulder, her expression sympathetic but a trace of her amusement still in her eyes, and heads off to continue her work, and I say to Vincente, "Should I leave?"

He starts to shake his head then looks back at his mother and the spectacle she's making of herself. "I don't know. I did wonder why she came to visit now, instead of after we'd been here a full two years as we'd planned, but she suddenly said she wanted to see us and of course I couldn't argue. It must have been after I mentioned you in my letter. She planned this all on her own, Papà had no idea... she thought you must be Italian and that since I mentioned you..." He does shake his head now. "She could be like this for hours."

I can't stand here and listen to her shouting about me for hours. "Then I should go."

He glances back at his mother, clearly torn between not wanting me around any longer and not wanting me to leave.

Why am I waiting for him to decide? I can make my own choices. Besides, his mother clearly hates me and my being here didn't help her accept Maria's death, so removing myself from Vincente's life makes sense. "I will go," I say, sorry I won't see him again but relieved to be about to escape the shouting. "Good luck, and take care."

I begin to walk away, but have managed only two steps when he calls, "Wait!" and his mother shrieks, "Rosie!" at the same moment.

Confused and surprised, I look back to find Vincente's mother staring at me. She says something in Italian, and Vincente blinks a few times before saying to me, "She says she wants to get to know you."

"She does?" She certainly didn't seem to a moment ago.

After more Italian from his mother, Vincente says, "You were Maria's friend. She says that's why."

That's true. I was, but—

Mrs. Cirrito grabs Vincente's arm and begins babbling away at him. I found English enough of a challenge; do I now need to learn Italian too?

"She wants us all to have dinner together tonight," Vincente translates for me. "So she can feed you, and you can tell her about Maria and the union and the fire."

Can't he do that himself? But no, I was there with Maria at the end. That's what his mother wants, I think, to learn what really happened to her daughter.

Even if she must learn it from the Jewish girl she thought would be her son's Italian bride.

CHAPTER FORTY

Rosie
April 13, 1911

A WEEK LATER, I sit in the entranceway of the union hall, waiting for Clara and feeling my corset pressing against my belly after yet another huge Italian dinner.

I did spend time with Vincente and his parents that first night we met, but conversation was slow because Vincente had to translate his mother's questions and my replies, and so his mother begged me to come back again. And again after the next night. I have had dinner with them nearly every day since they arrived, and we all spent Saturday afternoon together too, and she seems to be accepting now that I am Jewish and that I am not marrying Vincente.

Telling her about the fun things Maria and I, and Maria and I and Vincente, did together has been a joy, but tonight she wanted to know about the fire and I couldn't hold back the tears when she sobbed over the details. My crying was of sadness, like hers, but also of deep frustration and of fear.

The frustration is from not knowing how to make sure something like the fire never happens again. I still haven't seen the right way to reach that goal and I so want to.

The fear? In an hour I will stand before a group of rich ladies and try to convince them to donate money to the union. I have rehearsed what I want to say so many times in my mind, but even thinking about doing it makes me nervous sitting here in my chair. I'm wearing Maria's blue-glass ring, which I did try to offer to her mother yesterday but was told through Vincente that I should keep, and I hope some of my dear friend's strength and speaking ability managed to transfer themselves to it.

I don't believe that, but I do hope.

Another rehearsal of my planned speech seems likely to make me even more afraid, so I reach over to the small battered wooden table beside my chair and pick up yesterday's New-York Tribune. I've already read it once while waiting here, but the article that spreads across its first and second page did delight me so reading it again might calm my nerves.

The most important piece of the article is the first paragraph, which states that Mr. Harris and Mr. Blanck were both indicted on two counts of manslaughter for locking the doors that prevented their workers from escaping.

For some reason, the grand jury only charged them with the deaths of two girls even though 144 other people also died, but the article does say there could be more charges in the future, and they could each get twenty years in jail for each charge, which would be at least some punishment.

They both pled not guilty to the charges, according to the newspaper, but they shouldn't have and they know it.

Beside the article's second page is a huge picture of the ninth floor lock from the Washington Place side. The wooden door burned completely away around it, but the metal lock is intact and clearly has its locking pin sticking out. The article points out, correctly, that Mr. Blanck always locked the Washington Place door about an hour before closing time to make sure everyone went out through the Greene Street partition to be searched. No doubt he did so on that day as well, and the lock proves it. Amazing that something that cannot say a word speaks so loudly.

Did poor Maria stand at that door and desperately try to open it before realizing that her only escape route was the window? I hope not, but I'll never know.

To distract myself from that thought, I begin to read the article yet again but I'm caught this time by the boxed-off text at the top. In larger print, it talks about how the law will punish Mr. Harris and Mr. Blanck if a locked door caused even one of the deaths, but it doesn't consider that enough. I'm not sure I do either.

What if the jury at their trial doesn't believe the doors were locked? Wouldn't they then go free? Nothing will bring back the lost workers, of course, but I do want the bosses punished and I'm not certain it'll happen.

And they're only two bosses. Many, maybe even most, factories have the same sort of bosses and the same sort of attitude toward their workers. The fire happened to be at Triangle, but it could have been anywhere. Even if these two are sent to prison, what will stop the others?

More than punishment for the bosses, though, I want so badly to prevent a repeat disaster, but how can I make that happen? How can any one person make such a difference?

I glance back at the article's boxed text and realize it's wondering the same thing. At both the top and bottom it reads, in capital letters, "WHAT ARE YOU GOING TO DO?"

It's a fine question, and not one I know how to answer.

For anything.

The letter that arrived last night from my mother, for example.

Though I don't want to, I pull it from my pocketbook and read it once more, finding it only a little challenging to read Yiddish after an English newspaper. Mama's handwriting is at least larger than the newspaper's print.

Rosie,

We were overjoyed to receive your cable and to hear of your escape from the fire, but of course sorry about your friend and all the other girls and men who did not survive. From the articles about the fire in our newspaper here, it is clear that America is not the sanctuary for which we had hoped. We will therefore not move there as we planned, so you must come home.

This works well, actually, because your father has found a young man who will make you a good husband. His name is Samuel Seltzer and he is twenty-one years old and newly moved to a home a few away from ours with his parents. Old Mrs. Eisenberg has just passed away, so you will take over her grocery store and Samuel will study. It's wonderful that you have paid off your steamship ticket, as now we have been able to borrow for the ticket to bring you home to us and your safe life here.

Claim the money and purchase your ticket at the bank and then inform us of when you will be leaving America. It is not the place for you, or for us.

L'shalom,
Mama

In peace indeed. I do not feel peaceful and I have not since reading her letter. No matter how she signed it off, I know that she did not truly intend me to feel any peace. She intends me only to do what she wishes.

I put the letter away, not feeling any happier than I did the first time I read it, as the newspaper's question rings in my mind. What *am* I going to do? Go home and become a grocery store owner, married to a man I've never met? They didn't even ask me, they simply informed me I'd be going home to be a wife and mother. I didn't want that life, that safe life as my mother calls it, before I came here, and now that I have been living on my own for two years I want it even less.

But what do I do instead? Stay here and defy my parents? To do what? Be terrified about giving speeches?

To distract myself, I pick up a newspaper I haven't yet read from two days ago, and on the front page I discover that Mr. London was right in his speech a few weeks ago: a committee for safety has indeed been created. Men who know about architecture and engineering will run it, but not just them, as the article also says men in social work and labor will be included. I don't know what the men themselves will be doing, but they're going to hire a group of inspectors to look at factories and see what the conditions are like before making their recommendations.

Mr. London said the official government committee would be useless, and I believed him, but now it does sound like it might actually—

"Rosie?"

I look up, startled, to see Clara smiling at me.

I quickly tidy the newspaper and return it to its table as she says, "You read about the indictments, yes? Good to see those horrible men will be punished!"

"It is," I say, although I am still afraid they might not be. They'll have a jury of wealthy men, and will those men have any interest in protecting workers?

"I'm sorry for your wait," she says. "The organizing committee has an hour-long meeting every Thursday night at seven o'clock to try to keep up with everything we must decide on for the union, and even so we often run over our planned time. There's so much to do! But enough about that. Are you ready for your first speech?"

My stomach twists, but I make myself smile. "Yes, I'm so excited!"

If I can succeed at this, perhaps I truly can fill Maria's shoes.

AS CLARA FINISHES HER SPEECH, I clench my hands together through the folds of my skirt and stare at the longest shiniest table I've ever seen, made of some deep dark glowing wood I've never encountered before. It should have a tablecloth on it, but I understand why it doesn't: it's too pretty to cover.

Everywhere on the table are pure white china plates with gold trim, silver cutlery also trimmed in gold, and crystal glasses that catch and bounce the candlelight onto the rich red leather walls. Real leather, I am sure, not the painted burlap that tenements and theaters use to imitate it. Though the dark purple velvet drapes of the large dining room are mostly closed, the gap between them shows a sliver of the view of Central Park. What must it be like to live so close to such a beautiful *empty* green space?

Servants in black suits move silently around the room collecting used dishes and whisking them away and bringing new food, and I glance at one man and wonder how much more it costs to have men serving instead of girls.

Not that the lady of this house needs to worry about money.

Mrs. White wears a dress of the brightest reddish-pink I've ever seen, the fabric silk and clearly expensive to have been dyed so vibrantly, and her earlobes and throat bear large diamonds that sparkle more than all the crystal on her table.

She could probably give the union the money it needs for a whole year, all by herself. If she and the other twenty-odd women in the room each gave that much money...

As my nervousness rises, Clara says, "So now you understand," looking from face to face and keeping her chin high and her voice steady despite how powerful are the women to whom she's speaking, "how our union operates and what it does. I hope you can see why it matters?"

They all nod, smiling at her.

"Wonderful. Now, to give you another, perhaps more personal, view, I have brought Rosie Lehrer with me. Rosie came to America nearly two years ago, from Russia, and was in the Triangle factory on that horrible day. She will tell you how it was to work there, and why the union has become so very important to her."

Clara smiles at me and takes her seat, and I push myself up from mine feeling like my knees might collapse and spill me back down. I wobble, and Clara gives what sounds like a natural chuckle and says, "It's not always easy to rise after having your ankles crossed for a long time, is it?"

I didn't have mine crossed, and I suspect Clara knows it, but the ladies all chuckle too and that gives me the moment I need to rise properly and pull myself together.

"For Maria," I think to myself, and then I begin to speak.

I have been practicing this endlessly since Clara requested my presence. Not out loud, since I have no place where nobody could hear me, but I have whispered to myself as I bathed and mouthed the words while lying in bed and thought through them as I sewed waist after waist. I could not have practiced more.

"I... ladies, the fire was awful. So many girls were..." I can only think of the Yiddish word for 'trapped', so I stand frozen for a second then change to, "not able to get out. Some burned. And the bosses, they got out. They got out first and then..."

What is this stuttered mess? What happened to the speech I rehearsed?

"It's not right," I say, trying desperately to get back to something that will impress these ladies but seeing on their faces that I am not doing any such thing. Clara had them eating out of the palm of her hand. Me? They wouldn't eat from mine if they were starving to death. "I... the union! The union cares. It helped us strike, it... girls were buried from it after the fire. It cares."

My fury at how the bosses fled their burning factory and left us inside without so much as a thought is still with me, but I spoke about it in my mind far more eloquently before. Now I just have the fury and not the words. "The factory owners, rich men, they don't care if we live or die. Horrible men."

I hear Clara pull in a quick sharp breath, and I remember too late that several of these women, including Mrs. White, are married to factory owners.

"No, no, some, probably, they care," I blurt out. "Of course some must. But the others, they don't care how hard we work or what we—"

"Are you calling my husband horrible?" The woman who interrupted me stands and pushes her chair back so hard it falls over, the diamond drops of her earrings even larger than those of Mrs. White and trembling with her fury. Ignoring the servant who rushes to pick her chair up, she says, "He tries so hard to be fair to his workers but they waste time and cheat him and steal and... and I will not sit here and hear him insulted by a... a..." Unable to find a word to describe me, she waves her hand as if swatting away a fly and says, "*That.*"

"Neither will I," another says, getting to her feet as violently as the first did. "The workers are the problem, not the bosses!" she adds, then they both storm from the room as fast as their heavy silk dresses will allow.

"Anne, Mary, do come back and sit down," Mrs. White calls after them, but they either don't hear or don't care to do as she says. "Oh. Oh, my."

I stand shocked, the Italian food in my stomach churning even more than before, and for a brief terrible moment it rises in my throat and I'm afraid I'll vomit right onto the beautifully smooth hardwood floor.

Clara stands and takes a breath to speak, but before she can, a woman says to me, "The men *do* need to earn money, dear," a sneer in her voice even though she called me 'dear'. "If they had no money, they couldn't pay you anything. That doesn't make them 'horrible'. I hope you understand. Both of you. Or else I don't see the point in your being here. And I certainly don't see the point in asking us for money. Do you?"

My mind is empty of all words, English or Yiddish, and full only of horror. "I..."

Clara steps in. "We do understand that businessmen need to earn money," she says, sounding calm and as though she's happy to be having this conversation, neither of which can possibly be true. How does she *do* that? "I think Rosie meant that by leaving the factory and, as far as we can tell, not taking time to help their workers, Mr. Harris and Mr. Blanck gave the impression that the lives of their girls and men didn't matter to them. They may very well care, but it didn't appear that way." She gives me a sideways look. "Isn't that right, Rosie?"

"It is," I manage to say.

A lady at the back murmurs to her neighbor and both snicker softly. This feels like even more proof that I have done nothing but hurt the union, so I give up, drop into my chair, and bite my lip to keep the tears away.

"As you can see, Rosie feels very strongly about the union and how important it is," Clara says, almost as if she's pleased with what I said. "Please do not mistake her passion for a lack of understanding. We at the International Ladies' Garment Workers Union, and especially Local 25 of waist workers, know that businessmen are in business to make money, and by all means they should. We simply feel that workers should not be entirely shut out of that money, and of course we also believe that a fire like that at Triangle must never happen again. I'm sure you agree with that?"

She waits, and they agree with her, but not as enthusiastically as they did before. I want to run from the room but I can't risk causing even more trouble.

I know that our time with these ladies was supposed to end right here, with Clara asking for donations, but instead she clears her throat and goes on. "While all of the Triangle deaths are tragic, there are a few cases that make especially clear why we must prevent another fire, and I'd like to share them with you now. The mother of five who began working at Triangle two days before the fire, and has now left her motherless children and her husband struggling to survive. Another family which lost two sisters and a mother, a family of five turned to a son and father alone in moments. A girl newly engaged, about to embark on the wonderful journey of marriage and motherhood that you lucky women all know so well, snuffed out as her life truly began."

She pauses between each sad tale, letting them sink in, and the ladies murmur, without any of the amusement they'd directed at my pathetic speech, and one wipes her eyes.

That last victim Clara described is my friend Esther, I think. I picture the engagement ring somehow still sparkling on the burned ruin of her hand as she lay in the morgue, a tiny burst of beauty in the midst of such horror somehow making everything around it even more horrible, and I wish I could find the words to explain that to the ladies. But I know I can't. The thoughts are in my head but I don't know how to get them to come out of my mouth.

Maybe it's because I'm speaking English? What if I prepare my speech in Yiddish and say it to Clara so she can translate?

I try, in my mind, to describe that moment in Yiddish, but it's no better. I see the picture still, but no language seems to have the right words. Not for me, anyhow. Clara is doing it without even having rehearsed it, and all the time I spent rehearsing was a waste.

So I sit silent and listen as Clara goes on with the beautiful speech I so wish I could copy. "146 people died, each with their own story, and families here and around the world are suffering because of it. Local 25 is working for better laws and better law enforcement to ensure we never face such a tragedy again. Ladies, may we count on your support?"

Mrs. White says firmly, "Well, you can count on mine!"

I know that we've had hers all along or else we wouldn't be here, but Clara smiles as if shocked and delighted and says, "Thank you so much, Mrs. White. We truly appreciate that."

Mrs. White pulls a man's black silk hat from beneath the table. Reaching in, she draws out then drops back in a handful of money. "Hundred dollars here, ladies. Who will match me?"

A hundred dollars would pay for my ticket back to Russia twice over, and she can give it to us without a care. What must that be like?

She passes the hat around and they all drop in at least something, except of course for the two women who left during my speech. The others manage to move the hat past their empty chairs, but the room fills with awkwardness as they do and my eyes fill with tears.

I don't know whether they do all match her donation but several crow, "Hundred!" as they add their bills to the collection and one even says, "*Two* hundred, for me and for my sister who passed away last year." The others all applaud her, and Mrs. White looks a little put out but rearranges her face into a happy smile quickly.

Once the hat returns to its starting point, Mrs. White rises and gives it to Clara. "Thank you so much for joining us today," she says, extending her hand to Clara, who quickly moves the hat to her other hand so she can shake Mrs. White's. I look back and forth between them, the rich woman and the union girl, and wonder how much more these women could have afforded to give us.

Still, getting anything at all after my terrible speech is lucky.

Clara smiles and says, "Thank *you*. Thank you all. We will leave you to your book-club meeting now, and again, we appreciate your time and your support."

The ladies all applaud, and Clara leaves with me scurrying after her. As the dining room door closes behind us, the applause fades out and a rush of laughter takes its place.

I clap my hands over my mouth. "They're laughing at me," I say in Yiddish, again blinking back tears. "Oh, Clara, I'm so sorry."

She doesn't deny that they probably *are* laughing at me. She gives my shoulder a squeeze and says, "Well, at least they gave us money and they didn't all run away. And next time we'll make sure you practice first."

I sigh.

"What? I—" Her confusion fades and disappointment takes its place in her eyes. "Oh. You *did* practice."

I nod. "For hours and hours."

She sighs too, then begins pulling the bills from the hat and straightening them so they'll fit into the pay envelopes she brought. It takes six envelopes to hold everything, and as we fill them I think of the forelady not wanting to give Maria's final ten dollars to Vincente. We have so much more than that here, given freely, but if Maria had done this speech instead of me, I know we'd have had even more.

When we're finished and Clara's tucked the envelopes into her pocketbook, we leave the hat resting on the glossy hall table and head out onto the darkened street. Automobiles and expensive-looking carriages move in both directions, but without the pushcart vendors and the screaming children of the Lower East Side the night is quiet and peaceful. Nobody hangs out the windows of the elegant brownstone apartments the way they hang out of the tenements, and no laundry dangles between buildings.

It's like another world.

It's like what I thought America would be.

Clara and I walk in silence to the Sixty-Seventh Street subway station on the Third Avenue line. As we're about to head down the stairs, I can't stand it another moment. "Clara, I really am so sorry. I tried so hard. I thought I could do it, but...." Tears fill my eyes again.

She stops, and gives my shoulder a squeeze. "I know. So did I. Speaking just isn't right for everyone, though."

I nod. I could ask for another chance, but I would do no better.

So I won't be leaving my mark on the world as a fiery union girl.

How *will* I leave it?

CHAPTER FORTY-ONE

Rosie
April 14, 1911

FRIDAY NIGHT, AFTER YET ANOTHER DINNER with his parents, Vincente and I go out for a walk in Seward Park. As always when I eat with them, I can barely move.

"Your mother makes so much food," I say, wishing I could rub my belly but not wanting to embarrass myself. "I must have gained twenty pounds since she arrived."

He laughs. "Only twenty? She'd say you didn't eat enough. She worries you're too thin."

I roll my eyes. "If she fattens me up any more, is she going to pay for my new clothes?" My corset is barely holding me in enough for my skirt as it is.

"Probably not," he admits, tucking my arm into his. "Probably not."

We walk slowly along the wide flat path, occasionally glancing over at the boys playing baseball in the middle of the park and the men running along the track that encircles the ball area. "I couldn't do any of that if I wanted to," I say, pointing out a particularly enthusiastic man. "I can hardly breathe."

Vincente gives my arm a squeeze. "You'll learn to eat like a real Italian," he promises. "Now, tell me, why were you so quiet tonight?"

"Every time I opened my mouth your mother tried to put food in it?" I joke, surprised and touched that he noticed.

The truth is, I'm still devastated over my failure last night, and even more over what happened afterwards.

Clara and I returned to the union hall, for a brief meeting at which speakers would be assigned for a variety of events over the next few weeks. Before that meeting began, she pulled the organizer aside for a few words, and then during it everyone was given a speaking task, some of them multiple tasks because the union is so short on speakers.

Everyone, that is, but me.

It's the right thing after the mess I made, but being so completely unable to follow Maria's path hurts. Instead of a speaking task, I was given a stack of envelopes to stuff with letters to potential donors. Still useful work, but hardly fiery. Hardly something that'll change the world.

I have my own letter, in my pocketbook. To my parents. Saying I will come home.

I don't want to send it, and I cried writing it, but there's nothing left for me in America. My parents want me home, and anyone could stuff those union envelopes, so...

Vincente squeezes my arm again. "You're so quiet. Is it just being full, or is something wrong?"

I sigh. "My speech last night was... not good. Not good at all."

"I'm sure it wasn't so—"

"Two ladies walked out!"

Wisely, he doesn't say anything else.

"I really want to be a union girl, a great one, one who really makes a difference. But I can't do it, not in the way I want."

"And what way is that?"

"Well, the way Maria did. As a wonderful speaker."

"She was that," he says quietly. "She got all the words in the family."

I have to smile. "I think your mother got some too. Although I don't understand most of them."

"She learned 'more' and 'eat' and 'you're too skinny' in English pretty quickly," he says, smiling back. "As for the rest, I can translate."

He's been doing a lot of that, a good thing since I'd have no idea what's being said without his help. His mother often drags me into the kitchen to show what she's making, and of course he doesn't join us there, but she points at things and tells me what they're called, and when I repeat the names in Italian she's delighted. After her initial shock at Ellis Island over my being Jewish she's been nothing but sweet to me, even though we don't understand each other.

"Oh, I wish you could translate what's in my head into words. I think beautiful things but they won't come out. So the union has me stuffing envelopes, which is not at all what I want."

He smiles at me, but somehow it seems a nervous smile. "And what *do* you want?"

"I want to make a *difference*," I say, feeling foolish at saying it out loud. "Be important, do things that matter."

"You're important to me," he says, his smile widening. "And you matter to me. Doesn't that count?"

"Of course," I say, though it really doesn't. It's not enough, anyhow.

"Well, then. So you're not meant to be a brilliant public speaker. That's all right." He clears his throat. "Not a lot of need for that in Italy, you know."

"I suppose not," I say, then what he actually said sinks into my head. "Italy?" Why does what is needed in Italy matter to me?

Vincente takes a deep breath. "Rosie, we're going home. Next Friday."

I stare at him. "You're leaving? You and your parents? But they just got here! And you... I don't know what to say." I'll miss him, but I'm not sure I should say that. It feels too forward.

"They planned to... well, the original plan was for them to visit for a few months and then leave Maria and me here for another two years. But now, with Maria gone... I can't stay here any longer. Everything reminds me of her. And my parents don't want to stay either. Mamma, she thinks... well, she thinks you should come with us."

My heart races and my fingers go ice-cold. "Me? Go to Italy?"

He takes my hands, then frowns and rubs them. "Rosie, you're freezing! Here." He shrugs out of his coat and wraps it around me over my own coat.

"I'm not cold, I'm—" I don't know *what* I am so how can I tell him? "I don't understand."

"Mamma wants... no, it's not just her. She does, she's afraid of something awful happening to you like it did to Maria. But though it was her idea, it's not just her. It's me. *I* want you to come back with us. We can't take Maria home, can't protect her, but we can take you. I'll open a restaurant with the money I've saved, and you can do some sewing and also help me and we will be happy. It's a whole new life for us. Well, for you. For me it's going back home with the money to really make something of myself."

That's what he wants to make of himself? That's what matters to him? Running a restaurant?

I want so much more. I don't know exactly *what*, but I know that's not enough. And the idea that he and his mother have been talking about me going home with them, without so much as asking what I think, bothers me. Everyone tells me what to do and nobody listens to what matters to me.

"But I'm not... it's like your mother is trying to replace Maria with me. And I'm not her daughter."

He takes a step closer and brushes his fingers over my cheek. "No, you're not. But... you could be her daughter-in-law?"

I stare at him, shocked at his words and at how good the ripples from his caress feel. "I... are you..."

His mouth is so near mine now, and I can't think well enough to finish my sentence.

He strokes my face again, then his other arm goes around me as he closes the distance between us and kisses me.

I've never been kissed before but I can't imagine it could ever be better than this. His strong arms tight around me, his body pressed to mine, his lips and tongue making my heart race and my body pound... every second of it is bliss.

When our kiss ends, I can't do anything but stare up into his eyes. My knees are wobbly and my whole body is tingling, and looking at him makes all of that happen even more. He smiles and says, "Rosie, will you marry me?"

"Vincente, I..." With everything turned upside-down inside me, I don't know what to say. "I do like you, I do, but..."

He frowns, then his face clears. "You need me to ask your father. I'll send a cable tomorrow."

Of course he would have to ask my father, but I don't want him to. My father would say no anyhow, because he's found a Jewish husband for me.

Who I also don't want to marry.

I don't want to marry anyone right now. All of the lives marriage would lead me to would be lives in which I lose myself in my husband and what he wants me to be.

Vincente's mother's questions through him about my union work and how I spend my time have made it clear that she would not be happy if his wife worked other than in his home, and I sense that Vincente thinks keeping his Mamma happy is extremely important.

I do understand that, both because she is his mother and because when he wasn't hungry for the dinner she'd made yesterday, after he and I had eaten knishes on a walk together, she screamed at him so loudly I'm sure the whole street heard.

But the life she wants for him, with the devoted wife who raises his children and does whatever he says, that's not the life I want.

I don't want to lose myself. I want to find myself, find the place where I make a mark, and I can't do that married. Not to him, not to anyone.

I take a breath to tell him so, but what comes out is, "I don't know."

I am really not a good speaker.

"Your father..."

"It's not about him, it's about me. Truly, I... don't know."

"Is it because you're Jewish and I'm Catholic? Neither of us is very religious so I didn't think that would matter."

He's right that I'm not as observant as some, but being Jewish does matter to me. How would I be Jewish in Italy married to a Catholic man?

"It would be so exciting, bringing you there and showing you everything. And we could even bring your family to live near us too, if you thought they'd like it. The weather is beautiful, and Mount Vesuvius is nearby so I could take you there... it's a wonderful place to live."

I believe that. For Italians. But for me? And my family, they'd never go. America was one thing, but to leave Russia for a different country where nobody we know has ever moved? I can't imagine it.

But then, I would certainly be known. Vincente's Jewish wife, found in America. Is that the kind of "known" I want?

Vincente reaches out and touches my cheek again. "You're so quiet. Is Mamma wrong that you... tell me, Rosie, do you... care for me? At all?"

I nod. I don't know whether I love him as a wife should love a husband, and I don't know how much of my feelings for him come from our shared pain after Maria's death, but I do care. My reaction to his kiss tells me that.

He sighs. "Well, then, I can wait for your answer."

I start to smile, but it freezes when he adds, "Until next Friday at nine in the morning, when the ship leaves."

CHAPTER FORTY-TWO

Rosie
April 15, 1911

AS I TAKE OFF MY HAT IN THE DRESSING ROOM with the other girls the next morning Josephine says, "Rosie, those circles under your eyes look like my fingernail. See?"

I wave her pointer finger, the nail bruised purple-and-blue from when she accidentally sewed over it earlier in the week, away from my face. "They do not. My eyes are fine."

"Don't look it. Didn't you sleep last night?"

I sigh, setting down my pocketbook with the letter to my parents I never wanted to write still unmailed inside it. "Not much."

"What's wrong?"

I hadn't decided whether I'd tell anyone about Vincente's proposal, but suddenly the idea of deciding what to do all by myself is overwhelming. "Well, Vincente... he wants me to go to Italy with him next Friday. To stay. As his wife."

With each of my sentences the Italian girl nearest me gasps with excitement, and when I finish, she says, "You said yes, right?"

"I didn't say anything."

Several girls groan, and I say, "It's not that simple. I was about to go back to Russia. But instead I'd move to *Italy*."

The girl shrugs. "What's another country, especially with a new husband?"

"It's not America!"

"And has America been all that wonderful to us?" Another Italian girl, who like me lost her dearest friend in the fire, shakes her head. "No, I'd go. I'd go and become a fat happy housewife and raise lots of fat happy kids and leave all this factory work behind."

"Besides, a smart kind handsome one like that?" The first girl, who knows Vincente through Maria's union work, smiles at me. "If you don't want him, pass him along to me."

"He's not a hat or a pocketbook I could just give to you," I say, annoyed on Vincente's behalf.

"You could try," she says, giving me a nudge. As we all leave the dressing room to head for our work tables she adds, "Josephine, don't you agree she should go?"

Josephine, who's been staring at her bruised fingertip throughout all of this, looks over at me, and I'm surprised to see how sad her expression is. "It would probably be wonderful for you," she admits, "but oh, Rosie, I would—"

Loud laughter startles us, and Josephine gives a brief scream of surprise.

"Ignore us, girls," the boss says, and I glance over to see him standing with—

With Mr. Harris and Mr. Blanck.

I knew they'd been released on bail, which I hated, but to see them out in public, *laughing*, while their old factory lies in ruins and their old workers lie in their graves...

How can I move to Italy and do nothing about it?

Their trial won't be for months, the union says, not until December, and until then they walk around as free men and laugh. Laugh with my new boss, who is clearly anything but horrified at the way they locked their factory doors so their workers couldn't pilfer. A few possibly-stolen yards of lace are worth more than a worker's life to these men, and something must be done about that.

But what?

If all of the rich people like Mrs. White and her friends knew, if they could somehow all be told the real details of what life as a factory worker really is...

Self-hatred fills me as we girls move in silence to our tables and begin to work, because I could never tell those people. The words just don't come out properly. Clara and the others do their best, but they can't be everywhere, and I can't help.

But I have to, I *have* to, do something.

Or Maria and the others will have died in vain and I can't bear that.

AFTER WORK, WE PICK UP LUNCH at street vendors on our way to the union hall, where we join a group of girls who are stuffing envelopes and chattering away about the speeches they'll give and the work they'll do.

"And how was your first speech, Rosie?"

I flinch and shake my head.

"Oh, come now, I'm sure it was fine."

I shake my head again, and another girl says, "She must have used up all her words at the speech so she's got none left."

The others chuckle, but I don't.

"Or," the girl who was so excited about Vincente's proposal says, drawing the one word out to great length, "she's busy thinking about her fiancé."

The room explodes with questions, and I say over the noise, "I don't have one. Truly."

"Leave her alone, Laura," Josephine says as she elbows the excited one.

"What? I think it's great news. Isn't it? She can get married and go to Italy and have a wonderful life. Better than what we'll have."

Another girl says, "What exactly would you have, Maria? Who is he and what does he offer?"

All eyes turn to me, and I feel my cheeks going hot but I manage to stutter out an explanation of what Vincente and his mother want me to do and when I have to decide by.

Josephine sighs, but the girl who asked says to me, "Is that what you want?"

I shake my head. "I want to..." I sigh too. "I want to be Maria and I can't."

The group falls silent in memory of Maria, until Josephine says, in a strangled voice, "I think you should be you."

Surprised at her tone, I look over to see tears in her eyes. "What on earth—"

"You *saved* me," she says, the words bursting from her as though she's been holding onto them for years. "When that Mr. Rosenthal tried to... you saw it and you made him stop. Nobody else even noticed. I was so scared, I didn't want him touching me, and you helped me." She wipes away a few tears that have slipped down her cheeks. "Maria was wonderful, but so are you."

I do remember that moment when I called Josephine away from Mr. Rosenthal, but mostly what I remember is how I watched Clara arguing with the union man and knew I couldn't do what she was doing. I was so disappointed in myself, I didn't think I'd done anything at all.

"Well, I'm glad I was able to help you," I say, giving her shoulder a pat. "No girl deserves that from a boss." I sigh. "I just wish noticing things was enough to make a difference in other areas."

A thought strikes me like a slap. The committee for safety... if I became one of their investigators, I would go into the factories and notice things. I'd report those things, and they'd be fixed. My noticing would be perfect for that, and it *would* make a difference.

For one wonderful moment I know it's exactly what I am meant to do, and happiness fills me.

Then doubt pushes it out. How would a nobody like me get that job? Nobody on that committee would know me at all. Why would they let—

The union. The article I read said there are union men involved. If I report on my current factory, as though I'm an investigator already, I can present it to the union. If I do that well enough, they might let me be on the committee.

But how will I convince them if I have to *speak* to them?

And even if I somehow manage that, is this truly what I want? I still won't be known, won't be important.

My breath catches in my throat as something I've never understood before suddenly becomes so clear.

Those two things are not the same.

I can be important, I can matter, without anyone ever knowing my name.

I have always wanted to be known, as Clara is and Maria and Aunt Ida were. But making a difference, even if nobody ever knows it came from me, now feels much more important.

I'd be so good at it. Is it what I want? Is it what I can accept?

"So when do you need to answer Vincente?" Josephine asks, and I realize with amazement that all of this has run through my head in such a brief moment that nobody's noticed my silence. Everything has changed inside me, and they don't even know.

"She said next Friday," Laura answers for me. "That's when his ship leaves."

It is, but I don't need even another minute to make my decision.

CHAPTER FORTY-THREE

Rosie
April 14, 1911

VINCENTE IS GLAD TO SEE ME when I knock on his apartment door, but only for a moment. I see his face change as he looks at me, but all he says is, "Shall we walk?"

His mother claps her hands and says something excited in Italian as we leave. I don't ask Vincente what she said, because I think I can guess, and he doesn't offer a translation.

His first words to me, when we're nearly a block from his home, are, "You've decided."

I nod.

"Are you coming with us? Are you marrying me?"

I swallow hard. "No," I say. "No, I am not."

"Staying here and become a union leader? So everyone knows your name?"

The pain in his voice hurts me, but the hint of mockery hurts more. "No," I say again. "I'll never be a union leader. I am joining the committee for safety, as an investigator. I'm going to be one small part of changing the factories. At least, I will if they'll have me."

He shakes his head. "A small part? But you wanted—and the Triangle bosses' trial is coming up soon. Won't that change the factories?"

"The trial won't be until December, the union says, and if they're convicted it might change things, yes. But not enough. And if they're not..." I sigh. "Either way, there are so many things that are wrong. Fire safety, work hours, how the girls are paid less than the men and treated so much worse. And it's not just the waist factories, you know, it's all of them. And—"

Vincente's finger against my lips silences me. "You sound just like Maria."

I shake my head, and he moves his hand away as I say, "I don't. She was so strong, so good at speaking, like Clara and the others. I'm not like them. I wanted to be, but I'm not."

He grabs my shoulders. "Then come with me!"

I shut my eyes against the passion in his voice. If I doubted before that he cares about me, maybe even loves me, I don't now.

And I think I love him too.

So much of me wants to give in and go with him, be the good wife I was raised to be. Some smaller part of me also still wants to be known and talked about. Those parts are having to give up what they once thought was important, and it's hard. It's almost impossible.

But it's also easy.

With my eyes closed, I can see the girls falling from the windows because they had no other choice. I can see Maria with her skirt ablaze in the last moments of her life. And nothing is harder, nothing could ever be harder, than remembering these things and not trying to stop them happening again.

"No. I'm staying here and I will do what I can to make a difference. I will."

Vincente's hands slip away from me and I hear him turn and walk away.

When I've waited long enough that I'm sure he's gone, I open my eyes. Then I scrub away tears I didn't realize had fallen, and walk home, where I write a new letter to my parents.

Dear Mama and Tateh,

I have received your letter, but I am not coming back to Russia. I know you have picked a husband for me, but I will not be marrying him.

I don't want a husband until I have made the difference I've always dreamed of making. I thought I had to make that difference with loud words and meetings and arguments, as I've learned Aunt Ida did, but now I understand that there are many other ways. I will continue to work with the union here, as I have done all along even though I didn't admit it to you, but I will also work for a safety committee to help make the factories so much better for workers than they are now. It is what I am meant to do. And I will do it here, in America.

I understand if you still choose not to move here. I do think it's safer than Russia, so I think you should all come here and be with me, but of course it is your choice.

I also understand that you will be angry with me. You didn't want me involved with a union but I am, and you want me home but I will not be. I am sorry that I cannot do what you wish, but I am still staying here. That is my choice.

I love all of you, and I hope you can forgive me.

L'shalom,
Rosie

After wiping fresh tears from my eyes, I retrieve my old letter to my parents from my pocketbook and stare at it for a moment, then rip it in half.

My parents are going to be furious, not just angry. They will send me letter after letter telling me I'm wrong, and they might even come to America and attempt to take me home with them.

But they will fail. I *am* home, and I will stay here and do what matters, what I am meant to do.

I drop the halves of the letter onto my bedside table so I can fold the new letter, and the sight of them brings up the memory of my first day in this room.

As I did that day, I turn up the lamp and use my clothing to protect me as I remove its shade, and then I burn the halves of the letter I was going to send home.

I'm more careful than I was when I burned my father's letter on my first day, more aware now of just how much damage fire can do. But though this letter burns more slowly, it's gone even more completely at the end.

Once the lamp's shade is back on, I rub a few of the letter's ashes between my fingers. A tiny flame did this. I'm not fiery, but perhaps I can be a tiny flame?

Time to get started.

CHAPTER FORTY-FOUR

Rosie
April 20, 1911

THE FOLLOWING THURSDAY NIGHT, I stand before the closed door of the room where the union leaders are holding their weekly meeting, trying to stop shaking. In one trembling hand I clutch my report, ten pages long, and in the other is the single page that is my speech explaining what I've done and why.

Since I don't know what inspectors are required to focus on in their reports, I've spent every moment I could for the last week focusing on everything.

I took notice of the three days where the boss made us work an hour longer than we should have, and I tracked how our lunch "hour" was never more than fifty minutes and usually closer to forty.

I counted how many girls are crammed into the tight rows of tables, and I made myself look closely at exactly how dirty the two toilets provided for the ninety-three of us girl workers are.

I know how many electric lights hang over our heads and in which areas of the factory those bulbs shine directly into our eyes and make them even more tired, how often the six men who work as cutters smoke a cigarette each day and how they dispose of their ashes into the bins of fabric scraps just as the Triangle cutters did, and how many children work as thread trimmers even though all workers are supposed to be at least fourteen.

I was even lucky enough to have an official inspector appear yesterday, so I was able to add to my report the details of how the boss kept him occupied while the forelady hid the two tiny thread-trimmer girls in a large shipping box so the inspector wouldn't see them.

In short, I know the factory better than its owner does.

But is that enough?

I don't know.

But I could have done no more.

I take a deep breath, wishing my corset would let me take an even deeper one, and knock on the door with the hand holding my speech.

"Yes?"

Fighting the urge to run away, I open the door and pull it closed behind me, then freeze at the sight of so many faces turned in my direction. Mr. London the lawyer, Mr. Starr the man who wanted to marry Aunt Ida, at least fifteen men I know by sight but not by name... and Clara.

"Rosie, what on earth—"

I have been afraid of this moment for the last week, but I have thought it through so many times that I manage to raise my speech to my face and begin reading aloud. "I am Rosie Lehrer and I want to be part of the committee on safety. I work at Diamond Waist Company and I have been—"

"Young lady, this is a meeting, not a chance for you to give a speech," Mr. London scolds. "Plus, I can't hear you mumbling through that paper. Put it down and tell us what you want to say. But be quick about it."

When I lower the paper I see how annoyed he seems, and Mr. Starr is giving me a look that makes me think he's comparing me to Aunt Ida and wondering how someone like me could be related to someone like her. I open my mouth, trying to find the right words, but of course they don't appear in my mind so I can't say them.

"Rosie," Clara says quickly, "tell us why you're here."

"I—" I stare at her, feeling tears rising. No words come even when I focus only on her, so I bring the page back up so I can see it. But with the tears in my eyes, I can't tell where I left off.

"Really," Mr. London says, "this is completely—"

"Hush, Meyer!" Clara snaps at him. "Let Rosie speak."

But I cannot. I was so sure this was my path and I have failed because I cannot speak.

A sob bursts from me, and before I humiliate myself completely by crying in front of all these important people, I drop my papers so I can fling open the door and rush from the room.

CHAPTER FORTY-FIVE

Rosie
April 21, 1909

I CRIED MYSELF TO SLEEP LAST NIGHT, of course, and when I wake up this morning I want to cry again but I've got no tears left. I worked so hard, I was so sure my report was good, and I never even got to show it to the union leaders.

What do I do now?

Vincente flickers into my mind and I realize his ship is probably about to sail. Maybe I should have tried to join the committee *before* making my decision about him.

No, I know I did the right thing not going with him, but if I *had* gone, I wouldn't be feeling so awful now.

I force myself out of bed, though I want to lie there and mope forever, and dress myself for another day at the factory. I'll have to keep working there, at least until I can find another way to make a difference.

Even though I can't imagine what that way could possibly be.

I've dragged my sad confused self halfway down the stairs to the home's main floor when I hear a ferocious knocking on the front door.

"Goodness," the American girl who replaced Julia says, rushing over to open it. "Who could that be at this early hour?"

I stand on the stairs, not sure I want to leave her alone with the person who knocks so loudly, then gasp. "Clara!"

I want to run away, knowing how disappointed she must be with me, but I don't. She deserves the chance to tell me how I embarrassed her.

"Oh, Rosie," she says, hurrying inside, "I had to catch you before you went to work, you wonderful girl, you."

"I know, I'm so sorry," I begin even before she finishes, then I realize what she's actually saying. "I—wait. Pardon?"

She's in front of me now on the stairs, squeezing my hands tightly. "Your report! With no training! Meyer got his friend at the Labor Department to find the last official report on Diamond and you saw so many things the inspector didn't. And the little girls being hidden away! We all know it happens but it's never in reports. Of course. But you!"

I have never heard Clara speak in such a scrambled way. She sounds like me, almost. "What are you trying to—"

"You're an inspector, my dear! We all agreed, and that group never 'all' agrees on anything. Meyer's friend is a committee leader and he's going to make it official today."

Joy fills me, and I can't do anything but hug her.

She hugs me back, and says as she holds me, "Meyer read your speech to us, which he should have let you do, the fool, but he was in a terrible mood yesterday, and then parts of your report. I knew you were smart, Rosie, but the level of detail... we were all so impressed." She sets me back so she can see me and adds, "Sam Starr in particular—do you know him? He seemed to know you."

I nod. "He's from Belostok, like me. And he knew my aunt before she died."

"He said your aunt would be proud of you."

"Oh," I whisper, too overwhelmed to say anything else. I can't imagine a better compliment.

"Meyer's friend says the committee will send you to a different factory every few weeks so you can work there and learn about it then write your report. They were going to have only official inspectors, but after seeing how much you learned, they now also want regular working girls in the various industries they'll study. They'd like you to start at a new factory on Monday. Oh, and they can't pay you, but you'll earn money at the factories and you can keep that. Is that all right?"

I can't quite recover my senses enough to speak so I nod almost as furiously as she knocked on the door. I'd start right this second, never mind Monday.

Clara's smile fades away as if she's forcing it to. "There is one condition, though."

"Oh, no. What?"

She gives me a sly grin. "We all feel you need to submit your reports in writing only. *Never* as a speech."

I burst out laughing. "I agree, and I accept."

She hugs me again and whispers, "I'm so proud of you, Rosie. You're going to do so much good."

I'm feeling so many emotions that I can barely mumble, "Thank you." A thought occurs to me, and I clear my throat and add, "You told them to let me do it, didn't you? You convinced them."

She draws back and smiles at me, and I see that her eyes have tears in them too. "I would have, but I didn't need to. They all saw how perfect it is for you. Your papers convinced them all on their own. *You* convinced them." She gives my shoulders a squeeze. "I've got to go to a meeting now, but are you busy tomorrow afternoon? Meyer's friend wants to show you the important parts of the Labor Law so you'll know exactly what to look for. At the union hall at one?"

"I'll be there."

She gives me one last hug then hurries away, and I stand stunned in the open doorway for a moment then close the door and grab a roll from the dining room to eat on my way to work. I could just not go, but maybe there'll be something to notice that I missed.

I doubt it, though. I noticed everything. As I always do.

Loving how it feels to know I've found my way to make a difference, I rush out of the building while taking a huge bite from my roll. A young shlepper boy hauling bundles of black fabric is right there, and I bump into him but manage to steady his load before he drops it.

He skitters away, and I look after him.

I made a difference there. A tiny one, yes, and I'm the one who was in his way so clearly I *should* have made one.

But I saved him from dropping the fabric in the dirt.

Who knows what that one change will do?

Maybe nothing.

Maybe, somehow, everything.

I'll never have my name in a history book. I won't be talked about at meetings, or be mentioned in the newspapers or recognized on the streets.

But I'll visit factories and bring light to the dark corners and tell the committee what I see. Then they'll put my findings in their report, and that report will be used to make changes that will change the lives of workers.

And I will be one small part of that.

I can't be Clara, or Maria. Or Aunt Ida.

But I can be Rosie.

And that's enough.

Author's Note

I believe historical fiction should be as accurate as possible, so I have not knowingly changed any real-world facts or situations for "Fiery Girls". Dates and events are as accurate as I could make them.

Rosie and Maria and Vincente are fictional, but real people in this book include Fiorello La Guardia (an Ellis Island interpreter before he became New York City's Mayor in 1934), Clara Lemlich (such a union supporter that she organized the workers in her retirement home), and Cecilia Greenstone (one of many women who assisted immigrants at Ellis Island). As well, Yonah Schimmel, who sold Julia and Rosie a knish, created a shop in 1910 that's still open today.

My research found multiple reported versions of various speeches (especially Clara's that began the 1909 strike), so I combined them into my own version. Morris Hilquit's phrase of "what a tremendous difference between the captains of ships and the captains of industry" was too good not to include verbatim.

The committee on which Rosie finds her way to make a difference did exist (called the New York Factory Investigative Commission), and via the miracle of the Internet, I was able to find its 850-pages-long first-year report. When I discovered that Clara Lemlich served as an investigator, I knew I had the perfect role for Rosie.

Sadly, Rosie was correct that the trial of Harris and Blanck wouldn't result in huge changes; they were acquitted because jurors weren't convinced the ninth-floor door had been locked despite the evidence. Twenty-three individual civil suits were brought against the two men, which they settled for only $75 per worker killed.

But the Investigative Commission worked for four years, and thirty-six of the laws they drafted were eventually enacted by New York State and used as models by other states and on the federal level to protect workers.

Acknowledgements

When I attended the (online for 2020) Humber School for Writers Summer Workshop in Creative Writing, I hoped for a great week of learning about writing. I did get that, thanks to my fantastic instructor Alissa York, but to my surprise I gained a writing group too.

I now meet four wonderful women bi-weekly on Zoom, discussing each other's work, doing writing exercises, and talking about what it means to be a writer. Anne-Marie Mawhiney, Jacqui Morrison, Amy Pierrson, and Julianna Rutledge, I'm so grateful for your support and your encouragement, and of course your willingness to accept my inability to pay attention whenever I notice Julianna's cat. You're all marvelous and I'm so glad to have you in my life.

Amy Tipton, your interest in "Fiery Girls" even after you left the agenting world made such a difference to me. You picked me up when I wasn't sure if I could keep going with this book, and I thank you!

Scarlett Rugers, queen of book covers, you came through for me yet again, turning my vague suggestions into something beautiful and striking. I couldn't ask for a better cover designer, and I hope someday I make it to Australia so I can meet you in person.

Bev Katz Rosenbaum, editor extraordinaire, you have such a way of telling me everything that's wrong with a book while also convincing me I can fix it. Your detailed and insightful comments on the first two drafts of "Fiery Girls" made it a better book and made me more comfortable releasing my first historical novel.

My husband, without whom nothing I do would be possible, this is the twenty-second time I've thanked you in a book, and I still haven't so much as scratched the surface of how much I appreciate your support. Twenty-two books full of thanks wouldn't be enough.

And finally, I want to thank *you*! Whether this is your first book of mine or you've read them all, I am so very grateful to have you as a reader. Thank you for reading books in general and for reading mine specifically. :)

Resources for Further Reading

My list of resources I used for this book includes nine non-fiction books, seventy-five web pages, and fifteen multi-page newspaper articles from the time of the fire. Here are a few of the best.

First and foremost: Cornell University's Kheel Center, *The 1911 Triangle Factory Fire* (http://www.ilr.cornell.edu/index.html). This website has photos of the building before and after the fire, stories of survivors in their own words, and excerpts of out-of-print books, all of which was invaluable to me in understanding the fire and the world in which it happened.

The two classic non-fiction books on the fire are Leon Stein's "The Triangle Fire, Centennial Edition" (Cornell University Press, 2011) and David von Drehle's "Triangle: The Fire That Changed America" (Grove Press, 2004). There's a lot of overlap between them (a good thing since they're reporting on the same events!) but I used them to fact-check each other and to give me a more rounded picture.

Speaking of 'picture', I had so much fun reading "Women's fashions of the early 1900's: an unabridged republication of 'New York fashions, 1909'" (Dover Publications, 1992). As the title suggests, it's a reprint of a 1909 clothing catalogue. Seeing what my characters could have bought and what it would cost was wonderful.

Did you know 'skinny' has been used to describe thinness since about the year 1600? The Online Etymology Dictionary told me so, and it also stopped me using lots of other words that weren't of the time. Look up your favorite words at http://www.etymonline.com if you're weird like me and enjoy that sort of thing.

And finally, on the strike itself, I made use of the Jewish Women's Archive's article called "Uprising of 20,000 (1909)", which can be found at https://jwa.org/encyclopedia/article/uprising-of-20000-1909.

Things to See and Do in New York City

I was lucky enough to be able to make a visit to NYC purely for the purposes of researching this book, and here are the places I went. If you're already there, or are able to go, consider checking some of them out! (Most have virtual tours as well.)

The Tenement Museum is housed in two buildings on Orchard Street in the Lower East Side, and the apartments in those buildings have been kept as they were in the past. Seeing the narrow halls (with their red-painted burlap walls) and the various tiny rooms brought the Billotas' apartment to life for me. I did two tours and a discussion session, and all were fantastic.

I spent a day at Ellis Island, and I wish it could have been a week. The bravery and determination of the immigrants who passed through that vast building touched me deeply, and literally walking in their footsteps made my Ellis Island scenes more real. I also very strongly recommend the "Save Ellis Island" group's "Hard Hat Tour", where you'll see the old buildings of the Ellis Island Hospital Complex.

The New York Transit Museum, located in a decommissioned subway station in Brooklyn, let me see an actual subway car from the 1910s (yellow horsehair bench fabric!) and also gave me great information about how Vincente's work would have been done.

The Asch Building still stands, but it is now known as the Brown Building and is part of New York University. I wasn't able to get inside as I'm not a student, but I stood on the sidewalk and looked up at the ninth floor window and imagined what the girls must have felt that day, and even thinking of it now brings tears to my eyes.

On a happier note, don't miss Katz's Deli! Huge sandwiches and of course pickle slices.

Let's Stay in Touch

I so appreciate your reading "Fiery Girls" and I hope you enjoyed it. Book reviews are crucial, both for me as an author and for your fellow readers, so if you can spare a moment to leave a review at your favorite retailer that would be wonderful.

Visit www.heatherwardell.com to sign up to hear from me via email. You can choose announcements when I release new books, a monthly newsletter, or bi-monthly in-depth updates, as you see fit.

Prefer social media? You can find me on:

- Facebook (www.facebook.com/heather.wardell.author)
- Instagram (www.instagram.com/heatherwardellauthor/)
- Twitter (www.twitter.com/heatherwardell)

I love chatting with readers, so feel free to connect with me!

Thanks again, and happy reading!

Also by Heather Wardell

Stand-Alone
Holding Out for a Zero

Toronto Collection
Life, Love, and a Polar Bear Tattoo (free download!)
Go Small or Go Home
Planning to Live
Stir Until Thoroughly Confused
A Life That Fits
Live Out Loud
Blank Slate Kate
Finding My Happy Pace
All at Sea
Good to Myself
Pink is a Four-Letter Word
Everybody's Got a Story
Fifty Million Reasons
Plan Overboard
Safe Harbor?
Game of Pies
The Menopause Support Group

"Seven Exes" Series
Seven Exes Are Eight Too Many
Bad Will Hunting
Fifteen Minutes of Summer